In this wonderfully inventive debut novel from John Minichillo (a comedic, contemporary retelling of *Moby Dick*), a chance DNA test reveals to John Jacobs that he is in fact 37% Inuit. So begins the humorous, occasionally hilarious exploits of a man in search of genuine experience (which by his newly acquired tribal rights comes in the form of an Alaskan whale hunt). Whether in quaint suburbia or the frozen Chukchi Sea, human relationships are exposed. Minichillo's balance of satire and realism addresses issues of race, gender, class, and power. The search for the legendary white whale reveals underlying tensions about global warming and government intervention and their increasing impact on ancient customs and cultural relations. With palpable insecurities and unwavering commitment to what is an otherwise absurd cause, Minichillo has created in Jacobs an immensely endearing protagonist who grows more appealing as readers accompany him on his overwhelmingly personal and admirable pursuit. Packed with tongue-in-cheek observations, Minichillo has crafted a delightful tale that is subtle and outrageous in equal measure, and filled with "the wisdom of the-everything-and-the-nothing that is the Great Living Breath."

~ Publishers Weekly

ADVANCE PRAISE

"John Minichillo is a brilliant new writer whose first book is a wondrous contemporary refabrication, send-up, homage to and deconstruction of another whale of a novel from long ago. It's a stunning performance by an inventive writer at the top of his game, edgy and articulate, thoroughly imagined and peopled, funny as hell, a tricky story that's a marvelous read from beginning to end."

> — Frederick Barthelme, author of 16 books including *Elroy Nights*, a PEN/Faulkner Award finalist

"*The Snow Whale*, John Minichillo's quirky, comic first novel, is an American original. The ingenious way in which the story raises levels of social issues like identity politics and environmental concern, and seamlessly integrates them with an iconic literary text is a wonder and a delight."

> — Stuart Dybek, author of *I Sailed With Magellan*

"It takes a lot of guts to write a (post)modern retelling of Moby Dick, but that's exactly what John Minichillo does with *The Snow Whale*... The result is an auspicious and hilarious debut novel. I haven't chortled this much since Roger Boylan's *Killoyle*. For readers who want some laughter before the oceans rise."

> — Hey, Small Press! (July Book List)

"While a white whale is, indeed, at the heart of much action throughout the narrative, Minichillo also draws on the ethos of other classic works of American literature. Jack London's "To Build a Fire" and Ernest Hemingway's "The Short Happy Life of Francis Macomber" spring immediately to mind, for the novel is as much about survival – both physical and spiritual – as it is about whaling... Juxtaposing goofiness and grit, *The Snow Whale* gets at the heart of all that's amiss in our hyper-plastic consumer culture."

> — Marc Schuster, Small Press Reviews

THE SNOW WHALE

THE SNOW WHALE

A NOVEL

JOHN MINICHILLO

An Atticus Trade Paperback Original

Atticus Books LLC
3766 Howard Avenue, Suite 202
Kensington MD 20895
http://atticusbooksonline.com

The Jessica sections of Chapter 4 were coauthored by
Katrina Gray and appeared in *Emprise Review* 17 as
"Waltzing Birds."

ISBN-13: 978-0-9845105-9-7
ISBN-10: 0-9845105-9-1

Typeset in Melior
Cover design by Jamie Keenan

For Katrina

"It was the whiteness of the whale that above all things appalled me."

- Ishmael, Herman Melville's *Moby-Dick*

The Snow Whale

Prologue

Outside the Tikigaq School, a white Jeep Cherokee panted a thick white exhaust plume into the fierce cold dark Alaska morning. Tramping up the road to the school was an old man in a white parka, a legendary hunter and the clan leader. He stopped at the Jeep and tapped on the driver's side window. The woman inside, his daughter-in-law, pointed with her mittened hand at the passenger seat as a way of inviting him into the warm cab. But the chief preferred the elements, and so she reluctantly cracked open her window.

"I brought him his lunch," she said, "but the doors are locked."

"What did you bring?"

"Akmaaq," she said, "we go through this every time, and you eat it. I am under strict instructions not to give you this lunch."

"I can take it," he said. "That way you don't come out into the cold. What is it?"

"It's fish," she said. "It's always fish. And I can handle the cold."

Her father-in-law, the old hunter, stood straight, his form bulked up in the parka and caribou pants, his face wrapped with a scarf, so that all that was seen of him was the weather-beaten band of a raccoon's mask, with his glass eye and his good eye. The woman never felt comfortable talking to him for long. With her window only slightly open, the heat of the Jeep had rushed out, and she crossed her arms to give herself a hug.

"It really is cold," he said.

She rolled up the window, unlocked the doors, and pointed to a small Igloo cooler on the backseat, the cooler not to keep the lunch cool, but to keep it from freezing.

Akmaaq opened the door, took the cooler, and waved as he trudged through a snowdrift to the main entrance of the school, next to the tracks his daughter-in-law had made. He used to run with a harpoon down the halls of the school to chase the children. He used to call up the principal with a list of the boys who would be excused for months during the spring hunt. He used to head the tribal council meetings. At the door of the school, he took off a mitten and fumbled around for the key. He was the clan chief—no one would ever be able to take that from him—but these days his son was the council president, and his son was the one calling the shots.

Inside the school, Akmaaq took off the second mitten and rubbed his hands together. He scuffed his sealskin boots on the mat, removed them, and left them with the others lined up along the wall. He unzipped his parka, removed his hat, and loosened his scarf. Once the Jeep Cherokee had driven away, he sat on the floor, opened the Igloo cooler, took out the packet of fish wrapped in foil, pinched off a piece, and ate until it was all gone. Then he stood, dusted off the caribou pants, took the cooler by its handle, stopped at a water fountain for a long drink, and continued down the hall.

In the school library, the council sat around a large table, with Akmaaq's son at the head. There were open briefcases, laptops, coffee mugs, stacks of paperwork. One of the council members took notes. Upon Akmaaq's entrance, they all continued about their business, and his son tried to conduct the meeting as if the old man wasn't there. Akmaaq slowly removed his parka and his scarf, and he hung them from one of the pegs on the wall. He set the Igloo cooler in front of his son, who was speaking. His son stopped to look inside, took out the crumpled ball of foil, slammed the lid of the cooler shut, and said, "You ate it. You ate my lunch."

"Maybe your wife thinks you are getting fat."

The other council members, some of whom were closer in age to Akmaaq than to his son, laughed at this, and they were delighted the humdrum meeting had broken up because of his antics.

"Dad, you don't need to be here."

"I brought my petition," Akmaaq said.

"It's an application."

"When I was head of the council," Akmaaq said, "we didn't need no application. We just hunted."

"There wasn't an Endangered Species Act," his son said. "It's not my idea; it's the U.S. government. You want to whale? We have to send in the names."

Akmaaq went over to his parka, reached into the inside pocket and pulled out folded leafs of paper. He brought them over to his son, and not out of malice, but because of his poor depth perception, missed the table and dropped them on the floor. The nearest council member picked up the papers and gave them to Akmaaq's son for his approval.

"I can't read any of these names," his son said. "It's illegible."

"I can read them," Akmaaq said. "Just ask me."

"Harpooner?"

"*Akmaaq*. That's me."

"Who are these others? They all say *Akmaaq*. You need actual names of actual hunters. And you have to type them out."

"Who has a typewriter anymore?"

"*You* do," his son said.

"Just put it through," Akmaaq said. "I'll go alone. I'll bring in a whale by myself."

"I won't let you out there alone."

"I'm not asking you. I'm asking the council. Put it up for a vote. You can't deny me my *umiaq* this season and you know it. I'm your chief."

The son of the great hunter stared at the crumpled ball of foil on the table and he waited for a sign of what to do from the others in the room. "Show of hands?"

After a quiet moment a hand was raised and then another, until everyone but Akmaaq's son had consented.

"The council will put this through," he said. "But no one will let their sons go with you. And say what you want. You can't go out there alone."

Chapter 1

UniqCorps Plastics Division made what John Jacobs called desk doodles. They were clear plastic hourglasses filled with dyed water and a brightly colored copolymer solution, or "goo." When the toy was flipped over, the reservoir at the top dripped lazy liquid beads in an equidistant row that sank down a spiral maze, the effect mesmerizing. In the UniqCorps Plastics Division literature, desk doodles were known as "corporate novelties," and the official purpose was to inspire a childlike creativity in desk-bound employees. John Jacobs never felt anything close to childlike, though his cubicle space at UniqCorps was devoted to desk doodles. He didn't design them, he didn't test them, he didn't market them, though he was acquainted with the people who did.

John Jacobs and his fellow salesmen in the plastics division spent eight hours a day sending e-mails or talking on the phone to very rich and powerful people, the senior executives who gave their employees token gifts from the company each year—semiuseful things like stadium blankets, fold-up lawn chairs, can coolers, visors, or anything summery, fun, and costing less than twenty dollars per unit when bought in bulk. John Jacobs sold them desk doodles. His job was to convince the rich and powerful executives that profit and company pride were likely returns on the distribution of cases of corporate novelties stamped with the company logo. And all across the land, bank officers kept desk doodles prominently displayed, while bank customers yearned to set the goo in motion.

"We can stencil a quote on it," Jacobs had just been saying to the vice president of internal relations at a very large bank that had bought another very large bank as part of a high-profile acquisitions merger, with a lake of transitioning employees in need of the new logo. The SEC and both boards approved the collision of these two mountain ranges of money, and John Jacobs made phone calls to everyone at the top. He imagined that in the not-too-distant past the vice president of internal relations handed out real bonuses and patted workers on the back. Now the vice president bought into the desk doodles scheme—and the money the company saved on increasingly paltry gifts would earn the vice president a bonus of his own.

"*The creative mind is a happy mind*," Jacobs said, trying out one of the more popular quotes. There was silence on the phone.

"*The freedom to work is humankind's greatest gift to humanity*," Jacobs said, which was one he'd never sold, but he was going down the list.

"Sounds like what the Nazis used to put up in the camps," the vice president of internal relations said.

"I think that was *Freedom through work.*'"

"That's right," the vice president agreed. "Has a better ring, doesn't it?"

"Ours sounded OK before we stripped the sexism. Had been *man's* greatest gift."

"We probably can't go with that, though."

"Not if you've got women bosses," Jacobs said.

"You kidding me?" the vice president said. "It's the ones below me I worry about."

After a pause, he added, "And I *don't* have any women bosses if that's what you're thinking. It takes dedication and resolve to get here."

"I can only imagine," Jacobs said.

"Let's go with the first one," he said, trying to get Jacobs off the line. Time was important, and the running of the bank depended on him. The vice president had lost interest in the conversation, and sexism was something bankers didn't like to be reminded of. "Who said that, anyway?" he said.

"We did," Jacobs said.

It was the biggest-selling quote by far, *the creative mind*. Though no one in the plastics division was able to express creativity and no one was happy. Selling desk doodles was an embarrassment, with the single exception that it paid the bills.

When John Jacobs first got the job at UniqCorps, he set his student loans for automatic withdrawal, he went two weeks without a brown bag lunch, and he had his next car all picked out, the slightly indulgent Pontiac Sunfire. When his wife, Jessica, went on shopping sprees, he was proud to see her in new clothes and with the things she'd wanted. For a time, John Jacobs was the most nearly successful and practically contented person he knew. Until one evening when he overheard Jessica on the phone with her mother. This was before they'd gotten cell phones, and he often picked up the phone to discover Jessica on the line. She either didn't notice, or didn't care, so he listened. It was Jessica's mother who had said, "He's not much of a man, is he?"

But his wife didn't defend him, and she had said, "I made a mistake. I'd hoped he'd grow into it."

So what at first seemed a worthwhile compromise—financial stability for redundancy—was the longstanding character of their relationship, with his sacrifice no longer enough to keep the couple happy as Jacobs became suddenly aware that his life was small and his work unappreciated.

Recently, Jacobs had observed a change in Mike Schmidt, the salesman who occupied the cubicle next to his. He heard Mike make arrangements over the phone to fly to Ulaanbaatar, Mongolia, a trip that included an overland trek and would be paid for in installments. Mike Schmidt was excited, even giddy.

"I'm *from* there," Jacobs heard Mike tell the travel agent. And this was such an odd thing for Mike to say that Jacobs did something he almost never did. At lunch, instead of using his downtime to surf the Internet for news and celebrity gossip, he rolled his office chair out from behind his desk and took his brown bag over to Mike's cube.

"I couldn't help overhearing," Jacobs said. "You're going on a trip?"

"I found out the most amazing thing," Mike said. "I used to be like everyone else. But I sent away for a DNA test where they trace your ancestry." He pulled up the website and used the mouse to point with the cursor. "For two hundred dollars they extract your origins. They call them haplogroups and haplotypes, which come back probabilities and percentages—and it works. All very scientific. You find out what you are and where you came from.

"My ancestors roamed Mongolian plains," Mike con- tinued. "Or more likely they were savage barbarians sacking villages. It explains so much."

Jacobs stared at his coworker but saw no Asian traits in his face. He was pale, he was fair-haired, he was scrawny. Jacobs couldn't imagine Mike Schmidt doing any pillaging now or in any past incarnation. He let him talk.

"I've always felt a kinship with China," Mike said. "I love pandas, and I secretly root for their Olympic gymnasts over our own. The Dalai Lama is one of my all-time favorite spiritual leaders."

Jacobs thought Mike was confusing his countries, but he gave him the benefit of the doubt. There were like a billion Chinese, so what was crazy about Mike Schmidt being related to some of them? And why couldn't a mild- mannered desk doodle salesman like Mike be the recipient of the Genghis Khan gene?

"So you're going?" Jacobs asked.

"I need to be with my people," Mike said. "To walk knee- deep in Mongolian snows and breathe the free Mongolian air. Before this DNA test I was nobody. Did you know they drink oxblood and they have seventeen varieties of yogurt unique to the region?"

"You're always eating yogurt," Jacobs said.

"I know!" Mike said. "Now it all makes sense."

Later that day Jacobs logged on to the website Mike had shown him and he ordered his own DNA test kit. He charged the kit to his credit card but supplied his work address. There was no denying that what he had done was strictly against UniqCorps policy, and he could be fired for using company time and resources for personal expenditures. Except now Jacobs wanted what Mike had found. Mike sounded happy as he sold desk doodles the rest of the afternoon. Jacobs knew it was because of the DNA test and the upcoming excursion. Mike had a purpose now, something to look forward to, somewhere he was going to go. Mike researched Mongolian peoples and Mongolian culture, which he referred to as "we"—and all on company time.

"We were the first taxidermists," Mike said.

"Ghengis Khan had his own pony express," he said.

"We spread printing and gunpowder to the rest of the world," he said.

"We invented the longbow long before the Brits," he said.

"We race the Indy 500 on horses," he said. "Without saddles or bridles, and all the jockeys are kids."

Jacobs was envious, because Mike landed sale after sale the rest of the afternoon. The hawking of desk doodles came naturally all of a sudden, and Mike set about his phone calls like a Hun sacking executive offices. His attitude lifted, he pitched with aggression, and he enjoyed himself.

Jacobs remained leery. He hated his job but didn't know what else he might do. There were rumors the plastics division was going to transition into a defense contract, the desk doodle line changing over to manufacture a part for a cruise missile, something small and plastic, some kind of fluid switch that was important to the accuracy and smooth functioning of America's war on terror. The defense contract would be large and secure, and the sales department would cease to exist as soon as the paperwork was signed.

It was a believable scenario, but Jacobs knew the higher-ups sometimes started rumors facetiously, to keep everyone in line. And the rumor worked on Jacobs whether it was true or not, because he collapsed in his chair when he got the e-memo that a sales meeting was scheduled for later that day. He'd landed a very large desk doodle account that morning but wasn't confident he'd still have his job by midafternoon. If they called him out over surfing the Internet, he'd apologize and say he'd never do it again. He'd say the bank executive put the idea in his head by asking if he'd heard of these DNA ancestry kits. And so Jacobs convinced himself that he went to the website as a way of making better small talk for the follow-up call. It was a good-enough lie, something UniqCorps should *want* him doing. Besides, the company's Internet policy was draconian.

The meeting was not a rap session, or to hand out reprimands or pink slips, but to announce a new "corporate novelty," with a prototype arriving in a few days. And days went by, and the DNA test kit arrived, and John Jacobs felt like he'd gotten away with something.

Jacobs was superstitious about swabbing himself in the offices. He was afraid his state of mind would somehow affect the test results. But there was a free pick-up and express delivery service at work, and he also didn't want his wife to know. Jessica Jacobs had a way of multiplying anything he spent by four or five. Every time she saw something she wanted, she justified her whims with his.

"You spent two hundred dollars," he imagined her saying. "And I'm only spending ninety." But then she would use this excuse over and over so that Jacobs would never escape, with Jessica soon spending more than two hundred dollars: on dancing shoes, a riverboat ride, a horse-and-buggy tour, a psychic reading, a gym membership, a share in a grocer's co-op, a donation to the black swan exhibit at the zoo, a set of noise-canceling headphones, a kitchen appliance that made bread, or yet another women's magazine subscription. Jacobs decided not to tell Jessica about his DNA test. He would wait to see the results. Then maybe they would have that conversation.

In the bathroom at work, Jacobs went into the handicapped stall. It gave him more room to pace as he read the instructions. The swab wasn't a swab at all, but a piece of plastic that he ran along the inside of his cheeks. He did both cheeks for good measure. He put the swab in the test tube, sealed the tube with the stopper, and placed the test tube back in the Styrofoam packing. Then he flushed the toilet, in case anyone was listening. He set the small parcel on the counter as he washed up at the sink and he took a long look at himself in the mirror. It was like he didn't know the face staring back. There were red highlights in his brown hair and flecks of gray in his beard stubble. These features were written in him, and the sample of spit he'd carefully boxed up would tell him the origins.

Jacobs left the bathroom with the small parcel under his arm, and he dropped it in the outgoing mailbox on his way back to his cubicle. He felt the drip of perspiration from his armpits, and he was feverish, like he was in the midst of something sinful and forbidden. He had mailed off the question, and the two hundred dollars they had debited from his checking account ensured a detailed response. His cheek cells were FedExed that same day to a lab in Silicon Valley, where they would extract and decipher him. Translate him into geographic regions and bloodlines. Untangle him and tell him who made him. And within a margin of error of plus or minus 5 percent, Jacobs would finally know what his cells knew.

Back in his office he was distracted, and he foolishly surfed the Internet for the rest of the afternoon. If there had been a globe on his desk instead of all the useless doodles, he'd have sat there spinning it and imagining the places he might have come from. He noticed that a lot of websites promised to trace ancestry, but the most common method was through library research. He could hardly imagine anyone digging through a library for information anymore. There were easier, more reliable ways of finding things out. With science on our side, why would anyone take the time to look up marriage and death certificates? It seemed so limited, this idea of lives boiled down to publicly documented events. There were answers that he carried inside, and for two hundred dollars, he was given the key.

John Jacobs remembered his wife, Jessica, paying money every month to have her own website, and being proud.

"Now I have a web presence," she had said, showing him the Google search for her name. There were a lot of Jessica Jacobses out there, but one of them was his wife, and from that moment she had her own web page. He told her a MySpace page was free, but that didn't count in her mind as a web presence, and so he let it go.

Jacobs typed her name into the Google search and went to her page. She hadn't made any changes since she'd first set it up. There was a lone picture of her, where she smiled uneasily, and the photo was several years old. She looked younger and skinnier, and the light application of makeup seemed to complement her looks, while these days it detracted. She wanted strangers to know that she loved cats (though she couldn't bring herself to get another after Mittens was tragically run over), that Francis of Assisi was her favorite saint, that she was a certified ballroom dance instructor, and that she was helplessly paralyzed on the couch with buttered popcorn any time *Gone With the Wind* played on cable. John clicked the link of another Jessica Jacobs—who did have a MySpace page. This young woman was so different from his wife that one of them should be made to change her name. Everything his wife had on her website, that was costing them twenty-nine ninety-five per month, would easily fit into the categories of the MySpace template. He was depressed to realize, but not at all surprised to see, that this other Jessica Jacobs was younger, better looking, and probably more interesting than the one he shared his life with. He supposed there were more than a few John Jacobses out there too, and that his Jessica might also want to trade him in.

He could hardly bring himself to talk about work with her anymore. Mostly, they occupied the same house, slept in the same bed, and had the same conversations again and again.

Today, at least, he was paid by UniqCorps to sit and daydream. And when he left that evening, he was guiltless. He'd given too much of himself to the company for far too long. He hadn't done anything wrong, after all. He would continue to sell the desk doodles, but he was no longer compelled to. He would make the phone calls and send out the e-mails, but the job was no longer important to him. If they fired him, they freed him. If they found fault with his way of working, they could replace him easily, but he refused to give himself over. He wouldn't be cowed. He wouldn't kneel to the rich and powerful bank executives. He saw himself as their equal now, or perhaps their better. And he hoped that like Mike Schmidt he was also the recipient of the Genghis Khan gene. Because if it weren't for his obligations to Jessica and the bills she'd accumulated, he'd walk away from the job and never come back, wandering to a town under different stars, far enough away to leave the plastic world behind.

At home he didn't say anything about what he'd done. He noticed the parade of human variation on the TV, and he felt a kinship with people who looked nothing like him. Maybe I'm one of them, he thought. Maybe I've got some of that in me. Even if just a little.

What John Jacobs hadn't eavesdropped in Jessica's phone conversations with her mother were the times his mother-in-law defended John against Jessica, who liked to begin the call by saying, "I want a divorce."

Despite her frequent complaints against her husband, Jessica blamed her unhappiness on her mother, who had placated her with candy when she was a toddler, and all her life she was a touch overweight. When she was a child, Jessica's passion was a thing called a moonbike. They'd been made of plastic these past twenty years, but she had an aluminum one, a slim tricycle that Jessica loved and her mother considered dangerous. Her mother often told Jessica she was too old for the moonbike, which was meant for young children, and her mother didn't like the way she flew down the ramp of their driveway into the street. She wasn't a cautious child, and she might have gotten killed. Jessica knew the weight limit of the moonbike was seventy-five pounds, and still she rode it, and one day she broke it, and to make her feel better her mother bought candy.

Jessica Jacobs always dieted but never lost that last thirty pounds. She tried lettuce diets, grapefruit diets, fat-absorbing pills, taking the stairs, skipping meals for ice cream, the Slim-Fast cans, the celery diet, the Brazil nut diet, the glass of wine diet, the Diet Coke diet, which became the diet root beer diet, then the organic cane syrup pomegranate soda diet, and she also didn't see anything wrong with diet pills, they just didn't work for her. The only time she was happy growing up was the summer she swam at her grandmother's lake cottage while her parents fought for four months, what they called "working things out," but what became finalizing their divorce. Jessica met a boy while swimming, and he led her into the bushes where they lay on their towels. When the boy's vacation ended, they promised to stay in touch. Meanwhile Jessica brooded in her room, terrified that at fifteen she'd gotten pregnant. She wasn't, but she put back on the weight she'd lost swimming.

Before she'd met John, Jessica had dated other men, but ballroom dancing was the deal breaker. One refused to try, one tried but was embarrassed by his rigid body, one called it "flapper dancing," and one called it "ballet." The good one, the one she *really* liked—he let her down when he told her ballroom dance instruction didn't count as a career and that she lacked ambition. She read nine self-esteem books by PhDs before she got over that remark. Ballroom dancing was dignified, and the people who took classes came out of their shells. Ballroom dancing was exhilarating, and it was the only time she felt alive, like riding a moonbike she'd never outgrow. She'd always wanted to share that with the man in her life. When John came to the classes at the dance studio, he wasn't afraid to lead and the closed dance hold came naturally to him. He never divulged his secret but he'd learned ballroom style at some point, because he was no beginner. And for the cotillion at the end of the class, when Jessica always suggested the students dress up a little, John had rented a tux. She knew John Jacobs respected ritual and she thought maybe he had been a priest in a previous life, maybe even someone she'd known in one of her own past lives.

She'd learned to access her past lives during the three months she attended a group meditation at the dance studio that was followed by a free backrub. Jessica was given a window into her past lives, and they were fascinating. Once she even experienced her own death. Her husband in that life drove with excessive caution while her lover drove much too fast. Jessica was with the boyfriend in the vision, carefree and happy, when the memory was halted by the blinding instant of a side collision. This experience encouraged her toward restraint in three of her next four lives, what the meditation leader called "imprinting." She wouldn't even know why she was like that, but past lives shaped future selves. In one of her lives, she knows she was martyred, though she's never accessed the burned-at-the-stake execution, one of two such executions she'd suffered, because she'd also been a Salem witch. In that life she kept her petticoats clean, and when she was widowed, the neighbor accused her of witchery because he wanted the land. She often confused these past lives because in both she was beautiful and wrongfully burned at the stake.

Jessica's favorite things were ballroom dancing, late-night talk shows, anything with cheese baked inside, the black swan exhibit at the zoo, her personal relationship with God, her increasingly healthy attitude toward her body, her two standby perfumes, and her Waterford crystal punchbowl.

When the results of his test came back, Jacobs took the envelope into the bathroom to open alone and undisturbed. His data fit neatly on a two-page printout, with racial and ethnic categories and the probable geographic regions of his ancestors arranged in descending order. There were races he'd never heard of, but a letter accompanied his profile and explained that a detailed document at the website defined all terminology. At the top of Jacobs's genetic profile, in bold, he saw the word *Inuit*, with his lineage listed at 37 percent. The word was vaguely familiar but he couldn't place it: *Inuit*. He felt like running from the bathroom down the hall to the computer in his cubicle so he could look it up. He was more than a third, but less than a half Inuit, by far the most prominent category in his profile. Though he wasn't sure how comfortable he felt with this, whatever Inuit was, there was no denying what shouted out in his genetic code—because there it was at the top of the page.

He flushed the toilet, he washed up, and he walked down the hall as casually as he could muster. He looked over the other easily recognizable categories. He was four-tenths of a percent Tuscan, 3 percent Spanish Moor, 7 percent Danish, and one one-hundredth of a percent Egyptian. He had always liked the pyramids and mummy movies, but one one-hundredth was nothing to get too excited over. It was this Inuit category he needed to find out about.

He passed Mike Schmidt on his way to his cubicle, and for a moment they made eye contact. He could easily see Mike sitting at his desk wearing animal skins and furs. He thought maybe there was a slant to Mike's eyes and he imagined him with a thick black beard. Things had changed around the office for the two of them. Though Jacobs hadn't disclosed his purchase of the DNA test kit, they gave each other a knowing look and Mike slowly nodded. It was as if desk doodles, cubicles, company logos, and cruise missiles had never existed. As if their survival depended on something more basic and Mike and himself were brought together out of a primal bond. *Inuit, Inuit, Inuit*, Jacobs said to himself, searching his mind for some sense of the word's familiarity as he double-checked the spelling and typed it into a browser search.

He was taken to a page on racist language usage, the link highlighted because he had been to the page before. He recognized the page as the reference he'd used when he was told to eradicate sexist language from the list of desk doodle quotes. He never bothered to check his list against outdated racial and ethnic slurs, but they were listed at this same website. At first he was indignant, knowing instantly that the link to this page meant his people had suffered from racism, but when he saw the word—*Eskimo*—he felt a glowing kinship. And *Eskimo* was a word he was sure he was entitled to use. He was *Eskimo*. He sat there for a moment in front of his computer with his eyes closed, and his smile spread as he imagined an expanse of wild snow. There was a sense of serenity coupled with the nothingness in his mind as the walls of the cubicle vanished from his awareness and he felt finally and for the first time, at home.

As if to intentionally jar him awake, his desk phone rang, and it pulled him back to reality with each successive electronic trill. He picked up. It was the vice president of internal relations at the giant bank that had swallowed the other giant bank, and Jacobs was asked to change the order, because the vice president wanted to supply his own quote. The words seemed to pass through Jacobs, but he wrote the phrase on a pad so he wouldn't forget. "Yes, of course," he told the man. "Anything you want. I like it very much. This will make a nice gift."

Jacobs was sure no single quote mattered any more than any other in the whole history of time, and though the phrasing sounded vaguely familiar, he didn't really care to place it. Probably Shakespeare, or Churchill, or John Stuart Mill, and the executive on the line paused in order for him to guess.

"Done," Jacobs said, and he hung up, alienating the vice president who wasn't used to anyone being short with him, especially after he'd shown himself to be intellectual and special. The vice president was living proof that *the creative mind was a happy mind,* and one of the few bank employees with that kind of luxury.

The rest of the afternoon, Jacobs sat without using his computer, without eating, and without making or taking phone calls. At the end of the day, he went straight home to his wife, swept her off her feet, and carried her up to their bedroom.

She said things like, "What's gotten into you?" And: "Wait, wait. I need to go to the bathroom." But John Jacobs made love to his wife passionately for the first time in years, because their sex, like everything else, had conformed to a routine.

Afterwards, they lay in each other's arms and they talked freely. He told her about the DNA test kit and what he'd found out. He didn't care if she would use it as an excuse to spend money, because money didn't matter. At first she laughed, but then she saw he was serious, and the results were important to him.

When she came back from the bathroom, which she said could no longer wait, she asked, "What are you going to do?"

"What do you mean?" he said.

"You could join a tribe. There might be advantages. Maybe they have a casino. Maybe we can be Canadian. There must be something."

"I need to think about it," Jacobs said. "I need to find out."

"Thirty-seven percent is a lot," Jessica said. "Was there an Inuit mailman?"

Jacobs shot his wife a look that made clear she shouldn't joke, though she wasn't really joking. She was just trying to work out the details. She had known his family and they had lived in the lower forty-eight a long time. None of them had ever even been to Alaska or Canada. They had come over from Europe at some point, she couldn't remember when, but none of them were Native Americans.

"Do you think they got the tests mixed up?" she asked. "With a pregnancy test you do it twice just to make sure. When a doctor tells you you have cancer, you get a second opinion."

"I know this is true," Jacobs said. "I don't know how I know, but it's not for me to decide. This is who I am. It's where I come from. Remember how I told you my dad was always dragging the family off on camping trips?"

"You said even in winter," she added.

"*Especially* in winter. Mom thought he was crazy, but she went along. And once we were out there she seemed just fine. She was perfectly happy. Mostly, I think she worried what the neighbors thought."

"You could write poetry," Jessica said. "Don't Eskimos have more words?"

"One hundred words for snow," Jacobs said. "But I don't write poetry."

"I'm just saying if you felt like it. An Eskimo poet might get published."

"I'm also one one-hundredth Egyptian."

"I don't see how that helps you," his wife said. "Eskimo's better."

On camping trips with his family, Jacobs was the official wood gatherer. He collected kindling, he dragged logs, and he even cut down a tree. Jessica focused a week of meditations on her husband's past lives, and encountered caveman memories that were alike, and if she thought about it, might actually be her own. Though she also had a vision of her husband as a money counter. She saw through the eyes of a shorter version of John chained to a table of ducats he was indentured to count.

She understood that past lives affected us in the present, and that time wasn't a line, but all our lives were lived simultaneously. So there was a version of John in some parallel universe, all of the Johns and Jessicas alive at once, including a John who counts coins every day in a small room with the threat of death lingering. She knew, for example, that she'd lived seven full lives between 1945 and 1966, which was impossible, except in a quantum universe, and in most of her lives she was a dancer: flamenco, cabaret, and a-go-go.

On the phone, she told her mother she wished she'd known to concentrate on John's past lives before she'd married him. Had she been aware of his affinity for the caveman experience, and his fear of ducats, she would have had serious doubts.

That weekend the neighbors, Nat and Jodi Jorgansen, came over for barbecue. Winter was winding down, and though brisk, most days were pleasant enough that the smell of grilled meat returned to the Oaken Glens subdivision. The invitation had been made weeks ago, so there was no backing out. Jacobs was in a state of dread. He didn't want to be around people, especially white people, with the exception of Jessica. There was once a time when he found himself intoxicated by her bland looks, when he was in love with her, but now he *needed* her in order to procreate and he *needed* to procreate so the Jacobses might stand up, if even for a brief span, against the harsh arctic wilderness that would return and wipe out the modern world with the next ice age. He had thrown out Jessica's birth control pills, and when she asked if he knew where they were, he said he didn't see why she needed them. Jessica had always wanted a baby, and when she heard John say this, her lips curled into a half-smile.

"We can't afford it," she said, though her objection led to no further discussion. Her husband didn't know how to talk about money, and by default, she handled the finances. She might allow herself two casual spending days, which seemed the limit of leeway. Otherwise, purchases might threaten expenditures. Her most recent find was an electric space heater made by the Amish with a flickering light like fire that could be turned on without the heater running—and she just loved to bask in its soothing glow while the air conditioner purred. She convinced herself the space heater was for John, though she was the one who always turned it on.

John was certain Jessica would tell the Jorgansens about his lineage, and they would all have a laugh at his expense. Jessica would also tell Jodi, as soon as they were alone, that she and John were trying to "conceive." He hated the word, which sounded premeditated. He wanted to knock it from her mouth whenever she spoke it. But Jessica was his wife, and he endured many irritations for her sake.

When Nat and Jodi arrived, Jacobs felt Nat's eyes lingered on Jessica for too long, and their embrace was too familiar. Jacobs had known Nat to brush off adultery as the seven-year itch, and in the presence of his neighbor, Jacobs wanted to fight for Jessica. He wanted to knock his fist into Nat's jaw. Nat was an exaggerator, a braggart, and he liked to run the show. Jacobs wanted to protect Jessica and to take her away from Oaken Glens, where they had always lived and had been happy enough.

Jacobs used to enjoy a beer with Nat, but now he just wanted to avoid him. Jacobs tended the coals pulsing in the Weber grill, which saddened the wood gatherer in him as too hot and too modern an indulgence. So much *heat* and half-a-dozen burgers. He wished he could wash off the smoky petroleum smell that followed him back into the house. Jessica had prepared the patties and she was about to fry up some bacon to top the burgers with, when Jacobs picked up a raw strip and stared into it. The piece of fat was perfectly white and the smell made him salivate and tremble with hunger. To the surprise of his wife and friends, he put the piece of raw bacon in his mouth and slowly chewed.

"Good way to get trichinosis there, buddy," Nat said, and no one said anything else.

Jacobs continued to chew without swallowing, and when he reached for another raw slice, Jessica slapped his hand. He felt rejected and needed to get away, to start over with Jessica somewhere pure. More than anything, more than ever, they just needed to *go*.

Jacobs thought of libraries as repositories of old books collecting dust. Time capsules. Museums. When he found himself in a library he would check the cards to see how long since the books were last checked out. Two years, most books waited. And of these, he didn't understand why they hadn't just thrown them away.

When he was a child, his mother took him to the library to check out picture books. As a teen he wandered over to the adult side, and the sci-fi looked promising. But then those books were a chore and he wasn't happy in the library again until he discovered art books. They were extremely expensive unwieldy books he couldn't believe they would just let him borrow without a cent to his name. And when he went to college he studied the art books and wrote papers, but learned to think of the library as a place to stare at girls.

Now Jacobs discovered libraries were useful, at least as far as finding out about Eskimos was concerned. Eskimos had their own Dewey decimal, with a row of books in one section and a handful of books in another. There were

National Geographic videos he could take home and a vinyl LP with recordings of the spoken Eskimo dialects he could listen to on a turntable with bulky headphones. He was far from being an expert on the Inuit, but this was how Jacobs spent his free time, and with the days growing warmer he felt the energy sapped out of him.

Jessica was at first excited by John's interest in a baby, and she told him to bring home baby books from the library, which he did, but then she realized her husband was depressed, and she was afraid of what things might be like if a baby entered the picture. She restarted her birth control regimen without telling him and the days dragged on. He went to the library after work, and he wasn't assertive anymore, which depressed *her*. So their only interactions were to fight over things that didn't matter, and the fights took up the air in their lives. Which led her to spend money in order to feel better in the short term, though it made things worse with her husband overall.

"Maybe we *should* go somewhere," she said to him on a day when he'd called in sick. He hadn't sold any desk doodles in weeks, hadn't even said the words desk doodle in the house, and if he didn't snap out of it soon, he would lose his job.

As for Mike Schmidt, he had gone on his trip and come back with photos and stories. He had tried oxblood, against the advice of guidebooks and his physician, but he was fine afterwards. Eventually, as time wore on, Mike Schmidt went back to being his old self. He didn't talk about Mongolia or Genghis Khan and he was like he'd never had the DNA test in the first place. He became Mike Schmidt again, and Jacobs felt the man had betrayed himself. How could he learn something so significant and forget so easily? How could he choose to live a lie after he'd been shown the truth?

"Look," Jessica said, bringing John the laptop in bed. He sat up as she paged through the online brochure for an Alaskan cruise. "I think we can afford it," she said. "We should go."

But Jacobs was irritated by her use of the word *we.* She was the one who balanced the checkbook every month, but he was the one who worked for what they had, and besides, this was *his* journey, *his* ennui. He was mistaken when he had thought she might provide him with progeny, and he needed to find his own place on Earth, to escape the plastic and plenty, and to find his way back to a simple life. He would confront hostile elements and live or die—but he would never again question his purpose or his worth. He would be one with his environs. And he would win. The real John Jacobs was up north somewhere, and he was going to have to go up there, alone, to find himself.

"I want a divorce," he said, finally.

Jessica was as shocked as when he ate raw bacon. She walked away from their bedroom and left him with the laptop. She felt the shame of having said the exact thing to her mother on the phone countless times, and she wondered if he'd been listening. She blamed the outburst on his sour mood, and decided he would come around. Who did he think would want him? Not like this. He was losing it. He wouldn't want to go away if she lost that last thirty pounds. Or if she went with him on this trip, she could talk him into somewhere better. She wanted a night of Cajun dancing, a spa vacation in the Southwest, or an Amtrak ride across Montana. On a trip like that they could work out their differences. And it would be a step in the direction of the John Jacobs who had rented a tux to ballroom dance. Her all-time favorite trip would be to the Taj Mahal, while her *realistic* all-time favorite would be to the Empire State Building, though she didn't expect miracles.

He wanted a divorce? *He* was lucky *she* wasn't divorcing *him*.

Online, in bed, Jacobs came across a website he hadn't seen before, which was always a delight, because he had done all the Eskimo searches and had pored over the pages again and again. But on the PETA site he found an e-mail protest for an upcoming Inuit whale hunt. You could add your name to the list to ask the Inuit not to senselessly pursue the slaughter of as many as sixty of the few remaining bowhead whales. But the Eskimo had tribal rights, and once a year they were allowed to hunt, using centuries-old methods. Despite PETA's complaint, Jacobs knew the hunt was for the continuation of his culture. He knew instinctively that one whale would feed several families for months. He imagined chewing the raw meat and using the whale oil for light and for heat. His mood improved immediately, and he called to his wife as he read on.

"Look," he said, oblivious to her resentment because he'd threatened their marriage, "the Inuit are allowed to hunt whale."

"I'm supposed to care?" she muttered to herself.

"*I* want to hunt a whale. It's my right."

She stared at the lanky pale man who had been her husband for over a decade. People thought she settled when she married him, but he at least held more promise then. All her old ballroom dancing friends thought so. They called him light on his feet. They said he cut a nice figure. Now she was married to a desk doodle salesman and he was losing his mind. Ironically, the most exciting thing to ever happen to him was that he learned he might have Inuit blood—and it was tearing them apart. He was eccentric and she'd loved him anyway. Now she doubted their future.

"You think *you're* going to hunt a whale?"

"*This* is why I'm here," he said, pointing at the laptop's screen. "*This* is what I was meant to do."

She shook her head and walked away. She said, "I may not be here when you get back," but they both knew that wouldn't be true. She would take him back. Despite everything, she could hardly wait to take him back.

Chapter 2

The new desk doodle was mazeless. A stealthier goo escaped from a broader spout in a continuous stream that fell without impediment and collected at the bottom in a dancing snake, like squeezing a tube of toothpaste onto the floor. The dyed water was more diluted, the goo cheaper, and worst of all, there was no descending spiral staircase and no liquid beads. How was he supposed to sell that thing? Didn't they know he would be asked what it *did*? "It's fun to look at," he'd always said, and though there had been changes before, Jacobs had never been so let down as when the new desk doodle was brought in for a demonstration.

Things were changing around the office, with everyone using hand sanitizer, and maybe it was time for Jacobs to go.

At home, he surfed between The Discovery Channel and National Geographic looking for Arctic nature shows.

"Check the schedule," Jessica said.

"There's nothing on," John said. "There's never anything on."

"I want to watch *Scrubs*."

"I hate that show."

"You didn't used to hate it," Jessica said.

"I did. I just never said anything."

"What's wrong with *Scrubs*?" she said. "I think it's funny. It's original."

"It's smug."

"At least it's a show," Jessica said. "You keep flipping around."

"There's nothing on," John complained. "There's never anything on."

Jacobs was more single-minded, but also forgetful. A few days later he forgot to take his cell phone and Jessica answered an automated call to confirm John's flight reservations. He'd booked a first-class flight to Anchorage and Jessica boiled. She understood his desire to get away— but he had made plans to go without her, and he was being extravagant. She called the airline. She was armed with the credit card number, and if she cancelled within 24 hours they wouldn't be charged.

"I nixed your trip," Jessica said when he came home. "When were you planning on telling me?"

Jacobs was surprised. But when he realized what she was saying, his face became a mask, his fierceness suddenly on display. Jessica remembered his past-life experiences had been mostly caveman and she was afraid of her husband for maybe the first time. John didn't look at her like he loved her, or like he even knew her. But Jessica stood up to him and she let him know.

"If you go, we have to plan. We have to make room in the budget."

"It's my money."

"It's *our* money. We're married. That's our agreement."

"I'm going."

"If you take a trip," she said, "I get one too. And we have to budget."

"You're making things difficult."

"We've got joint accounts," Jessica said. "I can take the money same as you. I'll do it to protect myself. I can make things a whole lot more difficult."

"I need to walk," Jacobs said. "I need air."

And Jacobs left. He stood for a moment in front of his Pontiac Sunfire that was still cooling after his drive home from work. There were heat waves shimmering over the hood and the car gave off the smell of gas and hot plastic. He hardly recognized the hulking foreign object at rest on the strip of warm blacktop, a car he'd known so well, but an artificial beast in an artificial habitat. If Jacobs had a gun or a spear he might have tried to slay it. Instead he got in and drove away.

In the weeks since Jacobs had gotten the DNA test, Jessica had confided in Jodi Jorgenson. They were never good friends but Jodi had witnessed John's strange behavior, and so she seemed the logical person for Jessica to talk to.

"You've got our sympathies," Jodi said. "You know that, don't you, honey?"

And while they were still on the phone, Jacobs came home and parked in the drive. Jodi watched him through her dining room window and she narrated his movements to Jessica.

"He's getting a ladder," she said. "He's got cans of paint. He's putting the ladder against the side of the house. You better get out there, honey."

So Jessica hung up the phone and John was doing just as Jodi had said. By the time she'd gotten her shoes on and had gone outside, her husband was going over the brick

façade of their subdivision-style house with a roller and
white paint.

"What the hell are you doing?" she asked, though it was
obvious.

"If you aren't going to let me go," he said, "then I need to
feel comfortable here. I'm making the place livable."

"I live here too," she said. "This is something we should
talk about. Besides, it's getting dark and you've got work in
the morning. How much could you possibly hope to get
done?"

But she saw talking to him was pointless. He continued
to work as if he didn't hear her and he made good progress,
with a portion of their house turned white in no time.

"OK," she said, finally.

"OK, what?"

"You can go. Just book a cheaper flight. And write to the
tribe. Let them know you're coming. Maybe you can stay
with someone."

"You mean it?" John said, but he continued painting.

"You leave me no choice."

"I'll write them," he said, nodding once. "It's time for me
to introduce myself."

At work Jacobs found the website of a tribal council in
Alaska but decided an e-mail introduction from his work
address would get mistaken as spam. So he went down
into the basement of the UniqCorps offices, where one of
the janitors opened a storage room and he took out a
typewriter. It was an IBM Selectric, a very nice machine,
still functioning, though the ink had dried and he had to

find a box of replacement ribbons. The thing was cumbersome and heavy, but he carried it onto the elevator and up to his cubicle.

"Feeling nostalgic?" someone said to him in the elevator, and all Jacobs could think to say was "Yes."

The typewriter clattered off a letter to the tribal council. He attracted attention to himself on the floor, but Eskimos wouldn't be impressed by laser printing, and his handwriting was too loose and flow-y to be taken seriously. The IBM stamped his intention over the plain white surface of paper like footprints in an expanse of snow. Until he made a typo and began again. He repeated the letter, and it got better each time. Then he stopped, took the bottle of Wite-Out, and proceeded to Wite-Out rows of sentences. He stared into the drying white mass that reminded him of snow, so much Wite-Out the IBM's letter golfball became smudged with white glops when he typed again.

Jacobs knew what he wanted to say, but not how to get started. His tribe might not see things from his point of view. They might reject him. He was embarrassed because he couldn't talk to his people in his own tongue, and he knew nothing of them except what he'd seen on the nature shows. He'd been robbed of his culture and his language. By the end of the day, the carpet around his desk was crowded with paper wads and he hadn't made or answered a single call. But before he went home, and before the typewriter ribbon ran out, he'd written a letter he was confident he could send, and that they couldn't deny.

Brothers:
Enclosed is a DNA test that proves my identity as one of our people. Unfortunately, I was born and raised a white man and that's all I have known my entire life. I have also known

an unspoken longing, a feeling that my surroundings weren't real, and the notion that something very important had been taken from me. I'm as oppressed and kept down as our people were historically, but I have discovered my secret identity, and my day of liberation has come.

I intend to meet with you in person, and to join the whale hunt. While I have not, as yet, learned the significance of the whale hunt for our people, for me it will represent the end of the lie that I have lived and a rejection of the plastic culture that has stood as a cheap substitute for our centuries-old traditions and our language.

I am a man of humble means, but I will do anything I can to prepare appropriately. If there are camping supplies you might recommend, we have an REI where a knowledgeable staff will equip me. I have done Internet research, and there are several companies making high-quality products for subzero temperatures. Some of the people who work at REI have been ice climbing. That's considered a sport now, and they can give me pointers. I was thinking I would need a reliable sleeping bag, a heavy winter coat, and some top-notch boots. They make heated socks that you put batteries in, and I've seen thermal insulate that is lightweight and made of the same materials astronauts use.

In addition, if there are any products you have had difficulty obtaining that you would like me to bring, I would be more than happy to arrive with a care package. For example, I have a neighbor with cousins in Europe, and he tells me they can't get peanut butter. Every few years when he visits he takes a couple of jars, and they've become fond of the stuff. So if there's anything you would like me to pack: coffee, breakfast cereal, condoms, or anything, please don't hesitate to ask.

As for my accommodations, I hope you can put me up somewhere. If our people are living on a reservation, I will apply for my own habitation. However, I expect this will take time, and I think I would really enjoy sleeping in an igloo. If you know of any families that might put me up, I am polite, generally quiet, and I can pull my weight. I would keep to my own corner of the igloo.

If there are any good books or documentaries that you can recommend that would help me learn about our culture, I would appreciate a list of titles, and I will read them studiously and with pride. Although I am ignorant of our language, Spanish was my best subject in high school, so I feel I could learn quickly. Likewise, if there is an Eskimo-Aleut to English-language dictionary that you could recommend, I will be sure to obtain a copy before I arrive.

I am booking a flight for the first week in April, which should be two weeks before the whales run. I look forward to meeting my fellow Inuit, making preparations, and joining you in this festive time.

Your lost cousin,
John Jacobs

Jacobs hoped a response from the tribe would arrive in time to ease his mind. He planned on going whether the reply came or not. He had given them his home phone number, his work number, and his e-mail address. He imagined them writing back in the same fashion, using an obsolete typewriter, and the most difficult thing would be for him to go through the motions at the office while he waited. He had put in for vacation time, but he thought of his trip as one-way—leaving for good—because he didn't see how he could come back once he'd been whaling. He couldn't turn back into his old self as Mike Schmidt had done. He didn't want to be like Mike Schmidt, or like his old self, or like anyone that he knew. He wanted to be his real and better self, the noble Eskimo hunter.

He was careful not to talk to anyone about his trip, and when coworkers hinted Jacobs had been acting strange, he said, simply, "Headaches. From the fluorescent lights. And the computer screens."

Mike Schmidt had quickly cured himself of his Mongolian obsession by going there, but the people in the office wouldn't let him forget. They had started calling Mike "The Mighty Khan," and it had stuck and made him miserable. Although Jacobs despised the thought of going back to whom he'd been, or even who he was now, he at least wanted that option. More than anything he didn't want to be stuck in his job forever. But no one noticed him at least, and that was a luxury he wanted to be able to fall back into. If they started calling him Nanook at work he didn't know how he would cope. He had kept everything about his newfound identity secret, especially from Mike Schmidt, who longed for an ally.

An e-mail was waiting for Jacobs a few days later when he arrived at work in the morning. He was surprised to see it but also delighted, because an e-mail meant he could reply immediately:

Dear Mr. Jacobs:
In the same way that the US government and Greenpeace cannot deny us our culture, we cannot deny you yours. The news of your coming brings us trepidation, however. Please don't take this the wrong way, but also, please don't come.

We are a solitary and stoic people. There are no families who will take you in. We would have an obligation to treat you as an orphan and to ensure your survival, but we recommend against joining the whale hunt. It is an endeavor that is extremely dangerous, our boats are small, and there are limited seats. Men will take their sons only after years of preparation. As you aren't anyone's son, and you don't have any experience, no one would want you in their umiaq. You would be a liability and a deadweight. We wish you well as an Inuk, but if you are feeling suicidal please don't persist in taking any of us with you.

As for books, I recommend *Moby-Dick* by one Herman Melville, because you are trying to live some kind of fiction. All cultural studies, language dictionaries, and documentaries take the dominant white viewpoint. They see us as a subject, not a people, and we cannot recommend that you participate in that kind of racist objectification of the Inuit. Our ways aren't so much learned as lived. Our language isn't easily translated. And our people will always see you as a foreigner. It's nothing personal, Mr. Jacobs; I am only being honest.

Yes, the whale hunt is central to us as a people, and had you not somehow found yourself lost, we would welcome you. We recognize that this is not your fault. Some things aren't easily explained, but you also can't change the way you are. Surely, your life is not as empty as you make it out to be. You have peanut butter and you can shop at REI. You have easy access to coffee and condoms. You can have *anything*. We recommend that you enjoy your white American lifestyle to the fullest, and we would like to make your acquaintance should you choose to visit during the summer season—for a vacation—but please don't persist in your idea of going on the whale hunt.

Sincerely,
Yuq Junnaq, tribal representative and acting chief.

Despite tribal representative Yuq Junnaq's foreboding tone and the suggestion that dangers and distances outweighed soul-searching, what Jacobs got from the e-mail was an affirmation that if he wanted to go on the hunt, they wouldn't be able to stop him. He was being invited as a tourist, which is what ruined Mike Schmidt's odyssey. Jacobs would force himself on them and they couldn't deny him. He was an Inuk and he shared tribal rights. They might not like it, but he was one of them and he was going on the hunt.

The trip to REI let Jacobs know that being an Eskimo was going to be expensive. His only comfort was that Jessica had approved the trip. When he drove home down the winding avenue hours after he should have returned from work, he experienced a welling of joy at the way the white brick made their house stand out. He had painted the house every night until he finished, and applied a second coat because he wanted it thick. He supposed he should have called to tell Jessica he would be home late, but he didn't expect to be shopping into the evening, the store open until nine, and the mountain man salesman kept recommending products. The salesman was skinny, in his forties, but with long gray hair in a ponytail and a gray beard, his face weathered, and with nicks and scars on his nimble hands. He laced boots without looking, and his aqua-blue eyes were hypnotic. He never broke eye contact as more items were piled onto Jacobs's shopping cart. Jacobs was pleased to learn that they sold parkas, and he bought one with a fake-fur fringe around the beveled hood that he imagined winnowing in the frozen air.

He tried on sunglasses and was drawn to the most expensive pair, thick mirrored lenses like aviator goggles with leather guards that covered the eye sockets and kept out harsh winds. Jacobs looked in a mirror, and the reflected images of himself in the lens mirrors disappeared like long tunnels that bored through him and reached back.

"Excellent choice," the mountain man said. The sunglasses cost as much as the boots, parka, and battery-heated socks combined.

"The snow can be bright," Jacobs said.

"Snow blindness," the mountain man agreed.

Later Jacobs was haunted by something the mountain man salesman had said.

"How do I keep warm," Jacobs had asked, his face framed by the fake-fur parka hood and wearing the priceless snow goggles, "if I get wet?"

"Don't get wet," the man had said, as if it were that easy.

"But supposing I *do* get wet."

"Don't get wet."

Jacobs went ahead and bought all the things they'd picked out together: cases of Power Bars, wool undergarments, mini snowshoes, steel-toed Duratrack waterproof but breathable lambskin-lined Gore-Tex boots, a water filter and iodine tabs, a sleeping bag, a pup tent, a backpack. Jacobs knew he needed everything but felt what he really wanted was an Inuk salesman—someone who knew what to do when you got wet. Someone who'd survived. *Hypothermia, frostbite, dehydration, exhaustion.* There were things Jacobs needed to know. He wished he'd had an Inuk raise him. He was never even a Boy Scout. He'd been in a canoe, that was easy, but he'd also gotten wet. And even in the summer he felt miserable once his clothes were damp. *Don't get wet.*

At home Jessica was upset. They'd gotten a letter from the neighborhood association over his painting the house. It was something they weren't allowed to do. They'd signed a contract to that effect when they bought the place, and the neighbors had noticed. The president of the neighborhood association stopped by that afternoon and hand-delivered the letter so he could explain. The neighbors wanted Jacobs to restore his home to the original naked brick façade, and they had the law on their side. If he didn't make the changes himself, he was subject to a fine equal to the amount of the cost of sandblasting. The neighborhood association would take care of it, and they could do so without his consent. At the end of the letter, the president of the neighborhood association had said, "This can get very ugly. And you will lose. So please don't fight us."

"Wow," John said.

"He was actually pretty nice," Jessica said. "People had been calling, so he had to do something."

Jacobs thought the language in the letter was a lot like what the tribal representative had used in his e-mail, though this letter gave him a different feeling. He was emboldened by his rejection from the Inuit, and brought low by the letter from the neighborhood association.

"We have a neighborhood association?" John said.

"We pay dues," Jessica said. "Nobody wants to live next to an igloo."

"We can paint our own house."

"We can paint the trim, not the brick," she said. "There are approved renovations and a list of acceptable colors. It's all on the second page of the letter."

"We're moving," John said. "They can sandblast when we're gone."

"They can keep us from selling."

"I won't stay."

"What did you get?" Jessica said, and she peeked into his shopping bags.

"Supplies," he said. "But this cements it." He shook the letter. "I'm not coming back."

"You can't just leave," Jessica said, and she held up his new boots by their laces.

"When I get a place, I'll send for you."

"You want us to live on a reservation? In Alaska? Do they even have reservations? Are you insane?"

"We don't have to live like this. We can be with my people."

"Grow up, John," she said. "This is where we live. This is *how* we live. Oaken Glens is not a bad place. It suits us. We looked at a lot of places before we bought this house, remember? We get what we need here."

"I'm going whaling," he said. "You said I could go."

"Then buy life insurance," she said. "And *come back*."

There was a time in Jacobs's life when things were easy. He floated through school, he thought of job interviews as "fun," and when he landed one that paid well he settled into the ease of selling. There were enough bonus incentives from the desk doodles that Jessica didn't have to work. He was proud of this. For a man in the twenty-first century to be able to support his wife was rare. They *did* live comfortably. And they were happy until he questioned the foundation and asked about his origins. Just a few years ago he'd have left the notion alone. But he'd been shown how the answers were available. And he'd sent off for his ancestry on a whim, without realizing he might be unprepared for the truth.

Don't get wet.

He wouldn't worry about the house. They could punish him, but that would take time. He was going north, to be a warrior. He would deal with them later, and they would respect him. Though he also recognized he might need help. Like an immigration lawyer. Or a painter who knew a shade that looked enough like brick they'd leave him alone. In the meantime he could stall the neighborhood association. He would tell them what they wanted to hear, and they would believe him. He had to prepare for the hunt and there was too much to do. He had to research and get in better shape.

Yuq's e-mail got him thinking about bringing someone, not Jessica but a partner who would be of use to him. Yuq told Jacobs not to join the hunt, but he also said fathers could bring sons. So not only could they not keep him from whaling, but he could also bring someone. He might find an interpreter who would want to go, or an expert who had studied the Inuit ways and Eskimo dialects. Someone to help him communicate or at least tell him what to expect. Jacobs would become a man in the tradition of his people. He would venture back to his homeland, to a world with meaning. He would live where a day's work mattered. He'd gone into debt to study art history at the state college, and he'd wasted it selling desk doodles. He'd paid back his student loans bit by bit, but now he was waking up. There was a greater debt. An ongoing deficit. He was going to opt out.

Jacobs's life was just beginning.

As he went through the camping supplies Jacobs knew he'd bought more than he could carry. He added up the stock of Power Bars and there weren't enough to keep him fed. There was limited space in the backpack and he needed water too. Would there be snow dogs, he wondered? What would be provided for him and what wouldn't? Yuq's e-mail said they would be obligated to him as an orphan, but he had no idea what that meant. If they could kill a whale and carry it back, he knew they would also have room for him and a friend. He needed a partner.

He decided to halve what he'd bought the day before—so he loaded up the Sunfire and brought along his receipt. At REI he located the same salesman, the mountain man, and this time he was more specific about where he was going and why.

"You sold me too much," Jacobs said.

"I can help you scale down."

"Do you want to go?" Jacobs said. "I'm allowed to bring someone."

"What's the tour?"

"Alaska. To kill a whale."

"Killer whales?" the mountain man salesman said. "I've been whale watching. They take you in a boat. You'll love it. Unfortunately, you won't need all this. Just dress warm."

"*We* kill the whale. With harpoons. I'm Inuit."

"In little boats?" the salesman said. "Paddling in canoes?"

"I think so."

"And you thought *I* might want to go?"

"Chance of a lifetime."

"No fucking way," the man said, and he walked away. He went into the stockroom with the boxes of boots, and he didn't come back.

Jacobs nearly followed him but he was unsettled by the mountain man's reaction. Then he realized that even an outdoorsman wouldn't have, in a million years, agreed to do what Jacobs longed for. He saw now that the whale hunt was some kind of impossible fantasy he shouldn't pursue. But he couldn't help himself. He needed to kill a whale. He saw the rationality of the mountain man salesman's reaction—he understood—but he also couldn't turn back. He needed to prove himself to himself, to his wife, to his unborn children, to the planet, to the Great Spirit, and to the ages. He was going whaling, and he would come back successful or he would die. He was sure of this now and he also knew, despite his lack of experience, he had something the mountain man salesman could only pretend to. His sinews tightened, his thoughts focused, his vision was clear. Jacobs was already a man and already on the path.

He left half of his supplies in a heap inside the store and he walked out with the rest balled up in his arms. He knew what was essential now. And he walked back to his car self-assured. Yuq would respect his request to go on the hunt and the damned neighborhood association would leave him alone over the color of his house. Jessica was lucky to be partnered with him and their future children would rise like stars.

Jacobs didn't need an interpreter. He didn't need help. He needed a chronicler, a storyteller, like a TV reporter or a cameraman, someone to document what he was about to do. Yuq hadn't recommended any books or videos about Inuit whaling and Jacobs understood this was because there weren't any. He'd been doing his library research and he'd have surely come across one by now. He would be the narrator of his own documentary, in English, and his movie would play on the nature channels for the masses to marvel at. He would be an Inuk hero. He would bag a whale, legally, and the hunt would be captured on film. The mountain man salesman was a faker, an actor. He cultivated the look to sell camping products the same way Jacobs stockpiled sayings to sell desk doodles. Jacobs exposed him when he suggested the salesman go along, a mistake he wouldn't repeat. Jacobs needed a companion with nuts. And someone who owned a good camera.

On his way home, Jacobs decided he might bring along his own video camera, but he'd already gone way over budget. He knew there were twenty-four-hour pawnshops across the river and he went looking for a bargain. He parked in a lot in a part of town he almost never found himself in. Under streetlights, with the sound of sirens near, a black kid approached Jacobs's car and stopped to circle and get a look at the items inside. Jacobs wasn't racist, but the kid loitered outside the pawnshop and he was intimidating.

There were no other cars in the lot, but the small building was lit up and well-fortified. Payday loans and pawn loans were advertised in neon, with bars over the windows.

"Going camping?" the kid said.

"Something like that," Jacobs said. He hated this feeling of otherness, this gulf that was between them. He didn't have anything against blacks, though he had to admit he was uncomfortable around them. There were a few who worked at UniqCorps, a black man and two black women that he knew of. When he rode the elevator with them he didn't know what to say, especially if they were alone, though he always thought he should say something, no matter how trivial. Mostly, Jacobs felt blacks weren't interested in talking to him.

"They don't sell this shit here," the kid said. "They won't give you nothing."

"I need a video camera."

"*I* can get you a video camera."

"You sell stuff?" Jacobs asked.

"Maybe."

"They don't care?"

"Why you complaining? It's all the same."

"I'll decide for myself," Jacobs said. He locked his Sunfire and walked toward the entrance of what was one of the only businesses on the street. There were boarded-up and abandoned buildings and homeless bodies shuffling down the sidewalks. In another era, and if he were racist, he might have called them "spooks." The word came to him across time and against his better sensibilities. He supposed he might label them crackheads, or waifs. They wandered in the dark, at a distance, some keeping out of sight, but he was aware of them, his survival sense on alert. He watched their movement in his peripheral vision, and he also knew someone was behind him. A week ago he would have been afraid. Now he knew that if someone came at him, he'd stand up and fight, even if confronted by a black guy.

"I wouldn't leave all that in your car," the kid said.

Jacobs turned around, and though he knew there was truth in what the kid had said, the kid was also the most likely thief.

"I'll watch it for twenty bucks," he added.

Jacobs went back to his car and stood near the driver's door, unsure of what to do. He didn't need to buy a camera tonight, but he was intrigued by this black kid. He wanted to hear what he might say and see what kind of camera he might offer.

Before long a large man with a silver pistol came out of the shop and pointed it. *This* is why people go to Best Buy, Jacobs thought.

"Get the fuck out of here," the man shouted. "How many times I got to say it?"

The man from the pawnshop was the one Jacobs had felt watching him from behind, and he realized he had been safe all along, because this man was armed and he wanted to do business. But the black kid stood up to him. He poked a finger into the tall man's chest and he even twirled his finger around one of the proprietor's gold chains.

"I'm just walking home," he said. "I told you I live around here. People *do* live here, you know. This guy asked me questions, so I told him."

"He bothering you?" the man asked, and he took a step back, to keep the kid from grabbing at his gold.

"I was just leaving," Jacobs said. "He didn't bother me."

Jacobs was impressed with himself for not being afraid, and he was also impressed with the kid for standing up to the money bear with the gun.

"You want a ride?" Jacobs said.

"Yeah, we can ride."

"You steal my business," the man said, "and I will fucking kill you." He punctuated his anger with short jabs of his gun.

When Jacobs unlocked his car, the kid reached in and unlocked the backseat where he climbed in so he could rummage through the camping supplies.

"This is nice shit. You Ranger Rick or something?"

"I'm Eskimo. I'm going to Alaska."

As they rode away from the All-Nite Pawnshop, Jacobs took in the inner-city scene of stray paper wrappers and so much concrete. He imagined that when the ancients discovered cement it must have seemed wondrous. Liquid stone could be poured and shelters would harden against the elements. Now it was too easy a way to cover the earth.

There was desperation and desolation on this side of town. Jacobs tried to imagine what life was like for this hustler growing up, but he supposed the kid had never known anything else.

"Turn here," the kid said. "There ain't no such thing as Eskimos. That's cartoon shit. Like Smurfs."

"There are Eskimos. I am one."

"Pull up here and wait. I'll come down with the camera. It's real nice. I had it three years now."

"It's *your* camera?"

"Of course it's my camera. You think I stole it? I'm going to be the next Spike Lee."

"You know how to use it?"

"Point and shoot."

"How old are you?"

"You buy the camera, you do what you want. But that's on you and I ain't involved."

"I need someone to shoot for me. You want to go to Alaska?"

"You're making a film?"

"I'll get you gear. I'll get you a plane ticket. And I'll pay you. Are you eighteen?"

"Almost."

"Are you in school?"

"The alternative school. I don't really have to go. It's whether I pass the GED or not."

"What do your tattoos mean?"

"Kid's stuff," he said. "Gang shit. I don't do it much anymore."

"You got any felonies?"

"You're kind of rude."

"This is a job interview. Do you?"

"I'm a minor."

"You ever killed anybody?"

"Do you watch the news?"

"Of course," Jacobs said.

"Do I look familiar?"

"Kind of."

"If you're cool with me," the kid said, "I'm cool with you."

"So you'll go?" Jacobs said. "You'll be my guy?"

"Why the hell not?"

"What's your name?"

"Call me Q."

Back in the car, Q showed Jacobs the camera and said, "I guess you ain't buying, if you want me to go. But you got to talk to my mama. She says niggaz don't go camping. She thinks I'm bullshitting. *You* got to talk her into it."

Jacobs hesitated after he locked up his Sunfire on the street in front of Q's mama's house.

"Ain't nobody going to steal your shit," Q said.

Jacobs stopped in his tracks.

"I told you," Q said. "Pawnshops around here don't sell to Boy Scouts. And folks don't steal what won't sell."

"You wanted twenty bucks," Jacobs said.

"For real," Q said. "I get by."

Inside Q's mama's house a Pomeranian rushed forward with a torrent of barking, and Q pointed the camera to begin filming.

"See mama," he said. "I told you I met a white dude."

"Nice to meet you, mister," Q's mama said, and she extended her hand for a greeting.

Jacobs shook her hand, and everyone spoke over the barking dog.

"How did you meet?" she asked.

Q and Jacobs looked at each other, and Jacobs knew instinctively that the future of their partnership was going to consist of lies. "I took out an ad in the paper. I need a cameraman. If you'll let him go, that is."

"He don't read the paper."

"I do sometimes."

"I've never seen you with one."

"I didn't say I *paid* for it. I read when I'm out. I do like this... 'You through with that?' Or... 'Can I read your sports page?' I got manners."

"Why you want to film a camping trip?" Q's mama asked. "Nothing ever happens on one. You'd do better around here. Go on down to the church, or that city park. You walk around here; you'll find out."

"It's not really camping," Jacobs said. "We're going to Alaska."

"He don't got no passport," Q's mama said. "And we ain't got that kind of money."

"I'm taking him. I need an assistant."

"Not an *assistant*," Q said. "I'm your *director*. He's my *producer*, Mama."

"Don't you trust that boy," she said. "He'll quit on you."

"There's nowhere he could go," Jacobs said. "It's all snow."

Q's mama looked over at Q, then back at Jacobs. "He *is* good with a camera."

"I *told* you," Q said.

"You'll let him go?" Jacobs asked.

"You filming penguins?" Q's mama said.

"Eskimos," Jacobs said, and Q's mama smiled.

"Oh, I love them. I knew it had to be that."

"They rub noses and shit?" Q asked.

"We'll find out."

"That's how young people *should* be," Q's mama said.

"I *tried* that," Q said. "Still wound up the same place."

"You should have never sold your jacket," Q's mama said.

"He'll need all new stuff," Jacobs said.

"Why'd you pick him?" Q's mama wanted to know.

"He's got guts," Jacobs said. "He's quick on his feet."

"See, Mama, people *like* me."

"Give me your number," Q's mama said. "Or some way I can reach you."

"We'll be out of range," Jacobs said. "But we'll call when we can. And I can leave my wife's number."

"Bring me back something," Q's mama said.

"We ain't leaving tonight," Q said.

"Like a little painting or something I can hang on my wall. You know how I like penguins."

Once they were back outside, Q asked Jacobs, "So who told you you were an Eskimo?"

"It's in my DNA. I paid for one of those tests."

"You got scammed. You ever *seen* an Eskimo?"

"Not everyone who's black looks black," Jacobs countered.

"They look a little black," Q said.

"If we go out there," Jacobs said, "I'm telling people you're my son. You'll have to act Eskimo."

"Tell them I'm your *director*."

"It's for the hunt," Jacobs said. "You think a black guy can just get in a boat and go kill a whale?"

"They might actually believe there's Eskimo in me," Q said. "But you're about as white as they come. No offense."

"I'm not ashamed of being white," Jacobs said. "At least I wasn't. But I'm not white. Honestly. Truthfully. I'm Inuit."

"According to a blood test?"

"A spit test," Jacobs said, and Q laughed. "DNA is serious. You think I'm joking."

When Jacobs got home, Jessica handed him another letter. This one was from a North Alaskan tribe and was postmarked from Fairbanks. She was anxious for him to open it. The letter was typed on parchment, and this alone gave Jacobs an uplifted feeling. A typed letter was what he'd expected when he began the correspondence, and he was sure it had come from a like-minded Eskimo, maybe even a cousin:

Dear Mr. John Jacobs:

My son has informed me you are joining us this whaling season. While he may have been discouraging, please know that Yuq's isn't the only crew. As our most experienced whaler and tribal chief, I would be pleased to have you accompany me on this season's hunt. I expect, as an Inuk, you have a hardy constitution. I have been on fifty-seven successful hunts and have also witnessed the death of loved ones. We may be on the ice six weeks. We will spend hours at sea rowing in harsh conditions, without eating and without sleep. We look forward to this throughout the year and throughout our lives. It fills me with joy to know our dreams are also yours.

My son will no longer whale with me, and all my past crew teams have broken up. No matter, you and I are Inuk, and we could do it if even alone. Or with a boy of thirteen or so. You should bring one if you have children, maybe as young as ten or eleven. A kid comes in handy.

Arrive early so we can fit you. There's sealskin boots and fur coats for your use, but the women will need to alter them. Same for the kid. Bring two kids if you have them. If they can row, they can go. Except, no girls. I'm not superstitious, nor do I dislike girls. But I don't want any crying.

Yuq showed me your letter and he was laughing. He was fucking with you about the dictionary. It should be obvious to you by now that we speak English. The old ways have nearly vanished. This is one reason the whale hunt is so important. It connects us with our ancestors, the spirit winds who howl and speak to us in signs, and who sometimes take animal form. We are grateful to them and glad that you will be joining us in our endeavor. We need the whale, not just to remember who we are, but because everything in Point Halcyon is fucking expensive.

Foodstuffs would be appreciated, but we don't have the usual problems with spoilage, so get creative. Peanut butter is all right, though you shouldn't hesitate to try out your more refined tastes on us. I'm especially fond of chocolate.

And we need money. There's no bank in town but we have a store where you can cash traveler's checks. There aren't jobs, so I took an advance on my credit card as a down payment for this year's hunt. I'm not trying to make you feel guilty, just letting you know where things stand.

Also, please forward contact information. Someone we can call should you end up in the water, returning, like all of God's creatures, to the sea.

We look forward to your arrival, and I see your joining us as an answer to my prayers. Your coming means I don't have to occupy myself with *Law & Order* reruns, as they'd all hoped.

Don't expect much from Yuq. My son can't wait for me to die. He will deny it, but I see through him.

Your brother in Christ,
Akmaaq Junnaq, Captain and Chief

Jessica watched John from the kitchen table as he finished the letter. She had eaten and the dishwasher was running. She'd kept her hair short since they'd gotten married but also let it get bushy and she was in one of those phases. She got up from the table to heat up his portion of dinner. She leaned against the kitchen counter and watched him read as the carousel in the microwave turned.

"It's from the chief," John said. "He wants me to go."

Jessica embraced her husband. The changes had tested her. She knew the hunt was important and though she had been comfortable in their life together, she was also due for a change. John had rocked her sense of security but his leaving was for the better. They lived a lukewarm existence and had for too long. Their life was ordinary and the things they did, they'd done hundreds of times. There was no effort being exerted and her husband was at least breaking the pattern. There were people they'd known who reached a point in life where they ran marathons or got involved in charity, but John was now on a unique course. She couldn't quite grasp how dangerous things might get for him. She didn't really want to know. Like an army wife, she was better off numb. Jessica needed someone like John to prod her. She needed advice, companionship, and support. She was frightened by his leaving but felt a stirring inside at his becoming a man.

Chapter 3

At work Jacobs gave up trying to sell the new desk doodle and he surfed the Internet. He looked up the satellite image of Point Halcyon at Google Maps, a horn of black rock that jutted out into the icy sea at the top of the world, and he scrolled around the bumpy alien landscape. There were large faded-green, sulfurous-yellow, and coal-black lakes, the photo taken in spring or summer. Point Halcyon itself seemed to hang out over the edge of the world, the small landmass in the satellite image surrounded by an ocean of floating ice.

Because of the new desk doodle, everyone's sales were down, so for the time being Jacobs's inactivity went unnoticed, and since he didn't have six weeks of vacation time, he would have to resign soon anyway. He looked up weather reports and found a webcam with a live shot of what was supposed to be Mount McKinley from downtown Anchorage. He came back to the webcam every day but the view was always hazy, so he never saw the mountain, just wide city streets, dated office buildings, and a giant satellite dish. The Google Maps view of Anchorage was of houses in the characteristic curling clusters of subdivisions, complete with carefully placed shrubs and trees. Jacobs was glad he would travel beyond Anchorage, because he and Jessica could plop their home there and have the same life, except that things cost more and it got extremely cold.

The next day, Jacobs couldn't stand the thought of sitting at his work computer, so he called in sick. Jessica got up and left while he was still in bed and he wandered from room to room picking up useless object after useless object and taking it to the kitchen to throw away. Jessica had gone from recycling to composting, which made throwing anything in the trash complicated. He knew they took aluminum, and some plastics, but then what about a plastic screw-top lid, or a straw? What about tin? There were four trash containers in the kitchen and a metal bucket for food scraps, but only vegetable scraps. Meat went in the trash-trash, though sometimes he'd seen her send it down the sink disposal. He tried to remember to turn out the lights when he left a room, but his mind was occupied, and he couldn't see their contribution as important. There were probably two hundred houses in Oaken Glens, and theirs was the only one with a rotting mound of vegetable scraps in the backyard.

Jessica came home with a new hairstyle and a new pair of designer glasses. Her hair was shorter and dyed a glossy black, the rims of the glasses wide and black to match. He hoped she wouldn't buy ridiculous retro clothes to go with the new hair, and he was glad he wouldn't be around when her mousy roots grew in. Jessica came in through the door from the garage while John stood in the kitchen holding a crushed can of organic cane syrup pomegranate soda, a used paper napkin, a wadded bag of Doritos, and the bone from a chicken leg.

"I can never remember," he said, and he lifted the lid of each container.

"I numbered them for you," she said. She took the refuse and threw each in its place before he comprehended the distribution. Then she opened a lid and lifted out one of the useless objects.

She held the useless object as evidence and said, "This is my Turkish tea pot."

"Did I get it in the right one?"

"No," she said, but the brass gourd looked more worthless than ever. "This is mine. We're keeping it."

"You've never used it," he said.

"It's decorative. It's Turkish."

He knew he should have said something about her hair, that he liked it—no, that he *loved* it—but that moment had passed.

"Aren't you supposed to be at work?" she said.

"I'm staying home."

"You're going to get fired."

"I'm quitting."

"You *can't* quit."

"You said I could go. I have to go."

"We need money," she said.

"We can cancel cable."

"We need *income*," she said.

"You said I could do this," he said, and he went out the door into the garage. Jessica's car, her red Jetta, was always parked there while his car was parked in the drive. He hit the button for the garage door opener and ducked outside to get away from anything that reminded him of her. In the backyard, the grass was tall and the shrubs that bordered their property had grown shapeless and wild.

He went back to the garage and took out a pair of hedge
clippers, but the work was slow, so he retrieved the
hacksaw and cut branches at the base of one of the bushes.
He stood away and saw that while he'd saved time, the
bush was ransacked. The only solution was to finish the job
and cut off all the branches. After his second bush, he
dragged the branches to the front of the house where the
street crew would pick them up, and where Jodi Jorgenson
saw what he was doing, so she made a phone call to Jessica,
who came storming out to confront her husband.

"Have you lost your mind?"

"They'll grow back," he said. He walked to the backyard,
picked up the saw, and knelt in front of the next bush. He'd
worked up a sweat.

Jessica stood behind him and asked him to stop. She
knelt beside him in the grass and said, "Please, don't go.
I'm begging you. You can have anything you want. We'll
move. I'll go off the pill again. You can find another job. Just
don't go. Not now anyways."

And Jacobs stopped. He set the saw down and sat up. Not
because of anything she'd said but because he'd seen the
bush contained a nest of baby birds. He looked around for
the mother bird and didn't see her. What he did see was his
wife, who he almost didn't recognize with her hair dyed,
and she looked desperate. He listened and heard the baby
birds chirping, and the mother bird answered back from
one of the Jorgenson's sugar maples.

"What are you afraid of?" he said.

"It's because I love you," she said. "Can't you see that?"

But he didn't believe her. She was afraid for herself. He
had threatened her security and her well-being. She might
not see him as a man, but he'd made life easier, and she
understood he may not come back.

He looked at the row of overgrown bushes and decided to stop. He didn't know if the others had any birds' nests. He just knew he couldn't cut this one down and so why continue? He took the tools to the shed and Jessica turned around to see that Jodi Jorgenson was watching. Jessica waved and followed her husband back into the house.

He sat in front of the TV and flipped through the channels.

She wanted to tell him to put on a clean shirt. Instead, she said, "If we cancel cable, we won't get National Geographic."

He said, "There's never anything on."

He'd gone days without bathing. He would turn down the thermostat, and she would turn it up, so the setting went up and down without a word between them. For the first time since she'd known him, John focused on himself. A ballroom dance instructor always knows the next move and she hated not knowing what would happen. She'd heard of the midlife crisis, but this was different, and it was more than a spending binge. He'd always been predictable and what scared her most was that she would be forced to change too. She liked their life together. She knew it wouldn't appear like much, but there were homeless people who didn't have anything, or the underprivileged with their maladies and vices. Jessica and John were very nice people, and they knew nice people. She was proud of the way they lived. She loved their house and their things. She didn't know where John's tantrums might lead, but she didn't want to give up anything.

The next day Jacobs got up early for work and when Jessica awoke, she thought he might still be in the house, because his Sunfire was parked in the drive. But Jacobs walked to work, which meant stretches of highway where there was no sidewalk, with scattered fast-food litter and discarded liquor bottles, even a tire. The morning traffic occasionally veered onto the shoulder and threatened him, only to correct at the last moment and to honk at his boldness. Some drove as if their life depended on it, and there were more honks, as if Jacobs, the lone pedestrian, were the crazy one.

He also walked through a part of downtown where there were halfway houses and vagabonds loitering in front of rundown tenements. In one building a shirtless man leaned out of a third-story bedroom window and shouted at any passerby, "Has anybody got any smokes?"

There was a corner convenience store, so Jacobs popped in, paid an outrageous price for a pack, and he went back out and lit one up with the complimentary matches. He stood on the street and smoked while the man in the window continued to shout, "Has anybody got any smokes?"

Jacobs crossed the street and passed directly under the window where the man shouted, "Got any smokes? Hey *you.*"

Jacobs was doing what he wanted and he wasn't afraid. He felt akin to the seekers of another age. All he lacked was the opportunity.

At work they piped in white noise over the PA. According to a study the white noise promoted better concentration, but Jacobs couldn't shake the impression that the

UniqCorps building was a jetliner cruising at thirty thousand feet. He also thought the white noise sounded like the ventilation system had a leak and the continuous *f-f-f-f-f-f-f-f-f* was an omnipresent reminder of the artificiality of his work, and his life.

At his desk, he flipped through the Rolodex and called the vice president of internal relations at the very large bank that had swallowed the other very large bank.

"I'm wondering about dedication and resolve," Jacobs said.

"What about it," the vice president said.

"What's the formula," Jacobs said, "you know, to make it?"

"Are you mocking me?"

"I want to know."

"I've had two divorces," the vice president said. "Does that frame it?"

"Who divorced whom?"

"One was mine. One was hers."

"Has your order arrived?" Jacobs said. "Was everything satisfactory?"

"I don't know," he said. "You'll have to talk to my assistant. She keeps the spreadsheets."

"I have a spreadsheet?"

"I think you got a line," the vice president said.

"Been a pleasure doing business."

"Likewise," the vice president said, and he added, "Keep doing good work and you'll get there."

When Jacobs got home he heard a faint cry, in a high-pitched and meek nonhuman register. After a moment, he decided the sound came from under his Sunfire. He knelt and saw one of the baby birds mewling and trying to sit up by pinching its beak on the treads of a tire. Jacobs scooped the chick in a cupped hand and walked it over to the bush with the nest, but all the other birds were gone. He looked and listened for the mama, but there were no birds in the yard, no birds anywhere. The baby bird was exhausted and nearly dead, and he got the feeling that if he had driven to work, he would have run it over. Except for the beak that nipped at his palm, and the immature claws, everything about the bird was delicate and susceptible to injury.

He carried the chick into the kitchen where he grabbed a Tupperware bowl, then he went into his home office. He took paper batting from the shredder, filled the Tupperware bowl, and placed the infant bird in the makeshift nest. The little bird calmed and eventually quieted. Jacobs knew there was no divine intervention for chicks, and even if there were, this slight unfortunate hatchling had escaped the eye of God. But because he felt responsible, because the bird called out to him, and because it even seemed to *trust* him, he couldn't accept that the abandoned bird was doomed to die.

He left the bird in its modern condo of a nest and went back through the house into the yard, to the compost pile, which he knew to be teeming with worms. He pulled out two that looked tender and skinny. He took the worms into the kitchen, where Jessica stared into the open freezer, trying to imagine what she might cook. He held one of the worms on the cutting board and diced it to bits with Jessica's favorite chef's knife, while the other squirmed across the counter.

Jessica turned to say something but paused when she saw what he'd done.

He picked up the worm pieces, rolled them between thumb and finger, but he was unsatisfied. So he took the second worm, popped it in his mouth, chewed thoroughly, and spit the remains onto the cutting board. This, he was more pleased with. He brushed the chewed worm into his hand, which he was about to carry away, when Jessica said, "I was thinking we should go out next week. As a kind of send-off."

"Someplace I can get a steak," Jacobs said. "That sounds nice."

He supposed she had given up trying to dissuade him, and she used the excuse of this conversation to follow him back to the den. When she saw the baby bird, she gasped, and everything else escaped her mind while she reached down and stroked the feather nubbins that sprouted from its adorable head.

"Where did you find him?" she said.

"He's one of ours. He was in our bush."

Jacobs held a piece of the worm above the bird, who recognized the morsel but bobbed its head and kept its beak closed, only opening its mouth to cheep in protest of being harassed. The bird reacted positively to Jessica's touch, she smiled at the little fellow, and for a moment she and John were connected and close. There was no discussion about what they might do, but they were in agreement that for the bird's sake, they would sure as hell try.

The next day Jacobs walked to work again. When he got home, he looked under the Sunfire, and went inside to check on Jessica, who had been with the bird all day, watching TV in bed.

"He won't eat," she said. "But I got him to take water from a dropper. Maybe we can try a protein shake or something. I have some Slim-Fast."

This seemed as good a time as any to break the news, so John blurted out, "I'm taking someone with me, and we're buying his ticket."

"We can't afford it," Jessica said. "How did you get so generous all of a sudden? You never take me *anywhere.*"

"I need a partner," he said. "Someone to share the experience."

"A Batman to your Robin?"

"The other way around," he said, "but that's the idea, yes."

"Who are you taking? Nat, I suppose?"

"A kid I met. He's black. And he's not afraid."

"We don't know any black people. What makes you think it will work?"

"I have to try," John said. "I'm dying here."

"You think you're the only one?" she said. "What kind of satisfaction am I getting?"

Jacobs looked at his hands and noticed his fingernails had grown long. At some point during the conversation the baby bird had dozed off. John wanted to nudge it awake, just to be sure it hadn't died, but then he saw the chest rise and fall. He had just cut his nails, what seemed only days ago. Should he cut them again now, so they would grow back, or wait and cut them right before he leaves? His nails might be necessary in the wild, but what if they grew too long? He wasn't about to take a fingernail clipper with him and he had never been one to bite his nails. He didn't think he even knew how.

"You don't get satisfaction from our relationship?" John asked. "Or from modern life?"

"I don't have a problem with modern life," she said. "I *like* modern life."

"So it's me?"

"What do you even see in me?" she wondered. "Why are we together?"

More than anything he wanted to wake up the bird, to save himself from this line of questioning. He didn't know the answers, had never thought of their marriage in these terms. There weren't good answers. If he was honest, he wasn't happy with her, nor was she with him. But they couldn't really back out, at least not yet. They didn't fight, and he remembered how much he had been in love with her. That had to count for something.

"We haven't saved any money," she said, "and we can't keep living like this."

There wasn't a better job for John Jacobs. Not one that paid as well, and not one that he would find fulfilling. He didn't possess the skills to do anything else, at least not on paper, and there was no way he was going back to school. He was nostalgic about studying the art books, but after all the years of paychecks, he'd forgotten how.

"If I made more money?"

"Maybe."

"If I took you somewhere?"

"Yes."

"So it's the money?"

"We should go dancing. We should try one of those mystery theater dinners. We should get a dog."

"You aren't bored of dancing?"

"I *love* dancing."

"What kind of dog?"

"A poodle? No, a schnauzer."

"We can get two," he said.

"A poodle and a schnauzer, or two schnauzers?"

"Whatever will make you happy."

"We have to do better," she said. "We have to try and try and try."

Jacobs went looking for Q by driving around in the neighborhood near the pawnshop. He was surprised to notice trees, adolescent and bare trees, but trees. What drew the eye were the bright liquor stores and boarded-over and graffitied storefronts, the empty bottles in brown bags, and the long grass grown up through the cracks in acres of concrete. Jacobs didn't come across Q anywhere but he felt him, and he understood why Q would go, even to the Arctic. Jacobs could take him to the surface of the moon; it didn't matter. Somewhere no less deserted. No better and no worse. Jacobs had to get away *to* nothing and Q *from* nothing. He had found the right companion.

He stopped in front of Q's mama's house, on the same stretch of road where Q had shown him to park, and he went up and knocked on the door.

"He ain't here," his mama said, and she stepped out onto the stoop.

"It's going to be dangerous," Jacobs said. "And I can't pay much."

"Someone watches over him," she said. "He comes back."

"Can he swim?"

"You'll have to ask."

"You don't know? You're his mother."

"I don't swim," she said. "But he probably do."

Jacobs asked for his full name, so he could buy the plane ticket. She'd named him Trentonius Demetrius Compton. Like a gladiator, Jacobs thought, with no "Q" anywhere in the name. She gave Jacobs his cell phone number, which he tried, and Jacobs left Q a message to call back. They were leaving in a few days and he'd have to buy him supplies. He needed a snowsuit and the Gore-Tex boots. He needed a sleeping bag. They were going to do this, and the voyage would be dangerous and real.

"Even if he chickens out," Jacobs said, "tell him to call me."

"Not much chance of that," his mama said, and Jacobs didn't know if she meant he wouldn't chicken out or that he wouldn't call. He waited for her to say something else, but she went back inside and closed the door.

When the time came, Jacobs packed up his favorite desk doodles and he walked out of the UniqCorps building for the last time. There was no party, no gifts, and no send-off. He'd been asked to train his replacement, a fresh-faced kid straight from the nearest state university who picked up everything right away. The new kid knew not to take Mike Schmidt seriously, he knew to deepen his voice on the phone, he knew which receptionists and administrative assistants were single, and he knew how to surf websites without being detected by the company software, something Jacobs wished someone had shown him. They were allowed to surf at lunch, so it was as easy as resetting the clock on the control bar. The kid looked confident in Jacobs's cubicle. On his last day, Jacobs wanted to give the kid something he could keep in his salesman's arsenal as the years dripped by like beads of goo in a desk doodle maze.

"You probably think this is a dumb job," Jacobs began, "but there are good people here. And there are worse jobs."

The kid was like a boy in church, uncomfortable in his suit and tie, his hair still wet from his morning shower. He watched Jacobs like he was being accused of something.

"Worry less about single secretaries and more about your bosses," Jacobs said. "You can make good money here. Though there's a rumor they're getting rid of sales."

He thought that might stick. *Worry less about single secretaries...*

But the kid stared back with an impatient look. He was waiting for Jacobs to go away.

"If this job's so great," the new kid said, "then why'd you quit?"

Jacobs paused. He had wanted to give the kid some of his salesman's wisdom, but now he was being asked for something altogether different—the truth.

"I found some things out about myself," Jacobs said. "It was time to move on."

"Well, I hope you get there," the new kid said, and Jacobs felt he was being condescended to. "Everybody's got their something."

On his way out, Jacobs stopped by Mike's cubicle. He had the desire to disclose his secret, but since everyone at work called Mike "The Mighty Khan," and since everyone in the vicinity of the open cubicle could hear, Jacobs suggested they meet outside the office.

"Want to go for a drink?"

The Bennigan's was a popular lunch spot and this was Jacobs's last visit. Bennigan's, Friday's, Chili's, Applebee's—they were depressingly similar with the blended-ice drinks in separate flipbook menus, the abundance of TV screens, the colorful striped uniforms, the indoor neon, with street signs and all the faux-antique useless objects tacked to the wall. The meals consisted of small portions of skillet-grilled meat, melted cheese, and sides of fries or corn chips, depending. But Jacobs felt an overwhelming sense of calm. He was in the moment and he enjoyed himself. He was about to spill the beans to Mike Schmidt and the fake world around him seemed less substantial than ever.

"We weren't friends, but we were decent to each other," Mike said. "The new kid I can't trust. He wants to look at my accounts already. It's too soon and it should come from me."

"You may as well show him," Jacobs said. "He'll see them some way."

"I suppose. What will you do, now you're free?"

"I'm taking a trip. *You* showed me the way. I got the DNA test."

Mike perked up.

"I'm Eskimo."

"You're shitting me?"

"I think somewhere inside I knew all along," Jacobs said.

"Don't expect big answers. And don't count on people being nice."

"I'm going on a whale hunt," Jacobs said. "The chief invited me."

"It's not too late to get your job back," Mike said. "You don't have to go proving yourself. No one here will respect you either way."

"So what happened?" Jacobs asked.

"It was a big city with homeless people. They were my cousins, but I had no way of making them understand. Eventually, I stayed at the hotel and quit going out."

"My chief speaks English," Jacobs said. "He made it sound like they all do."

"In that case," Mike said, "if you are dead-set on it, the Mongolians have a saying: *While horse is strong, travel and see.*"

"They told you that?"

"I Googled it. What do you know about this whale hunt? What kind of boats?"

"I don't know."

"Maybe you should find out. The Mongolians have another saying: *Don't begin if afraid. Once begun, don't be afraid.*"

"Have you been selling these?"

"Bankers want poets and politicians," Mike said.

"Have you tried?" Jacobs said. "They think investing is courageous. I sold the Churchill quote."

"*The only thing to fear?* That's FDR."

"No," Jacobs said. "Maybe it was MLK. *Something* about fear."

"*There's nothing more dangerous than sincere ignorance and conscientious stupidity?*"

"It was on the list," Jacobs said. "It had the word 'fear' in it."

"I may not get there with you, but as a people we will, so I'm happy. I'm not worried about anything. I'm not fearing any man."

"Is that MLK?" Jacobs asked.

"I'm paraphrasing, but that's his last speech. And not on our list."

"I didn't know you were a fan."

"Isn't everyone?"

"Not really," Jacobs said. "A lot of people don't see it as their cause."

"Human rights?" Mike asked.

"Civil rights. They admire his courage but see the struggle as a thing of the past."

"And what about you?"

"I'm not white," Jacobs said. "So it's my cause too."

"But don't you see us all as the same?" Mike asked.

"I used to. On a good day. But that was talk. PR. A con job."

"I hope you don't really believe that," Mike said. "And I hope you come back around. I did."

On the drive home Jacobs felt a romantic longing for his wife, and he became nostalgic for the early days of their marriage. They dated at the chain restaurants on this strip near the mall, and he didn't think badly of them then. Time cheapened the places as the menus and the clientele stayed the same, but he got older. And time put distance between himself and Jessica. After the first few years there was nothing new. Habits became friends. And they didn't keep secrets from each other, but secretly, they derided each other. Jacobs was softening as he drove past the old places he used to take her. When she wore a skirt for him. When he opened doors for her. He missed that sweeter younger version of himself and wished he could go back. He picked up the phone to call her and saw there was a message from Q. He told Jessica he'd stopped for a drink with a coworker but he needed to go meet his partner before he came home.

"Thanks for calling," she said. She recognized he'd made the effort but she also didn't care one way or the other. He was leaving in a few days and hadn't yet made her understand. He'd changed but she remained the same. He recognized her funk, and they were mostly swinging at each other and missing. He wanted her to know that he needed her and that even though he wasn't coming straight home, he remembered happier times. He searched for the words but she'd hung up, probably because of something on TV—one of her shows.

He nearly turned the wheel and headed back home, but he really needed to find his cameraman, Q. He listened to the message, which told him to stop by Q's mama's, and when Jacobs got there, Q waited on the front stoop.

"Do you know that MLK quote," Jacobs said. "The one about fear?"

"*All we got to fear is fear itself,*" Q said.

"That's FDR."

"No," Q said, "It's Martin. My mama's got it on a record."

"He was quoting," Jacobs said.

"No, it's on there. He said it."

"So you're not afraid?" Jacobs said. "You still want to go?"

"If you ain't scared," Q said, "then I sure as hell ain't."

At home Jessica sat up watching late-night TV. She'd been talking on the phone, and she hadn't missed him. The baby bird was dead or asleep in its Tupperware bowl on her nightstand. Jacobs undressed and crawled into bed with her.

"You smell like beer," she said. This signaled her lack of desire. He shouldn't expect to get intimate. Not tonight.

"I *am* beer." This was an old joke of theirs and she smiled. His jokes were never funny and she couldn't remember when this one began, but it was one of their ways of talking to each other, at least familiar, nothing at all like the Eskimo hunter who came home most nights.

"Did you have fun with your coworker?"

"I wouldn't say *fun*," John said. "I'll probably never see the guy again. He's the one who told me about the test."

"The DNA test?" she said. "Give me his name, so I can shoot him."

"Haven't you wanted one?" John said. "Don't you want to know where you're from?"

"I'm from Ohio."

"I mean before that. Way back. Before history even."

"Ohio's all the history I need."

"But where do you think you might be from?" John asked. "Where would you *want* to be from?"

"Atlantis."

"They're all dead," John said. "Or mythical."

"*I* would have escaped."

"Of course. Pick somewhere else. Someplace on a map."

"Key Largo."

"People don't come from Key Largo," he said. "It has to be a civilization."

"You asked me to choose. I choose Key Largo."

"Is this Jay, or some other show?"

"It's Jay, but he's on vacation. They got this guy—I don't know who he is. He's some comedian but I don't think he's funny."

"Do you want to do it?"

"OK."

This was their lexicon and Jacobs supposed a lot of other couples' too, a direct way of saying that was harmless but gave him permission to move. She wasn't too much into it but she let him have his way, which they both saw as an act of kindness on this particular night, a need that Jacobs had after his last day as a desk doodle salesman, with no sure sense of what the weeks would bring. He held Jessica tightly after a quick release, then he started to roll into her again, slowly at first, so she didn't realize. But he gained momentum, until she said, "Oh my...," and he rocked the bed.

After shouting out and settling his face calmly into her chest a second time, Jacobs said, "I really *do* love you."

"I know," Jessica said. "And you won't stay gone. No matter what you say. You'll be back."

Chapter 4

On the flight to LA, and then on the flight to Anchorage, Jacobs watched Q, who looked out the window. Jacobs had gone back to REI and bought him an outfit exactly like his own, only slimmer. They were dressed like white and black twins but were supposed to be father and son. Jacobs wanted the window seat but the kid had never flown. He wondered what Q thought as he looked down on puffy clouds for the first time and saw mountain ranges extend in ripples in every direction, or when he spotted the tenuous, jagged sandy line where the Pacific met the California coast. Jacobs had brought along a book, a survival guide, but there was only one chapter that covered snowy climates. He was sleepy and it was a dry read. Mostly, he watched Q gaze out the small window and take everything in. The kid was quiet but sharp. Jacobs told the people they'd met they were whalers, but Q said they were a documentary film crew.

When he gave Q the plane ticket, Jacobs was reminded of Q's real name, so he asked about Mr. Compton. What had happened to him, or was he still in the picture?

"Compton is a place," Q explained. "And now you know as much as me."

"I didn't mean to pry," Jacobs said.

"You just didn't expect the answer you got."

"I'm glad," Jacobs said, "that we can talk about things."

"Talk is easy."

"The saying is *talk is cheap.*"

"Whatever."

"You never heard that?"

Q stared at Jacobs and held eye contact as a way of expressing exasperation at something old, unimportant, and better left unsaid.

From the air, Anchorage was beautiful, nestled in the bay with white mountains rising and Mount McKinley in the background. The sun lingered, and everywhere dusk roses and magentas reflected in water and snow. It was the beginning of the tourist season, but the streets were clear of cars.

"Nice view," Q said.

"It's gorgeous," Jacobs agreed.

After collecting their gear from the baggage claim, they went out to the curb to catch a cab, loaded down with backpacks, duffel bags, and John and Jessica's rolling suitcases. Q walked slowly with his arms folded, his posture stiff, and he took small steps.

"I'm fucking freezing."

"You're supposed to be Eskimo," Jacobs said. "You don't have to like the cold, but you can't gripe. It's going to get a lot colder where we're going."

"You didn't tell me about the cold."

"You're in Alaska. What did you expect?"

"Maybe I'm a warm-weather Eskimo. Mostly African."

"Act like an Eskimo."

"Don't act black?"

"That's not what I said. You're supposed to be my son."

When the cabbie drove up, Jacobs and Q looked hopelessly at their mound of gear, but the guy got most of it in the trunk and the rest in the front passenger seat. There was a heater vent in the back Q huddled into, and before long they were riding through downtown. Jacobs hadn't made reservations and he asked the driver to take them somewhere safe but cheap.

"How safe?" the cabbie wanted to know.

"Mostly cheap," Jacobs said.

"Hell isn't fire and brimstone," Q said. "It's cold. Damned dark and cold."

Tourists snapped photos as they walked from their hotels to the seafood restaurants. They were as over-bundled as Jacobs and Q, and the cabbie cursed when they sometimes wandered into the road. He apparently didn't care that he was also hauling tourists.

A couple walked and held hands wearing thick ski gloves. Jacobs wanted the cabbie to know he belonged, that he had more right to the place than they did, but he also craved a steaming cup of chowder and a plate of fish. He envied their leisure but was living a life of purpose. Then, as they drove, Jacobs looked for the familiar view from the webcam. The days were longer and the ice had thawed, though it felt like the snowy dead of winter, even colder. The tourists shuffled in their boots and they exhaled white puffs.

The Starlight Motel had vacancies, though the guy at the desk didn't give that impression.

"Too many sailors looking for work," he said. "But we've got a single."

"Are there jobs?" Jacobs asked.

"You're not sailors."

The Starlight was middling, the décor of their room like the basement apartment of a chain-smoking uncle with no cares but the time clock and paydays, game shows and college sports, cop shows and Judge Judy. Q claimed his side of the bed and flicked on the TV with the remote. The desk clerk loitered in the doorway of the room and waited for a tip.

"You've got to be kidding me," Jacobs said. He had helped them with their bags, but they were a short distance down the hall from the office.

"See if you get a wake-up call," the man said as he turned and left.

Jacobs and Q had traveled all day, and they were finally at rest and alone. If they were going to get to know each other, this would be the time. They watched hockey instead. Q undressed and made himself comfortable while Jacobs slouched at the end of the bed in his snow gear. The semipro Anchorage beat Manitoba 4-2, and shouts were heard from the rooms when a goal was scored. With the lights out, Q rolled on his side and Jacobs lay on his back on top of the bedspread, still in the parka and snow pants. He stared at the ceiling in the darkness.

"You finally home?" Q said.

"Not yet," Jacobs said. "Still as far as from Atlanta to Chicago."

"It's the North Pole to me."

"*The world is a book*," Jacobs said. "*And those who don't travel read only one page.* That's Seneca. Or Shakespeare. Or Saint Augustine. One of the S's—I can't remember."

"It's not wisdom if you don't know the source," Q said. "That's from *me*."

"We used sayings at my old job," Jacobs said. "And my head is filled."

"What'd you do?'

"What does anyone do? We sold stuff."

"Give me another," Q said.

"*Manners are the hypocrisy of a nation.*"

"I meant something apropos," Q said. "We're on a big adventure here."

"*Travelers never think that* they *are the foreigners.*"

"And how did that help you sell stuff?"

"Most of them didn't," Jacobs said. "But we looked them up just the same. Gave us a feeling of being in control."

"I got one," Q said. "*Spike Lee isn't saying African American culture is just for black people. Culture is for everybody.*"

"We probably could have used that, if you took out Spike Lee and African American. If it was just, *Culture is for everybody.*"

"Then it's generic."

"*There is no truth,*" Jacobs said. "*There is only perception.*"

"You're going to get boring if you keep doing that."

"I *was* boring. That used to be my job."

"Sounds to me like you *liked* it."

"Some days I did," Jacobs said. "And I liked the paycheck."

"When Spike Lee made his first film, he financed it with a credit card."

"That's what we're doing. Only this is real."

"*There is no real,*" Q said. "*Only entrepreneuritudiniza-tion.*"

"If you make up sayings, they have to at least sound believable."

"Authenticity," Q said. "I know my film theory. Verisimilitude."

"So who are we?" Jacobs wanted to know. "What would they say about the film of us?"

"An unlikely pairing. The long shot. The underdogs."

"Sounds like sports talk."

"They speak the same language," Q said.

"Entrepreneuritudinization?"

"You got it."

Jessica loved being alone in the house. She didn't have to bite her lip when John flipped through channels, or sit through nature shows just for snow. She watched her own shows and ate whatever she wanted, whenever she wanted, without counting calories and without doing the dishes, because her own mess was no mess at all. Even after a day, she'd been freed from picking up after, putting up with, and even making conversation with her caveman husband. If she didn't feed the bird—who would sometimes take raw hamburger from chopsticks if she timed it right—she didn't feel guilty, because no one else knew. She didn't have a dance class at the studio that afternoon, and she stayed on the couch in her satin nightie. Though she might stop by the studio later to see if any of the girls would go out for a glass of wine.

John had gotten testy, he'd gotten messy, and he'd gotten strange. But then when the sun went down, Jessica wanted him home for dinner. He'd have eaten the extra biscuits and she'd have given him the nicer of the ham steaks. When the baby bird stood up and took a few steps around the Tupperware bowl, she even shouted for John to come look. And when she tried to sleep in their bed, she was apprehensive, having realized that at night their house was empty and dark. The worst part about missing her husband wasn't that his quest had taken him so far away, but that it occupied his imagination, and he probably didn't miss her at all.

In the morning, a chartered single-prop plane took Jacobs and Q across Alaska and up the coast past the Bering Strait to Point Halcyon, an old whaling port where fanatical missionaries and white whalers had a sundry history, with the Inuit the point of contact. The place was a narrow peninsula that jutted out into the Chukchi Sea, and a naval outpost sonar station rotated a small crew to monitor submarine traffic.

"What do you want there?" the desk clerk asked as they checked out. He added, "That's the middle of nowhere," not recognizing that to most people *anywhere* in Alaska, even Anchorage, was the middle of nowhere.

"We're a film crew," Jacobs said, having learned Q's trick. It was better not to talk about the details and to leave people to their assumptions. "This is my director."

"Where's your shit?" the clerk asked.

"Shoestring budget," Jacobs said.

The clerk eyed them suspiciously and nodded. There were certainly people who came to Alaska to avoid the law. Jacobs and Q were a strange enough pair, but they were also leaving.

"You'll be getting up there while it's still light," the clerk said. "And not quite as God-forsaken cold."

The first Inuk they met was the charter pilot, a cowboy-hatted kid not much older than Q. At the municipal airport on the other side of Anchorage, he trudged across the melting slush of the parking lot in cowboy boots, and he walked them to his plane, a Beaver on floats older than its pilot. The hangar was open with the Beaver in front, parked there overnight to keep out of the weather, with landing wheels beneath the pontoons.

They were headed north, where the days would be longer. Jacobs had the feeling the weather had gotten warmer, but everything was relative, and though the ice was melting, they were caught in a cycle of melt and freeze.

He extended a hand to the young pilot, who saw him as a white man, and Jacobs knew this was how he'd always be seen, no matter what he felt inside.

"I'm flying you to Point Halcyon?" the kid said.

His features looked foreign, though Jacobs knew that at Point Halcyon the Inuit would outnumber everybody else, and he and Q would be the outsiders. What white luxury—to be on the kid's own turf and see him as foreign, to judge his looks against some white ideal—even here. And Jacobs realized he hadn't shed his white point of view entirely. He wondered about Q's perspective and what he thought about the encounter.

But as soon as the kid walked off to sign out at the office, Q clued him in: "I hope he can fly."

The cab of the Beaver was smaller than the inside of a VW Bug, which was about all Jacobs had to compare it with. He had never flown in anything other than a commercial airliner, and this was the first signal that they were leaving the farthest outpost for the last frontier. Inside the cockpit were a hanging rosary and a statuette of Saint Christopher. The kid took off his cowboy hat to put on a headset and a pair of mirrored sunglasses before putting the hat back on.

"Point Halcyon?" the kid said in the moments before he fired up the engine. He looked down at his clipboard. "There's nothing there. Are you a teacher or something? A missionary?"

"I'm Inuit," Jacobs said.

The kid scrutinized Jacobs and then looked at Q. "Him too?"

"No, he's American."

"I'm black," Q said.

"I thought you was whitey," the pilot said to Jacobs. "I don't like whitey. Nothing personal."

"None taken," Jacobs said. "I thought I was whitey myself."

"You could sure pass," the pilot agreed. "So why you up here? You a teacher or something?"

"Film crew," Q said. "He's my producer."

"I'm Inuit," Jacobs added.

"Right," the pilot said. "Well, hang on tight. We'll get you there."

At the push of a button the engine coughed and the propeller turned until the entire plane was shaking and all they heard was a steady roar. The plane pulled out of the hangar slowly into sunlight, where it slid uneasily on wet ice. They turned and crawled the length of the runway, then turned back, and the pilot throttled up. The world outside seemed to vibrate while the steering wheel shook violently and resisted the kid's grip. Soon they moved along the runway, which was short, and the pilot corrected as they veered sideways. The wheels remained in contact until the last moment, when they rushed toward a line of trees and a pile of snow. Then they gently lifted and tilted back over the small airport.

Jacobs held on to his seat and wondered if Q saw him. The Beaver was nothing at all like the jet planes Jacobs had flown in, and he felt the pull of the earth more acutely. He decided he'd never really flown, and the wings of the plane, for just a moment, were an extension of himself. He remembered dreams he'd had as a kid when he could fly by breast-stroking in the air. He would swim to climb above a game of tag or to escape the pursuit of a stray dog. His arms and legs pumped and pulled as he lifted higher over his yard, sometimes too high for comfort, and he woke up from the dream the second he realized he couldn't really fly, because it was impossible, and then he tumbled and dropped. Jacobs felt that way now, as if their lifting off the earth was daring and dangerous. Like in the dreams, when all he had to do was believe. But if he remembered flying was impossible, they were doomed to fall.

Jacobs also had the sense of going back in time, to when the frontiers of the globe had been reached and white men turned their thoughts to flight. A time when the technology was unsure and the machines that defied gravity were by no means standard, akin to the beasts ridden before them, machines that needed to be tamed. Then, as they gained the height of clouds, Jacobs knew the pilot would depend entirely on the dials and gauges of his instruments, with the clouds white, the sky white, the ground white. He wondered how bewilderingly white it must all be in the midst of a snowstorm and figured this young pilot had probably flown in snowy conditions more often than not. Jacobs wondered how many Eskimo words the kid knew for the snow he'd flown in, and he decided they were safer with him than any gray-haired commercial airlines commodore. The kid had experience and knew his flight path.

After three hours aloft, with the same beautiful rolling scenery, at least when it could be distinguished from white on white, the kid indicated the coastline and beyond it,

Russia. Point Halcyon looked a lot like the satellite map, with the landing strip completely traversing the tip of the small peninsula, and the runway appeared short from this altitude. The pilot spoke into his headset and started his descent.

He held out his index finger near the window to compare his hand to the black land of Point Halcyon that jutted out into the sea ice. "They call it *Tikigaq*. It means finger-pointing. But they also say it looks like a raven's bill, or a harpoon tip. It points to the sea."

"It points out *into* the sea," Q said.

"It's not really land," the pilot said.

Point Halcyon was detached from the mainland with lakes and ponds separating Tikigaq, and only a thin line of beaches connected it to the coast.

"The old legend," the pilot continued, "is that Tikigaq was a whale. The first hunter killed him, and that line of beaches are the harpoon line. They call Point Halcyon *the animal.* It is alive and also dead. The spirits of whales live there. It's a sacred place."

"Like the elephants' graveyard?" Q said.

"You'll find whale bones and Inupiat bones," the pilot said. "It's the oldest continuously populated village in North America. Tikigaq is thousands of years old, and the Inupiat who live there now are descendants."

"What's the difference?" Jacobs said. "Inuit or Inupiat?"

"I thought you were Inuit?" the pilot asked.

"I *am.*"

"Inuit is more generalized. We're Inuit all across the Arctic. Inupiat are the people from the North Slope—the whalers."

From the air, the town looked modern, rectangular houses laid out in a square grid.

"What do you want in Tikigaq, anyway?" the pilot said. "You a teacher or something?"

The pilot dipped the plane into a nosedive as he aimed for the short landing strip, with the frozen ocean at both ends. Jacobs had never known a fear of flying but he'd also never been shown such a clear view of the danger. He felt dizzy and he struggled to breathe. There had been a kind of helplessness throughout most of his life, but the sight of the black living landmass coming at them put him in the grip of something terrifying. Tikigaq *was* an animal. Merciless and unthinking, the place would devour them.

Relieved to be on the ground, Jacobs crunched across ice and gravel. He carried his share of gear in a daze. He scanned the white horizon and the earth seemed a slick black skin in the places where the snow had thawed. He got the impression they walked on the carcass of a long-dead leviathan that once breathed life. Tikigaq, the first whale, the animal, was fed whalebones and Inupiat bones for centuries. And Tikigaq was hungry. The alien landscape gave Jacobs the uneasy feeling the whale might roll them off its back.

Q continued to walk with half steps, arms folded.

"Stop shivering," Jacobs said.

"I'm fucking freezing."

"Act Eskimo."

"What does that even mean?"

"This is the thaw. This should be warm for you."

"So you're the white guy giving the black guy advice?"

"I'm the older guy giving the younger guy advice. If they don't believe us, the whole trip is wasted. No whaling and no film."

"OK," Q said. "I'll do it for the film. But I'm fucking freezing."

Yuq drove a white Jeep Cherokee and wore a white parka. His frame was sturdy, his smile dotted with a golden molar. There were bags of groceries in the front seat of the SUV. Yuq rearranged the gear to fit and Q and Jacobs sat on the wide backseat.

"You're staying with my father," Yuq said. "I'm taking you there."

There was snow and slush along the roads and Jacobs and Q couldn't see through windows that had instantly fogged opaque when the doors opened and the warm air escaped from the Jeep. In a flash the windows frosted white, and Yuq drove much too fast. They were close to the edge where the land ice met the sea ice, and a strong steady wind blew in from the expanse of ice-covered water. Yuq passed a small scraper to Q, who understood the game and cleaned a spot in the middle of his window, then he passed the scraper to Jacobs, who was bemused that Yuq was either too polite or too ballsy to use the scraper first himself, the front windshield blinded with frost. Q prodded Jacobs to work quickly, and when Yuq was handed the scraper back, he set it on the dash. Q moved the bags of groceries, climbed into the front passenger seat, and scraped the frosted windshield furiously. Yuq saw they would soon drive off the icy gravel road, and he calmly corrected their course.

"Stop scraping," he said. "I like to let the defroster do it. You'll leave streaks."

They passed a schoolyard where snow blanketed the basketball court, the swing sets were empty, and the kids surrounded a snow whale they had collectively built, a mound of snow that reared up with the characteristic striped smile of a baleen-feeding bowhead whale. The schoolchildren took turns hurling a broomstick like a harpoon, and they all cheered when it struck.

"The celebration is in June," Yuq said, "but last year there was no catch. Imagine Christmas without presents, Thanksgiving without turkey, and Fourth of July without fireworks, combined. It's been hard. Akmaaq's my father, I will always respect him, but some of us don't get along."

"Was it his fault?" Q said.

"He's set in his ways," Yuq said. "Stubborn."

Jacobs said, "He gives the orders, right? He's the old sea captain."

"You two are his only crew. And you should know, if you go on the water with him, he thinks he's going to save the world with his white whale bullshit. He's suicidal, and it's how he wants to die."

"He's your father," Jacobs said.

"He's a coconut."

Jacobs realized Akmaaq's letter was nonchalant about the possibility they might not come back, *returning like all of God's creatures*.... The old sea captain hadn't given instructions about what to wear or how to survive. And suddenly John missed Jessica. He wanted to call her and tell her he'd arrived safely, and though he hadn't thought of it until now, he wanted to live through this, if only to hold her again, to listen to her romantic notions, and to fall asleep in their bed. He remembered serving her first at the table, standing behind her in line, and holding doors, each gesture packed with love. When they were younger there were no TV talk shows and no desk doodles. He'd made her homemade soup when she got sick, he'd brought home flowers in the middle of the week, he turned commercial jingles into love songs for her, and he hand-washed her delicates. He could be like that. He knew *how* to be like that. He would be like that again.

At the airport Jessica gave him a peck on the cheek, the same as their humdrum days. He wondered if she understood she might never see him again. She knew this, but did she *feel* it? She was disappointed in their attempt at composting and was thinking of teaching him the new rules upon his return. Jacobs thought his wife should have shown more affection. He was left wanting her. He was sulking, and there was more he could have done to encourage her, but she should have at least hugged him like she meant it. She should have sent him off with a kiss.

"This is a time for prayer," Yuq said. "Do you believe in God? Do you believe in Jesus?"

"Sure as Mama raised me," Q said.

Jacobs was unsure but felt the need to explain. "I believe we come from *somewhere.*"

"Search yourself," Yuq said. "There's no shame if you don't get in the boat. One must be pure. The whale knows. If we are deserving, he offers himself. He sheds his body and returns to the spirit. His remains go in the ground of the first whale. We return the head to the sea so he can reincarnate. In this way we help each other. There is no death. Only gifts of life."

"What happened last year?" Jacobs said.

"Pridefulness, brother versus brother, backbiting, pettiness, in-battles, faithlessness, a modern disregard of *Sila*, and turning our backs on God."

"Y'all sound Baptist," Q said.

"*Piskipulut*," Yuq said. "Mixed with our own traditions."

"I knew you were Protestant," Q said.

"The air around us and the heavens have never stilled. The Great Living Breath is eternal—what we call Sila. Ancestor spirits walk among us. Their breath continues, for we speak their names."

"How should we pray?" Jacobs asked.

"Make offerings to the ancestors and to the whale," Yuq said. "And be creative. Because once you are out on the ice, you have nothing left to give, and you pray for your lives."

When Jessica fed the bird in the afternoon, it waltzed. *One-two-three, one-two-three.* The moves were unmistakable. It waltzed for its water, and it waltzed for its raw hamburger, the bird slightly better than Jessica's worst student, and she spent the rest of the afternoon trying to capture the surprising phenomenon on her camera phone. But when she held the phone close to the Tupperware nest, the little guy froze, wide-eyed. Or the one time she thought she'd gotten him, she'd blotted out the tiny lens with her thumb. The prospects of saving him were slim, but she'd refused to give up. Now she couldn't help but think the baby bird would waltz all night while she was at the open house.

The Mavis Erlewine School of Dance Spring Open House was a big deal. A good portion of Jessica's repeating students had come from the open houses, and Mavis Erlewine herself would make an appearance, which was also a big deal. Mavis lost her lesbian lover and both legs in a car wreck in the late eighties, and the studio was locally famous because same-sex couples danced together long before that sort of thing was kind of normal. So there were people who would show up to be looky-loos. But there would also be people to meet who mattered, people who wanted to learn to dance. Jessica would debut her new hair color, and she also got to bring out her Waterford crystal punchbowl.

Jessica unlocked and opened the glass door at the front of the Mavis Erlewine School of Dance, and the small cowbell and clapper Mavis had secured inside the door decades ago answered with a clankety-clunk, the same sound no matter how the door was opened, and the *first* thing Jessica would replace if the studio were hers, to something light and bright, because as much as she loved dancing, the cowbell always reminded her this was a job.

The calligraphy painted on the large storefront window advertised the Free Spring Dance Open House, Saturday, April 4, and she'd felt the weight of those words for weeks, with the day finally here, and Jessica, for the first time, in charge.

The folding chairs were already lined up along the mirrored walls, and all that was left for her to do was to bring in the refreshments and set up the coat check. She floated across the familiar dance floor and paused as her feet met the painted footprints that mapped out the fox-trot. She danced a few bars, the eight-count musical in her head, and she skipped to the kitchen counter in the back of the long room where she unlocked and rolled up the aluminum shutter at the service window. The small kitchen would serve as refreshment stand and coat check, a change this year. It might get claustrophobic, but doubling up at the service counter saved them the dance-floor space of people loitering at a table, and Jessica's plan was to look through the women's purses as she pretended to tray more cupcakes. That way she'd know for sure who lied when they said they'd forgotten to bring the checkbook. She imagined these women accepted the free dance lesson with an easy conscience, but this was her livelihood, and her peace of mind, and her magazine subscriptions depended upon it.

Being in charge this year meant that Jessica could choose the music. Mose Allison did not make people want to dance; he made them want to drink and smoke. Chet Baker was too sad. She wanted something hipper and more modern. She still did not have an iPod—which was embarrassing—so she dragged along a stack of CDs from her collection: Riverdance, Celine Dion, Michael Bolton, and, of course, Coolio. She put them all on rotation in the CD changer. The Tom Jones remake of Prince's "Kiss" was up first, and it instantly put Jessica in a party mood.

Audrey Vance's car pulled up as soon as the music was pumping.

Audrey taught contra and line dancing, and she wore tight jeans over her giant bottom, which was out of proportion with the rest of her petite body. She liked tee shirts, but Mavis had asked her to show some class and not wear the ones with outdated sayings: *If Mama Ain't Happy, Ain't Nobody Happy. Love Machine. Disco Sucks. I Just Stole Your Boyfriend.*

"This is way better than that other shit," Audrey said when she came through the door.

Jessica shushed her. "Mavis will be here any minute."

"Shit!" Audrey said, and she looked around. She crunched the end of a granola bar and wiped the crumbs from her plain black tee shirt.

Shit was Audrey's favorite word, and Jessica thought she probably owned a tee shirt that said just that.

"Ready Freddy?" Jessica said.

Audrey rolled her eyes. "I guess. Always feels like a waste of time."

And she was probably right. Out of all the classes, contra and line were the bottom two as far as enrollment went, and Audrey was nervous about getting fired.

Audrey sauntered to the kitchen to see what snacks there were. Jessica, unable to think of anything else that needed to be done, stared out the window. It was just starting to stay light out past dinnertime, and she wondered if that meant all daylight all the time in Alaska. She knew people went crazy from it, and she hoped John would remember to get a good night's rest. As for herself, she could write her follow-up thank-you notes while she watched *The Tonight Show*, but tomorrow there was nothing to do except feed the bird, and so she planned to sleep in.

Mavis's van pulled into the lot. Jessica moved away from the window and waited.

She called to Audrey that Mavis had arrived.

"Oh, shit," Audrey said, and she stayed in the kitchen.

The access ramp was in back but Mavis appeared at the front door, and when she walked in, it was like witnessing a miracle. Sometime between today and the last open house, Mavis had ditched the wheelchair. She wore pants and moved on stilts.

Jessica gasped. "Ms. Erlewine!"

"Hi, dear," said Mavis, upright on two prosthetic legs. She leaned over and kissed Jessica on the cheek. "Sounds like a party in here."

"I think it's fun," Jessica said. She didn't know whether to mention the legs or not, or if she did, what she might say. And then she realized, with Mavis Erlewine walking, no one would notice what she'd done with her hair.

Audrey poked her head in. "Shit, Mavis! You got legs!"

Mavis wrinkled her brow but moved across the floor like a toddler to give Audrey a kiss on the cheek too.

Mavis exhaled and sat in one of the folding chairs. "Somewhere in this city lives my anonymous benefactor," she said. "I told the salesman if I can't dance, I'm sending them back, benefactor or not. He said we've made incredible advances. I said I didn't need charity. He said I should accept them and they just might change my life."

Jessica knew Mavis spent very little time around other people, and that changing her life would be more difficult than getting up and walking around.

The shoes were black orthopedic-looking things, the kind nurses wore. They made a shuffling sound, but Jessica could forgive the shoes, since artificial legs were probably hard to fit at Nine West. Or maybe they weren't, if what the salesman had told Mavis had been true. Sometimes, Jessica felt sorry for herself for what she'd endured in all her past lives, sorry that she'd been made to live with superstition and so few technological advances. How many times had she upped and died for lack of penicillin?

Libby, the quintessential ballerina, with her brown hair pinned in a bun, was next to arrive, her compact frame swallowed by the khaki raincoat she wore on this perfectly lovely sunny afternoon. Libby was the newest hire, since the de facto boss, Bethany, quit and left town to get married. Bethany was the only instructor at the studio since before the accident, and so she stood in as Mavis for all those years. Once Bethany was really gone, Jessica daydreamed about owning the place herself.

Within minutes, the other instructors came through the door. Rachel, the short, spunky red-haired jazz teacher. And Katrin, the lumbering blonde German salsa and tango teacher who wore high heels and a red dress. No one knew how to properly react to Mavis's legs, but Mavis put them at ease.

"Listen, girls," she said. "Someone paid for these things. The least I can do is give it a shot. Jessica, you're going to lead me in a rumba."

Jessica was giddy. All the other girls looked at her, relieved that their only role was to watch, and Jessica mistook their relief for jealousy, which made her even more giddy.

"Girl," said Audrey, "I'd need a drink after that."

"I could use one anyway," said Jessica. "Want to go somewhere after?"

They made plans and asked the others, who each said they'd think about it.

Soon, the students drifted in. There were more women than men, the women also better dressed. There was an April chill in the air, but not enough for heavy coats. The coat check was so the women wouldn't have to worry about their purses while they danced.

Jessica greeted everyone individually, and she guided them toward a seated Mavis, who spoke in a storytime voice about the refinement of the discipline. Libby stood with her toes apart, and she nodded in recognition of each high point in the evolution of choreography while Audrey, Katrin, and Rachel all looked bored.

Jessica ducked into the kitchen to check on the damage to the sweets, and she scanned the purses under the counter: Louis Vuitton knockoffs, an old Dooney & Bourke, and off-brands from T.J. Maxx. The best one was an Oroton shoulder bag that still smelled like cow. A cell phone vibrated. It came from the only heavy coat on the rack, a Jackie Kennedy leopard-skin coat that belonged to a frail old lady who had shown up at every open house but never signed up for lessons, saying, as she walked off, that she would give it serious consideration. Her coat was too young-looking for a white-haired woman with off-kilter lip liner, and Jessica was dying to rifle through her pockets, but she knew, from that angle, that someone might see.

The first bag Jessica opened was the Oroton. The checkbook was in the front of a full-sized wallet, the checks stately, with a regal-script, gold-leaf "P" in the corner. *Mr. and Mrs. Calvin Phillips.* And they lived in one of the subdivisions where the utility lines were buried. Not a gated community, but almost. Jessica liked the idea of a single gold "J," but disliked the plainness of checks without pictures.

She had long been unsatisfied with the checks she and John used, with a small shaded silhouette of square dancers. She knew they were square dancers by the position of the figures' arms, but no one else was able to really tell. They were the only checks with dancers and she wanted something that symbolized her passion.

She sifted through a green Dooney & Bourke with beige trim. The end of a checkbook stuck out, in a matching D&B cover, with the miniature duck emblem in the middle. *Connie Gaylord.* Now Connie had some personality. Her checks were printed with a coffee cup ring in the middle, so it looked like a mug had been set on the checks because there was so much other stuff on her desk—the checks of someone who thought it was funny to pretend to be busy. The checks made Jessica giggle, though she supposed by the time she reached check #541, this joke would grow stale.

Jessica worried people might get suspicious, so she replenished the tray of cupcakes on the counter, and, while taking her time, she made sure she appeared to be working.

Mavis tended to overemphasize the influence of the Peloponnesians, and Jessica figured she had time for one more purse. A flashy red one impressed her, and she went for it. The zipper was loud, so she moved it slowly, and the purse was deep; she had to dig around. There was an Elizabeth Arden lipstick; she could tell from the gold tube. She fished out a case that held white plastic sunglasses. Then she found the checks, with endangered wildcats in the center. She also found a flipbook of family photos and was surprised to realize she'd been rummaging through a black woman's purse. If this was true, she would be the first, and Jessica couldn't believe she hadn't seen her come in.

She put the wallet away and just before she could zip the purse closed, a prospective student stood at the door, licked blue icing off a cupcake, and said, "I love your purse!" Then she moved in closer and whispered, "Tell me, is it Hermés?"

Jessica was still recovering from shock when she answered. "No," she said, "not Hermés." But she liked the feeling of someone thinking she might own one. She had wanted to answer yes.

"I still like it," said the lady, and she winked. "I'm Carla, by the way. Carla Phillips."

The gold cursive "P" checks.

The woman never actually bit into the cupcake. Once the icing was gone, she tossed it into the garbage, reached past Jessica, and grabbed another. Jessica wondered if this was some new diet she hadn't heard of, and she entertained the idea of doing the same. She introduced herself and saw an opportunity to snag a client.

"I teach beginning through advanced ballroom," she said.

Carla covered her heart with her free hand. "I just *love* ballroom dancing!"

Jessica tried not to stare into Carla's mouth as she spoke, at her very blue tongue. She decided every diet had drawbacks and she guided Carla back to Mavis.

The crowd divided into groups based on preference of dance types. Audrey had three students, which thrilled her, and one of them was the black lady, which put Jessica at ease. Rachel snagged some spunky twenty-somethings. Katrin took most of the men, as usual, and Libby got the younger women and children. Jessica—whose typical clients were groups of girlfriends looking to try something new, singles looking for spouses, or wives dragging their husbands along because of a lost bet—did not get many men at all, which disappointed the women, who had to dance together, and Jessica made the point of saying this was not the usual setup, that in her classes there would be men to dance with.

"Single men?" asked one.

"I hope so," said Carla, who Jessica knew was married to *Mr. Calvin Phillips*.

"Yes, single ones *and* married ones," said Jessica.

"I'll take the married ones!" yelled a large lady, and the women laughed.

Jessica wished there were more men: she was feeling open to anything. When she showered that morning, she shaved her legs. She also fished out a push-up bra in a last-minute wardrobe change. She was looking pretty good.

Jessica offered them a mixed bag. She led them in a waltz first, then a fox-trot. They still had energy left, so she taught them the cha-cha too. They were having a blast, and Jessica knew there would be at least a couple of sign-ups. Good. She needed the money. She thought she might pay one credit card's bill with another.

Then, as she was in the middle of breaking down the moves, she looked up and saw the black lady had joined her group. She wondered if Audrey had said something to turn her off. She knew the woman's name was Trinity and that she had three daughters. Maybe she was checking out the studio for them, but she moved on to another group before Jessica even had a chance to make eye contact. So she was having herself the free smorgasbord of dance, and Jessica supposed Trinity would work her way around to all of the groups before they were done.

And sure enough, by 8 p.m., when Jessica gave her usual speech about how she'd be in the back hall signing people up, and how she'd love to "guide everyone on the exciting journey toward effortless ballroom dancing," this black woman had even made it around to Libby's group.

A few of the freeloaders, and the black lady, snuck out soon after. But most everyone stuck around.

"Can you believe the nerve?" Jessica said to Mavis later.

But Mavis disagreed, and seemed to think maybe that was the way they should do it from then on, to let people sample all the dances.

And when the open house was nearly done, everyone gathered around the coat check and cupcake counter, while Mavis staggered to the center of the dance floor.

Mavis nodded to Jessica that she was ready, and she had Katrin queue "Antillana." Jessica held Mavis's waist with one hand, and they raised their opposing hands above their heads.

Mavis's feet stuttered at first, but Jessica made sure they picked up the next bar, and they really got going after that. Mavis smiled at Jessica, who was only inches from her face. She could feel Mavis's breath, which smelled like licorice and alcohol. Jessica concentrated on Mavis's legs, and she had to alter the dance, but not much. Mavis's eyes were childlike, and they were glued on Jessica's.

Jessica felt rattled by this, and her mind wandered. She realized with Mavis dancing again that any hope of getting a business loan and buying the studio was dashed. She supposed she should be happy for the lonely old eccentric, and she was reminded of her dancing bird. His immature legs and large watery eyes were entrusted to her by some large force, something big, and she may never encounter anything so delicate ever again. But she would still go out and have a vodka tonic and if the bird were meant to live, then it would live. And if it didn't, she would accept that too.

The heavy plaster legs shuffled from spot to spot, and by the end of the song, Mavis had put her head on Jessica's shoulder. Jessica wasn't expecting this, and she didn't think that Mavis expected it either. The room applauded. The large woman cried. Jessica had done well. She had done her job. And there were cupcakes left over—cupcakes that she would usually take home to John, but tonight she encouraged all the new students to take them. She licked the icing off the ones that were left, and stacked the empty dishes.

Mavis and everyone else all thought Bethany would just take over entirely one day. No one thought Harvey would turn out to be that important to her. But when Bethany left, she looked at herself in the mirrored wall and said, "People can be surprising."

Akmaaq's home was dug into a hill. There were two poles out front with whale baleen splayed at the top like palm fronds for the visual joke of palm trees in the Arctic, and snow everywhere. Three huskies bounded over to greet Yuq, and the men followed the dogs down a short set of log stairs, then through a tunnel to where a whale jaw formed an archway and another set of stairs led back up to a second door. Inside was a round room with a stove, a picnic table, and a few unmatched chairs. It was like walking into the belly of the whale with a windowpane at the top, and the large room was stuffy, cluttered, and warm. The old man reclined in a rocker with an unlit pipe that dangled from his mouth.

After a few trips to the car, all of Jacobs and Q's equipment was in a pile between what served as the kitchen and a rolltop desk covered with magazines and newspaper clippings. Yuq had brought in one of the bags of groceries to give to Akmaaq, and he set it on the table.

"Welcome to my igloo," Akmaaq said, and he extended a hand but overshot and gripped Jacobs's forearm. Jacobs noticed Akmaaq's glass eye, and supposed it accounted for his lack of depth perception. The eye stared back unknowing. It was a porcelain ball with a ring of bright gypsum around a coal-black dot. His glass eye didn't match the real one in size or color, but it was close enough and not as unsettling as a pirate's patch.

Thinking the old man was joking, Jacobs said, "I haven't seen an igloo."

"*Igloo* is the word for *house*," Yuq said. "When trappers and whalers came they learned our skill of making shelters out of snow, and they thought the snow houses were how we lived. We slept in them when we hunted, which is how they always thought of us, so the word stuck when really it just means *house*."

"Nobody even makes them anymore," Akmaaq said. "When I was a boy, we had a dance every winter and the men built a snow house big enough for the clan. Got so warm in there from body heat, you had to take off your parka."

This was the same feeling in Akmaaq's sod house. The fire in the stove burned low, and everyone took off their coats.

"We didn't have much wood," Akmaaq said. "Only driftwood. But we didn't need it."

"People buy wood now," Yuq said, "though it's too expensive."

"So what do you burn?" Q said.

Yuq said, "Trash, seal oil, food scraps, whatever burns."

"Dog shit," Akmaaq qualified.

With everyone seated, Jacobs and Q had a chance to take in the room. They noticed Akmaaq's bedroll and the lack of space for much else, the room cramped.

"You grew up here?" Q asked Yuq.

"Naw," Akmaaq said. "He lived with his mom. Inupiat didn't divorce until the missionaries came. We've got them to thank."

"He blames white people for everything," Yuq said.

"Family is family," Akmaaq said. "You tough it out."

"I brought you some things," Yuq said. "I've got to make more rounds. See you in church."

"I need a ride later," Akmaaq said. "And I need something to drink."

"I'm not buying your alcohol," Yuq said.

"It's for the women," Akmaaq said. "They're sewing for us. Least we can do."

"I'll give you a ride," Yuq said. "And I'll get you something for the women. But don't expect me to drive you around if all you do is get drunk."

"Used to be we respected elders," Akmaaq said to Yuq's back as he walked out. But once Yuq was gone the old man's demeanor changed, and he said, "Let's see what we got. You two bring any food?"

"We've only just got here," Q said.

"We had limited packing space," Jacobs said. "But I brought this." He went over and produced a jar of Peter Pan extra crunchy.

"Save that for later," Akmaaq said. "Maybe it burns. Maybe it will make seal bait."

"I need to call my mom," Q said.

"And may I call my wife?" Jacobs said.

"No phone," Akmaaq said. "But I got Internet." He cleared a stack of magazines from the rolltop desk to reveal a computer monitor and, next to it, a manual-key typewriter. He flicked a switch with his foot to turn on the power bar and the PC came to life.

"Why did you send a letter if you had e-mail?" Jacobs said.

"Because you sent a letter," Akmaaq said.

Once Windows booted, the characteristic sound of a dial-up modem could be heard, and Jacobs objected, "You said you didn't have a phone."

"You see any phone?" Akmaaq said.

"You've got a phone *line.*"

"I like to look at the Internet."

"My mom doesn't have a computer," Q said. "She can't get e-mail."

"Even if we had a phone there's no long distance," Akmaaq said. "You can call from the neighbor's, but they don't talk to me."

"There's a way to call over the Internet," Jacobs said. "We'd need a microphone, but we could figure it out."

"Not tonight," Akmaaq said. "Tonight we're going drinking with some girls."

"I'm married," Jacobs said, "and he's seventeen."

"What are you afraid of? Inupiat women are like nothing else. You do what you want. But these are the women sewing your boots and your snow pants. I'd recommend you come along so they get the right measurements."

Akmaaq took the bag of groceries and put it in his refrigerator. "The girls will cook," he said.

Jacobs sat at the computer and tried to type something meaningful to his wife. He thought about how awfully far away he was. How she was already in bed and curled up watching one of her shows. Jay had come back from vacation, so things were back to normal on *The Tonight Show*. She wouldn't see his e-mail until morning, and he wanted to whisper to her before she slept. He had seen where Point Halcyon jutted out into the Chukchi Sea, and he had trusted that warmth and shelter would be provided. He had met and been welcomed by his chief, and he was going to be fitted for the hunt. Tonight he would sleep in Akmaaq's sod house, in the Alaskan earth, an igloo with an entrance decorated with a whale trophy. He realized he hadn't paid enough attention to the whale as he came inside, with everything new and his senses overwhelmed. So he got up from the computer with only his first sentence composed: "Jess, we've arrived."

He opened the door and he was surprised a breeze didn't blow in, but the dropped passage kept out most of the wind. The whale jawbone was thick and smooth. He ran his hands along one edge, then another. And he said the first prayer in about as long as he could remember. He used to pray before he married Jessica, and it was a habit he kept for a year or two. He would ask God to help him provide for her and keep her happy. To help him get the job and afford a new car. Then the habit fell away. They did fine, they were settled, and they were immersed in the everyday.

Now Jacobs spoke to the whale. He searched his heart and his motives, and the word yes came to his lips. He may have even said it aloud because Akmaaq and Q both watched as he stared into the white whale jawbone. A descendant of this whale was beginning its last migration, on his way to them. They would meet here on Earth, and they would meet again in the spirit realm. It would fall upon the loser to thank the living now, and later, when they met again, the thanks would come from the one who'd lived. Jacobs wondered as he ran his hand over the long smooth bone, what kind of gift is life? Had he lived fully and to his potential? Had he been good? He had heard the word yes well up from within, but it wasn't in answer to any question. They would meet, yes. There was more living for him to do, yes. He would learn quickly or die, yes.

He went back to the computer and finished his letter. "More later. Got to go. Love you, bye."

The American Frontier and Bread Baking Company was open late without the smokiness, dirty carpet, dim lights, and loud men of all the sports bars and pickup places Audrey had suggested. She was craving jalapeno poppers but Jessica convinced her the cracked-pepper bagel with ricotta and spinach would make a nice health-conscious substitute.

The walls were contoured and papered with blown-up photos of life-sized Americans from another era, in brimmed hats and hooped skirts, with suffering children and antique implements. A woman posed with a broom so flopsy she'd probably fashioned it herself. A gentleman's pants hung at a sharp angle from his waist as he stared at the camera dour-faced. Everyone wore dark clothes. Everyone had dark hair.

By contrast, the wares of The American Frontier and Bread Baking Company were colorful and decadent-looking in the long glass counter: cheese-filled turnovers, frosting-covered croissants, kiwi-coconut fruit salads, and a wide assortment of sample sandwiches on signature whole-grain breads sliced open to display the generous portions of deli meats. There was no line at the register, and Jessica and Audrey were poured drinks at a café counter where the barista was also the bartender. The American Frontier and Bread Baking Company wasn't really a drinking establishment, and the alcohol was mostly for business lunches or to add kick to the coffees. The barista handed them a draft beer and a vodka tonic in plastic cups, each with a small square drink napkin and on an orange tray. The sandwiches had names like The Manifest Destiny B.L.T, Where the Roast Beefalo Roam, and the Homestead Ham and Swiss. Audrey opted for the Gold Rush Turkey Melt with a side of grilled vegetables while Jessica decided to let her cupcakes settle. The kid at the counter gave them a plastic number and said he'd bring the sandwich as soon as he had a chance to pop it into the microwave.

Audrey carried their tray, set it on a table, and slumped into a booth. "I don't know about you," she said, "but I'm pooped."

Jessica sat across from Audrey and she rifled through her bag for some ChapStick. "I'm pumped," she said, and she was. She wasn't tired at all.

"Mavis might have bit herself in the ass tonight," Audrey said.

Jessica looked up. "Yeah?"

"Now she has to wear those legs everywhere."

"But she doesn't *go* anywhere," Jessica said.

"She kind of has to now."

"You think she'll come around the studio more?"

Audrey leaned in like she was going to tell Jessica a secret, but her voice got louder. "Dancing is like sex. You get a taste for it.

"Speaking of," she said. "Have you heard from John?"

"Not really."

"Either you have or you haven't."

"I don't know *what* he's doing."

"Doesn't it bug you? I mean, he's up there where you can't keep an eye on him."

Jessica took a drink and a deep breath. She shrugged her shoulders and hoped Audrey would leave it alone. She hadn't told many people about what John was doing. She'd told Audrey because she knew so many of her secrets that it only seemed fair to reciprocate with something so big.

"At my house," Audrey said, "I have to be the one to start it. But most men *want* sex. Am I right?"

Audrey was on her fourth husband and by the way she talked about him, Jessica didn't suppose it would be too long before he was gone too.

"Caroline I can put in her room with the TV on, but Sarah wants a story, and Jimmy sneaks downstairs to play video games. By the time they're all settled, I'm exhausted. Except I still want to. He's not even thinking I could get it somewhere else."

Jessica couldn't remember Audrey's husband's name, and she was not about to guess, because with her luck she'd remember one of the exes.

"But *would* you?" Jessica said.

Audrey slid her beer to the middle of the table. "Sometimes a girl gets desperate."

"I thought you were Catholic," Jessica said. "It's against your religion."

"So is divorce," Audrey said. "I'm not into the dogma. I like how the Mass is old-fashioned. And how it's the one true church."

Jessica was astounded that so many people juggled full-time jobs, churches, children, and hobbies when she couldn't manage to do anything other than what *had* to be done. And when things were done, she was happy to just watch television.

"I *love* John," Jessica said. "Shouldn't that be enough? We don't always have to be *doing it.*"

"It's what we're here for," Audrey said. "God wants us to. It's in the commandments."

Jessica stared at a photo of a blown-up frontier couple on the far wall. The woman was a head shorter than her husband and they stood before a plowed plot of land, a torn-up square of dirt that belonged to them simply because they'd built a log house. They were going to make a go at it, to grow some food and live with each other on the lonesome plain. Jessica wondered if they met at a barn dance, if they were betrothed to each other through an arrangement of their parents, or if they were cousins. She wished John had felt the same sense of obligation to her, so that they needed each other like air and he would never dream of leaving. And if she were more necessary, he might also be better at putting her in the mood. Or if they had been Catholic, devout to some strict denomination with rules about staying together, then she wouldn't have to worry about getting in the mood. Their religion would keep him faithful and she could just be herself.

Audrey's turkey melt was brought to the table. She took two bites, and as she chewed she said, "I've had enough of this place. Let's go somewhere fun."

"I have to go home," Jessica said.

"You said you were pumped. John's gone. You can do what you want."

Jessica felt guilty about the bird. She had missed two or three feedings already and couldn't stand the thought of it dying for the sake of Audrey's dissatisfaction with her husband. Jessica knew she couldn't stay out any later, but she also didn't think Audrey would understand. Audrey had kids. The whole episode with the baby bird would sound silly to her. Even Jessica knew she'd only been prolonging the inevitable.

"Some other time," she said. "I really have to go."

Jessica hadn't sipped much of her vodka tonic, although she'd been looking forward to it. She'd thought the drink would make her feel like a single woman, or like someone on TV, but now she felt flat and lifeless. If the bird were dead she didn't know what she would do. She hated the idea of going home to an empty house with an empty bed. She missed the casual physical contact of her husband. Touching each other was natural yet unexpected, even on the boring days: John's palm rested on her shoulder as he squeezed by her in the kitchen, or as their feet nestled in bed, forgettable, unremarkable gestures that she was aware of now and feeling lonely about. Those times were more important to her than sex, and she wished John were here so she could tell him.

"I have to go home because I'm married."

"I hope your husband feels the same."

Jessica didn't know if he did or he didn't. He'd been through a lot of changes.

"We feel the same," she said. "I'm sure of it."

Yuq returned with his parka unzipped. He informed them the temperature was *only* fifteen degrees, so the old man insisted on going out without one, while Jacobs and Q both bundled up in their gear from REI. In the Jeep Cherokee Akmaaq took a pint of schnapps from its brown bag and said, "Is that all you got?"

"The shit is expensive," Yuq countered. "Marta will have something."

"You got any pot?" Akmaaq said.

"You know I don't smoke anymore."

"But have you got any?"

"If you want pot," Yuq said, "you have to pay for it. And you have to pay someone who has it."

"Marta might."

"Marta doesn't have any pot," Yuq said.

"How you know?"

"She's got kids," Yuq said.

"Doesn't stop her drinking."

"She's got kids."

"Put the kids to bed is what I say."

"That's your solution to everything."

"Toni will have some," Akmaaq said.

"Toni's got kids too," Yuq said. "They live in the same house."

"This generation," Akmaaq said, and he shook his head. "We didn't need laws. At least we didn't need *their* laws. What do they care what we do?"

"Peter Pence is one of us," Yuq said. "Jamo is one of us."

"We got Inupiat cops, so what?" Akmaaq said. "Inupiat don't need laws."

"If he gets too drunk," Yuq said to Jacobs and Q in the backseat, "then he walks home. I'll come get you two so you don't freeze, but *he* needs to walk it off. He acts like he's already drunk."

"You'd make an old man walk?" Akmaaq said.

"If you can get drunk, you can walk. If you can whale, you can walk."

"*We* respected our elders," Akmaaq said, "drunk or not. *This* generation. *We* never had a season without bringing back a whale."

"There were more whales then," Yuq said. "There were no government allotments. There were more Inupiat. Boys didn't grow up just to leave."

"We weren't excuse makers," Akmaaq said. "We just did it."

"You sound like a Nike ad."

"You say that to me?" Akmaaq said.

"It *is* a Nike ad," Q agreed.

"*We're not excuse makers*?" Akmaaq said. "I guess it is a catchy slogan. I guess that *would* make me want to buy jogging shoes. I thought of it first though. I been saying that for years."

Chapter 5

Driving back through Point Halcyon, Jacobs grasped the town in its entirety. Houses were arranged in a grid, trailer homes or model 1940s ranch houses with ramshackle additions. There was no discernable downtown, the businesses and municipal buildings sprinkled among the residences, the businesses only distinguished by a sign or by the vehicles parked in front. Marta and Toni's house looked the same as the rest, with the exception that all the lights were on and one of the cars on the street in front of their house was idling, the tailpipe sending up a cloud of exhaust.

"They just leave it going with the keys in?" Q asked.

On the screened porch, there were boots, jackets, and bags of dog food strewn about.

"Winter habit," Akmaaq said. "When it's cold enough you let the car run overnight. Probably, she forgot."

Inside, the house was humid. There were children and toys that made traversing the carpet difficult. Two malamutes raised their ears but didn't get up from where they lay in front of the couch while a third came bounding in, and he barked. The dog was formidable, with green eyes that hinted at a human soul. He poked Q with his snout and he growled.

"That dog's racist," Akmaaq said. "He don't like strangers."

Q moved cautiously into the room and the dog went over to Jacobs. It gave him two sniffs then walked off, signaling approval, though the dog kept an eye on Q from then on. Marta and Toni came over, hugged the old man, and Toni took his bottle. The TV blared cartoons from a DVD player and two of the four kids were transfixed. The other two went from living room to kitchen to bathroom seeking something to do. With Jacobs and Q in their house, the two kids stared for a moment, then they continued to wander, occasionally stopping to turn over a toy.

"Toni's husband was a good captain," Akmaaq said. "He is at peace, and his boys will be whalers."

There were pictures of him about the room, all of them black and white, as if from another era. Toni's husband was young but had a weathered stoic face, his parka hood pulled back to reveal a tangled mess of matted black hair, and he held a harpoon.

"We sure miss him around here," Marta said. "Can't say the same for mine. I *wish* he were dead."

"Marta's husband left for Seattle," Akmaaq said.

"He sent checks at first," Marta said. "Then the well dried. He got lazy. Met a girl. Got arrested. He was no good. He better never try and come back."

"You want mixers?" Toni said. "We got juice and Coke."

"The captain likes juice," Akmaaq said, referring to himself. Q and Jacobs shook their heads but accepted coffee cups half-filled with schnapps.

Akmaaq went over to the refrigerator and opened the freezer. "Maybe these guys are hungry," he said, and he took out some frozen fish. He produced a knife from his pocket, carved shavings from the frozen carcass, popped them into his mouth, and chewed.

"Maybe they like it cooked," Toni said. "We got seal fat, we can fry some."

"You like fried fish?" Marta asked.

"Yes, ma'am," Q said, and he took off his coat. He sat at the table and nursed his cup. He crossed his legs, eager to be served.

"I like him," Marta said.

"You like them young," Toni said.

"He's your son?" Marta asked Jacobs.

"He favors his mother," Jacobs said.

"I'm his director," Q said. "He's my producer."

Toni took a pat of seal blubber from a jar that had been sitting out, she dropped a dab into the frying pan, and when the oil was bubbling she threw in the frozen fish, which hissed and spat. Jacobs licked his lips. The smell of food weakened him and he was impatient to finally eat. Toni dipped her finger into the soft blubber and held it out to Jacobs.

"Try it," she said.

Q winced, and she laughed.

"It's good," she said, and she licked her own finger clean. "I thought you were Inuit," she countered. She dipped her finger again and put it in Jacobs's mouth. She kept her finger there for too long, letting the digit linger in a way intended to be sexual.

"I like this one," Toni said. "He really *is* Inuit."

"What about the captain?" Akmaaq said. "Who's going to take care of the captain?"

"The captain's old," Marta said, and she ran a hand over his balding head. "We keep telling him and he keeps coming back."

"You're the only single girls. I got hope."

"There's others," Toni said.

"You're the only ones who'll have anything to do with me."

"Does that say something about us?" Marta said.

"It says something about *him*," Toni said.

The three men ate heaping servings of the steaming white meat. Then Jacobs and Q sat back, feeling sated.

"Eat now," Akmaaq said. "On the water, we don't stop. And no fires on the ice. So no hot drinks and no hot meals."

"For them, it's like giving birth," Marta said. "All their stories of hardship."

"Closest they come," Toni said.

"My man couldn't hack it. Gave him nightmares."

"That's why people say he left," Toni said. "Afraid of the shifting ice. Afraid of black waters."

"That ain't why," Marta said. "TV is why. They made Seattle look damn good."

"I been there," Akmaaq said. "Three words: salmon, coffee, and computers."

The schnapps only made it once around, so Toni took an unlabeled jar of yellow liquid from a cabinet and poured out seconds. The yellow liquor was decidedly stiff, and Jacobs choked it down.

"I want to show you something," Akmaaq said, and he led his crew into the garage through a door in the kitchen. There was an umiaq upside-down on sawhorses that took most of the space. The umiaq was large enough for a crew of ten men, an open boat with a whalebone frame. Several sealskins were sewn together and stretched across it. There were steel oarlocks screwed into the whalebone but no oars, only a set of long canoe paddles that had been waxed to look like new. There were harpoons, spears, and long knives that all leaned against the wall and smelled like grease.

"The women have sealed our canoe and polished our implements. If we look snappy, the whale will come and take a look."

"The three of us can row this thing?" Jacobs said.

"*I* could row it," Akmaaq said. "But I'm the harpooner."

Back in the house, Marta and Q snuck off to cuddle on the couch while the kids crawled around or zoned out watching TV. Marta stood up and declared, "Let's get you measured," and she took Q into another room.

"Yes," Toni agreed, and she tugged at Jacobs, who hadn't finished his drink and who didn't want to get up from the table. "You need to get measured."

Against his will, Jacobs found himself in Toni's bedroom. There was another photo of her dead husband on the nightstand. He looked at the couple like a disapproving father.

"Strip," Toni said. "Caribou snow pants fit on tight."

"I can wear underwear, can't I?" Jacobs said.

"Strip."

Jacobs took off his clothes and sat on the bed. Toni got down and took a pair of old sealskin boots from under the bed. She slipped them over Jacobs's feet and she was immodest about the fact that her face was close to his exposed lap. She stared right at him.

"I'm married," Jacobs said.

"I am too," Toni said. She took out a long piece of twine, ran it along his arms and legs, and tied knots to mark the lengths. She reached around him to measure his waist, and he flinched.

"I'm only trying to measure you," she said, and so he relaxed, but as soon as his guard was down she pushed him onto the bed and tried to kiss him.

"I can't," Jacobs said.

"It's been too long," Toni said, not letting up. "I need it."

"I have a wife," Jacobs said.

Toni leaned back but didn't release her grip. She tried a different tactic.

"You could die out there," she said. "This could be your last chance to be with me."

Jacobs was shocked, not at what she was saying, but at himself and the way he had brought up his wife. Two weeks ago all he wanted was to get away from her and he'd kicked around the idea of leaving for good. He had resented her trying to hold him back and was disappointed they hadn't had any children.

"Are you on the pill?" Jacobs asked.

"Eskimo women don't need the pill. There are twenty-five or twenty-six days you can do it."

"That works?" Jacobs said. He remembered all the kids running around in the other room.

"Of course it works. You don't have to take no pill. Those pills are bad for you."

"My wife..."

"...is crazy from hormones," Toni said. "She don't know up from down."

"The pill was more sure."

"Inupiat girls learn," Toni said. "And then it's easy."

"I can't do this," Jacobs said.

"We don't have to. Your wife is probably pretty."

"She's OK," Jacobs said, and that's what he'd always felt. Then, because he knew Toni would have no way of knowing, and it was best to let her believe what she believed, he added, "She's beautiful."

"That must be really nice for you," Toni said.

"It's nice."

"We got to act like we did it though," Toni said. "Or the captain won't respect you." She started to fake an orgasm as she bounced on the bed. Jacobs joined in and they were both laughing. He was surprised at himself, but he really enjoyed bouncing on the bed and grunting in time next to her. As they moaned back and forth into a climax, the door opened and one of Toni's kids stood holding the doorknob.

Jacobs tried to cover himself but they were on top of the bedspread and it was too late, the child had seen.

"Mom," she said. "They won't let me watch *Teletubbies*."

"You already saw *Teletubbies*," Toni said, and she kept bouncing on the edge of the bed to keep up the momentum.

"That was yesterday."

"No, it was today," Toni said. "Remember, the one with the cement truck?"

"Oh yeah," the child said, and she closed the door behind her. A moment later the same child could be heard saying to the kids in the living room, "You were right, they *were* doing it."

When Jacobs and Toni came out of the bedroom, the children all ran at them holding what looked like giant puffer fish with teeth bared. Jacobs ran back into the bedroom before he realized what was happening, and Toni called to him, "Come on out, great white hunter. Those seals are dead. They're drag-floats for your harpoons."

He had taken off Toni's husband's boots to get dressed and then slipped them back on. They fit loosely and he nearly tripped as he ran into the bedroom.

Jacobs took one of the overlarge footballs and inspected it. The float was a single sealskin sewn together whole and inflated like a balloon.

"A bowhead might be sixty feet," Akmaaq said. "You rarely kill him with one strike. You have to chase him and wear him out. They swim fast and dive deep. Stick a few of these in him and he slows down. And if you kill him, if you are lucky enough to get him, the drag-floats keep him from sinking."

Akmaaq sat at the table emptying gunpowder from rifle shells onto a sheet of paper. His head was turned to the side so he could see what he was doing with his good eye. "When he surfaces," Akmaaq said, "you jab him in the heart with one of these." He held up what looked like a homemade stick of dynamite tied to a harpoon head with a long fuse. It made Jacobs uneasy to see Akmaaq playing with explosives, but he figured the old man knew what he was doing. The Inupiat had ushered in the modern age long ago and Akmaaq had witnessed it. There was no disgrace in foreshortening the agony of the whale with a homemade bomb. The carcass was eaten just the same.

"You sure he's a man?" Akmaaq said to Toni. Marta and Q were still in the other bedroom, and Akmaaq meant that Q had outlasted him.

"He's man enough," Toni said. Then she added, *"I'd rather be a brave man's widow than a coward's wife."*

It sounded like a familiar saying and Jacobs searched himself but he was never good at placing quotes, he just sold them.

He didn't really like how easily Akmaaq accepted Toni's truism. Living had its advantages too. He gave the blown-up seal back to one of the kids, who lined up in front of the other bedroom because they heard the door unlock and the doorknob turned. When they ran at Q with the seal buoys, he wasn't surprised or taken aback and Q chased the kids with his arms over his head. They loved him and spun in circles, giggling. Q had obviously been around kids, and he wasn't too much scared of anything.

"The captain was there when my husband died," Toni said.

"Tell it, tell it, tell it!" the kids all said in unison, and they jumped up and down.

"I don't want to give anybody nightmares," Akmaaq said.

"They've all heard it," Toni said.

"I need tobacco for my pipe," Akmaaq said.

"We don't have tobacco," Marta said. "What gave you that idea?"

"You know what I mean," Akmaaq said, and he winked with his good eye.

Toni said, "I've got what you want." She took his pipe back into the bedroom and returned with it filled, the contents of the bowl a bright green. Akmaaq puffed until a cloud of pungent blue smoke permeated the room.

Q said, "Give me a hit of that," but the old man ignored him. Akmaaq paused and held the smoke in his lungs. Then he exhaled slowly and started to talk.

Evening fell over the land like a curtain. I was with Toni's husband, Captain Ilguq, and my son, Captain Yuq. There were others of us along the ice shelf, boats ready. We were silent. We were waiting. A shout went up in one of the nearby camps. There had been a sighting. We all took to the water, where we encountered thin ice and floating ice. Fish were jumping and three whales spouted in a patch of open water. If we missed these whales more would follow.

We paddled our umiaqs in fading light and the spouts were farther off. Ilguq, Yuq, and I were the strongest paddlers, but other boats among us had the advantage of setting out sooner, or of starting from a nearer vantage point.

The harpooner with the first strike kept the first share. As a hunter, you pray for it. Everyone rejoices in the sharing of the whale, but the first portion is best. Secretly, I sometimes wished another hunter would strike and kill the whale, or that my son would. But in those days, when I had two eyes, I was the surest mark and the most successful harpooner. The best hope lay on me.

After pursuing the whales out to sea and following for an hour, it had gotten dark, but we could see where the whale might surface. We were eventually near enough to strike. There was much sea-ice, but with open patches and wide rivulets. My dart rifle was loaded and ready. I stood in the boat, released the safety, and waited. A bowhead breached near us, and just as I shot I could feel our umiaq turn and rise as a second whale surfaced beneath us. Females will travel in a pod if one is pregnant or they will swim with their young, but this was a lone adult closely trailed by another. Bowhead follow each other and surface in the same places, but they are a solitary species and they migrate alone.

At first this second whale seemed a block of ice that floated up from below. He was a white whale, the snow whale, and when he surfaced from under us I saw the tail and his open mouth. Belugas are white and not uncommon, but they precede the bowhead migration; it's how we know when to wait on the ice. This animal was much too large for a beluga, with thirty feet of head and trunk floating above the water. He was a whale sixty to seventy-five feet long. He looked at me with his black eye and the vision of this whale was disorienting because he was all white, his mouth wide open—not a baleen-feeder, but he had teeth. The white whale had seen me take aim at the bowhead and knew what I was about to do. He had come at us in the bowhead's defense and it was why he traveled with them. As large as the bowheads are, they won't actively try to sink the umiaq. They are passive. Mostly, they try to get away. But the snow whale reared and threatened to swallow our skin-boat.

When I realized what had happened, I dropped the dart gun, took up a harpoon, and thrust it into the creature's mouth. The giant bit down on the line and dove deep. We held on as he pulled us away from the other boats, and farther from shore. He pulled us into the lead, the wide channel with floating sea ice that opened to sea silence and to our deaths at sea. He took us to where the sea met the night. We held on to the rope, the umiaq pulled over ice and water, and we left a wake as we were dragged, the strength of a whale like an ocean liner. Then the rope went lax and there was play in the line. We knew we had to take up the slack or he might get free. But we couldn't keep up and we felt the sea rise. We held on to the sides of the boat, he struck us from below, and Captain Ilguq was flung into the water. You can only live a minute in freezing water. An Eskimo need not know how to swim.

Yuq reached for Ilguq with a paddle and I had the instinct to grab one of the harpoons. That night we witnessed something unnatural. This whale wasn't simply protecting the bowhead, he was being more than defensive—*he* was hunting *us*. He'd known we would come out to meet bowheads, and he had been waiting. He wanted us dead and he wanted us to suffer. He surfaced next to Ilguq, he twisted in the water, and he clamped his mouth over the poor captain, disappearing with him under dark water, with only his booted leg left floating, the same leg we brought back for the funeral, all that was left to bury in the cemetery, the rest of him carried to the bottom of the sea. Ilguq was chewed and spit out by the devil whale, an evil white incarnation like none ever seen.

The snow whale is still out there and he also took my eye. We will meet again, here or in the afterworld. We are indebted to each other.

Ilguq was a good man. He was my friend and a friend to my son. They were the same age and grew up together. I taught them both to hunt. I taught them their prayers and to dip bread in warm blubber. Yuq, my son, has said to me many times that we set out that day without giving thanks and he believes this creature was sent in answer of our pride. He feels that for many years the whites had done too much damage to the whale population, and now *we* were being punished. The snow whale was the devil guardian sent from the underworld to answer our weaknesses and unfortunate alliances.

Yuq will also tell you we never saw it, and that I was dreaming and drunk. He'll tell you Ilguq fell from the boat and froze to death in the waters without molestation. He'll tell you he fell out and that's all there was. But we came back with Ilguq's leg, and only his leg. Yuq's afraid if he speaks of the snow whale it will come looking for him. And this is also why he will never again whale with me. But he was there, and he knows.

When the creature returned and made a third pass, we were ready with our harpoons, both of us fearing for our lives, maybe for the first time since we started to hunt together. And so it was my last hunt with my son and the last hunt with both eyes. I had lit the fuse of one of my bombs, I stood up with the harpoon reared, and I struck the animal when he was near. When I hit him, the snow whale turned to show me another harpoon blade in his side. The creature was bragging. He seemed to say he had been struck before and he could absorb our blows. Another harpoon blade was lodged in his side, the spot swollen with layers of hide that had since puckered around the old implement.

When he twisted back, I saw where I had hit him, and the bomb exploded in front of me. Splinters of spear shaft were thrown into my face and a piece of wood stuck in my eye. Yuq sat down in the boat and chanted to the winds. I had taught him the old songs, and he cried out to the ancestors to come to our aide. When he stopped there was silence. We only heard the sound of waves lapped against the umiaq and chunks of ice rubbing together farther out in the darkened sea. We scooped up Ilguq's leg and rowed back toward shore, to where the reflected moonlight from the snow-covered land was brightest, which we knew to be Tikigaq. Yuq told me to lay back and to rest, but I continued to row. You can hardly maneuver a skin-boat with just one paddler, so I leaned over the side and I also rowed—all the while with a splinter of wood in my bleeding eye.

At some point in the telling, as the tale became somber and serious, Akmaaq turned his head and removed his glass eye without the children noticing. When he got to the end of his tale, he put his pipe into the eye cavity so the pipe stem stuck out and smoke seeped from his eye socket. He hunched over and nearly whispered by the end of his story. Then he turned to face them and shouted the final sentence: "*With a splinter of wood in my bleeding eye,*" and he showed the kids his smoking eyehole with the pipe stem sticking out. They ran screaming and he chased them around the room. Jacobs jumped, and so did Q. Marta and Toni had known this was coming, as the kids must have too, and they all laughed and gathered the children for bed.

The old man was drunk, and it was time to walk home. Jacobs wore Captain Ilguq's boots, knowing they weren't the ill-fated pair, since they *were* a pair.

"Wear extra socks," Toni had said when Jacobs complained the boots were loose, but that wouldn't be enough.

"Stuff newspapers in them," Marta said, but that wasn't a solution either. So much for having his gear fitted. The women seemed to want to avoid any sewing, though they were more than happy to try to get Q and Jacobs into bed. As the captain announced he was leaving, Toni pulled on Jacobs as she had before.

"You can stay," she pleaded. "We don't have to do it. But you should stay."

On the phone with her mother, Jessica was conflicted. She expressed her truth, which was that she missed her husband, but since she'd long been in the habit of calling up her mother to complain about him, she felt like a fraud. All the hours where she'd spoken of his shortcomings, his mediocrity, his indifference. How she was uninspired and embarrassed by him. She meant all that. She felt it. The annoying sounds he made when he ate. The way he never had anything interesting or important to say. Yet, she wholly and absolutely missed him so completely that she walked into his closet as she talked, to retrieve some sense of him.

He didn't own enough clothes. He had shoes where a hole had worn through the sole, and socks with holes that matched. Four suits were hung there: brown, beige, and two blue. They were nice suits, expensive suits, but he'd kept them too many years and didn't dry clean them often enough. His silk ties were in beautiful patterns. He had an eye for color and contrast, but he only owned a handful, so they seemed common. She ran her hand over the fabrics and found even his casual clothes elegant, but worn too often. She closed her eyes and pressed into them, surrounded by notes of dried perspiration, stagnant dry cleaning, old leather, dust—and from somewhere in the closet, she also smelled wool.

"*Why* is he in Alaska?" Jessica's mother wanted to know.

"Because I couldn't keep him here."

"You can't go blaming yourself," her mother said.

"He thinks he's an Eskimo."

"I remember."

"I have no idea when he's coming back," Jessica said. "Weeks."

"You two needed a break anyway."

"Did Dad ever do anything like this?"

"Your father?" Jessica's mother said, and it was a way of sending the question back to Jessica, who had been there and should have known. Her father had been an accountant. He read the newspaper every day. He required quiet in the house when he listened to his Tchaikovsky. Jessica remembered her father's records played loud, but still he wanted quiet.

"Dad never left us," she said.

"He *did*. He went inside. At least your husband is coming back."

"Dad made me feel guilty for wanting attention," Jessica said. "I always thought it was my fault. That I was boring. Or that he didn't want to spend time with me because I wasn't pretty."

"And now you feel the same from John?"

"Mom, you're supposed to say, 'You *were* pretty.'"

"I'm your mother. It doesn't count. I see what others can't."

"I guess I don't need that feeling from my husband of all people."

"He *loves* you. He *adores* you."

Jessica walked back out of her husband's closet. She had felt sorry for herself and had wanted her mother to encourage her sentimentality. She'd wanted to be indulged. But all the things she'd complained about with regard to her husband, all the things that had made him unattractive and nothing to brag about, those same attributes assured John's return. And when he got back, she would work on him then. Who knew? Maybe he'd come back in better physical shape. Maybe he'd find passion and return to her reinvigorated and interesting. This Alaska trip might be good for them both.

"You really think so, Mom? You think he *adores* me?"

"I don't think," she said. "I *know*."

In the middle of the night, Jacobs woke up disoriented and sweating. He remembered he was in Toni's bed. He slept in his boxers and they had kept to themselves, as promised. Toni was at the end of the bed and sobbing. He tried to ignore her, and he rolled over to show her his back, but when she sensed he was awake she latched on to his feet through the covers.

"You don't belong here," she said. "You shouldn't go whaling."

Jacobs didn't say anything. Toni slept in an empty bed, with a lonely heart, and if it weren't for Marta being in similar straits, the children would overrun her.

Jessica had never been a crier, so Jacobs was unsure of what to do. It was clear Toni wouldn't let him sleep. He had to say something. He sat up and took her in his arms. She was naked, and he suspected she hoped he might change his mind about her, though she insisted she always slept that way. She collapsed into his chest and cried. He ran a hand up and down her back and said, "There, there. It's OK. It's going to be OK."

He didn't know what, specifically, was making her cry: the death of her husband, the fatigue of her circumstances, or the fact that he too might soon be dead. Jacobs hadn't thought enough about dying, and he'd been too trusting. He *didn't* know it would be OK. But that was what was said when someone cried. Jacobs knew to sound sure, to act like he knew. Yet, he lacked the capacity to imagine his own quick death in ice-cold water here at the top of the world—and *he* should have been the one crying.

"Do you blame the captain?" he said, and as soon as he said it he knew there might be confusion over which captain he meant.

"It's what they do. You can't keep them from it."

"Do you believe Akmaaq's story?"

"There are those who think Akmaaq is a liar. Either way, he's brought division and has failed us as a leader."

"Can a chief retire?"

"He wants to die," she said. "His pride won't let him show it, but he's unhappy. He hates not being in charge."

"Yuq told me to pray," Jacobs said. "Teach me."

"You know 'Hail Mary'?" she said. "That's a good one."

"I want to pray like our people. Not like white people."

"We're Christian," Toni said. "Those are our prayers too."

"I guess I thought there would be prayers for hunting, and prayers for facing the unknown."

"Pray how you want," Toni said. "If there's a God, He'll listen. Come with us tomorrow to church."

"Won't I stand out?"

"This is a small town," she said. "You think people don't know you're here?"

"I guess I'm anxious. I want to be accepted."

"Don't worry about them," she said. "They don't much like anybody. Not even themselves."

In the morning Toni dressed Jacobs in a suit of her husband's that fit well enough. She let him use her phone, which he thought was generous since he'd rebuffed her advances.

"Did you get my e-mail?" John said.

"I was glad you arrived OK," Jessica said.

"This is the first chance I've had to call."

"What are the people like?" she wanted to know.

"It's cold and it's dark," John said. "They like to drink. They're like a big extended family. We're going to church."

"I went too," Jessica said.

"*To church?*"

"The bird died," she said, "and I felt I had to say something."

"I'm sorry," John said.

"Not as sorry as I was. I mean, we both knew there wasn't a chance, but when I saw him all flopped over in his nest my heart sank, and I cried."

"Everyone goes to church here, I think."

"Have you met Santa Claus?"

"I met the chief. We're staying at his place, sort of."

"What do you mean, sort of?"

"I need to keep this short. It's an expensive call."

"I can call you back," she suggested.

"We're running late. I just wanted to say I've missed you and I can't wait to see you."

"Really?" Jessica said. "I thought you wanted to get away."

"It wasn't you," John said. "I just needed to find out about myself. It was never you."

"You've had me going up and down."

"I know," John said. "And I'm sorry."

"I lit a candle for you," she said. "One for the bird. One for you."

"You went to the *Catholic* church?"

"Why not?"

"Because they're Catholic, that's why not."

"Eskimos aren't Catholic?"

"We're Piskipulut."

"Episcopalian?" she said. "Light *me* a candle. If they have them. One for us."

"They might not. But I will if you want me to."

Jessica sealed the lid on the bird's Tupperware bowl and knew just where to bury him, but she doubted her ability to loosen the hard-packed soil. She called Jodi, explained John was out of town, and asked if she would send Nat over for a few odd jobs. There was just the one, but "odd job" sounded funny, or maybe even vulgar, in the singular. She tried to think of something else Nat might do and then she regretted calling, because Nat and Jodi were bound to ask questions. She decided she would say John went up to witness the whale migration, because that sounded interesting. She had no idea what the odds of actually *catching* a whale were, but she'd been fishing, and remembered that the bigger the fish, the slimmer the chance. If he came back unsuccessful he might never mention whales again. However, if he—if *they*—bagged a whale, he would brag to everyone, especially Nat, who was no hunter, but the kind of man to appreciate the primitive arts. Killing a whale, though, was more of a transgression than shooting a bald eagle. Worse than killing a monkey.

Nat had combed his hair and he was wearing a dress shirt that looked ironed. When Jodi explained what she wanted done, Nat rolled up his sleeves, and his shirt came untucked, but in a matter of minutes the baby bird was in the ground. Nat didn't ask where John had gone, or why, and when he stood too close to Jessica his nostrils flared in response to her old standby perfume number two.

Jessica was sad for the occasion, but grateful to Nat, so she asked him into the house for a drink. She had in mind iced tea or lemonade, but Nat helped himself to a can of beer. He relaxed on the living room sofa, which Jessica worried he might soil with his sweat. So she asked if he'd help her hang a framed playbill of *Phantom*, which had come through on a Broadway tour over a year ago, when she'd convinced John to go. She remembered talking on the way about the chandelier—would they be able to drop it? And John had said the university auditorium was too small, maybe if they performed *Phantom* at the basketball stadium. The theater had empty seats and a chandelier was dropped, but it looked miniature and not much of an effect. John held her hand through the performance, and afterwards he bought the framed playbill, which cost less than the prints but more than she expected he'd spend without prodding.

Jessica found herself chatting as she went up to the bedroom closet to fetch the framed playbill, and Nat followed, without a word. She was jittery with him in the house, and while she had always been sure she wasn't attracted to him, she wasn't so sure, because she shouldn't have been nervous. She knew Jodi waited and was maybe even looking out their dining room window.

Nat stood behind Jessica as she dug around in her cluttered closet, and when she came out with the framed playbill, which was a lot smaller than she remembered, he set his beer on the nightstand and held her at the wrist.

"You wanted to show me your prints?" Nat said with a knowing smile.

"No, it's not like that," Jessica said, but Nat put his arm around her.

She dropped the framed playbill on the bed and, in a moment of panic, she led Nat in a cha-cha around the bedroom as she counted out, "*Rock. Step. Cha-cha-cha. Rock. Step. Cha-cha-cha.*" Nat gave Jessica more space because her behavior was weird, but when he decided to go for it, he became harder to lead. Despite Jessica's attempts, and her counting louder, Nat managed to cha-cha her back to the bed, where he shoved her and she fell back on it. Before she could sit up, he crawled on top of her, and before she could protest, they were kissing.

Jodi Jorgenson, by instinct, knew just when to call, and Jessica's cell phone was heard ringing downstairs. Nat also knew what this meant, so he got up, downed the rest of his beer, and wagged a finger at Jessica before he left.

Jessica knew Nat would see her as the instigator, and she wondered if maybe she was. She'd hoped her salon makeover would have had this effect on her husband, but she'd attracted the wrong man. Could that have happened if she hadn't wanted it to? She couldn't remember the last time she'd been so *desired*. Maybe she'd been discouraging toward her husband these last few years, but even when he'd come straight home and carried her up the stairs, John didn't look at her as Nat just had.

Jodi wasn't the one on the phone, however. It was Q's mother, who hadn't heard anything since her son had left. She wanted to know if they'd arrived OK, if there were penguins, and if they'd begun filming. Jessica could hardly believe John had found someone naïve enough to go along with him, and here she was speaking to the naïve person's mother.

"What did my husband tell you?" Jessica asked.

"They're making a film," Q's mother said. "My boy is the director."

"He wants to kill a whale."

"*Kill* it?" Q's mother said. "Why?"

Jessica wanted to say, "To prove he's not white," and while she knew this was the simple truth, she also knew she couldn't say it to Q's mother. Instead she said, "I don't know. Why do men do half the things they do?"

In his borrowed suit and the sealskin boots, Jacobs walked with Toni and her two children along the slushy gravel road to the Point Halcyon Piskipulut Church. Q and the captain walked home late last night, but they would meet up at the service. The sky was an overcast steel gray and the wind blew in from the sea. As if he had been waiting, a police cruiser came up the road behind them, drove past, and slowed for them to catch up. The passenger's side window was rolled down and the fat Inupiat cop shouted, "You're not from around here!" Toni's kids continued ahead, as if being followed by the police wasn't unusual, while Toni and Jacobs instinctively met the pace of the car.

"Jamo," Toni said, "leave him alone. We're on our way to church, for Christ's sake."

"I'm not talking to you, Toni," he said. "I don't much like the looks of him."

"You've seen white people before," she said.

"I didn't say he was white," the cop said. "I said he wasn't from around here."

"There's whites at the sonar post and you don't bug them."

"They're here for a reason. The government has a contract. They spend their money. They're good for the economy."

"He's here for a reason too. And he's more Inupiaq than you. He's whaling at least."

"Somebody's got to keep order," Jamo said. "If I go whaling, who enforces the law?"

"Try it and you'll see," Toni said. "We'd be fine without you. We don't need you prowling the streets."

The couple continued to walk, with Jacobs's gaze on the road ahead as the fat cop glared at him with an unwelcome stare. A squirrel ran across his path and Jacobs was surprised to see it—a creature familiar to his subdivision.

"I could take you in for jaywalking," Jamo shouted.

"There's no sidewalk," Toni said.

"I could get you for trespassing."

"We're walking by the side of the road," Toni said. "This is public property."

"I can see where your tracks crossed over into the Nunanuq's yard."

"We're on our way to church, Jamo."

"Jump in," he said. "I'll give you a ride."

Jacobs moved in the direction of the rolling police cruiser, but Toni pulled him away. "Don't you get in that car," she said. "No telling what he might do."

"I'm offering a ride."

"Where to is the question," Toni said, and she encouraged Jacobs to walk faster by pulling him along by the hand.

Chapter 6

Point Halcyon Piskipulut was a small stone church like many Jacobs had seen throughout his life, except the cemetery was surrounded by a picket fence made of whale jaw. Graves had been recently visited, with tracks in the snow and headstones dusted off. Toni's kids threw snowballs at these markers, and they cheered whenever one stuck. There were several snowmobiles and cars parked along the gravel road. Jamo sat in his police cruiser and idled. He sent up a cloud of exhaust.

Jacobs and Toni went in through the side entrance of the church, which made them conspicuous. The pastor was speaking, and the rows of round beige faces watched Jacobs as he and Toni moved to a second-row pew. Jacobs wondered who among them might be cousins. They looked alike to him, and so they might all be relations, their moon faces smiling. They appeared fun-loving and friendly. Jacobs might be stereotyping, but it also couldn't be denied—a crowd of jolly Eskimos stared back with black eyes. He wanted a brotherly connection, but he was self-conscious and anxious.

Q, Marta, her two kids, and the captain were in the back of the church, but Toni waved and they all came to join Jacobs and Toni in the second row. Toni's two kids went to sit in the back, in the space cleared when Q, Akmaaq, and Marta came up front. Akmaaq made a special point of sitting next to Jacobs, and once they were seated, he slapped Jacobs's thigh in a gesture of friendship. The captain signaled his acceptance of the white Eskimo to the rest of the clan and hoped to gain something from it.

In the remaining Sundays before the hunt, prayers were said for the men and boys, with their names read off. When the list was completed without Akmaaq's name being called, he cleared his throat, his eyes closed and his head lowered in prayer. The sound carried across the congregation and drew attention. At which point the pastor named him too, and Akmaaq smiled, because the pastor referred to him as captain and chief.

Yuq was in the front row, and though he also sat with head bowed and eyes closed, the display from his father made him bristle, and he felt the eyes of everyone on him. Next to Yuq was his beautiful wife. Her posture, her awareness, and her fine clothes all suggested she was the wife of the acting chief. Jacobs was drawn to her radiant grace and earthy sexuality.

Akmaaq cleared his throat again. The pastor tried to continue uninterrupted. So Akmaaq cleared his throat a third time. And the pastor understood, though he didn't know their names. He asked everyone to pray for the two visitors, who had graciously agreed to join the hunt, with the hope of bringing in a whale for the sake of the clan.

"May we be grateful for the bounty of the sea," the pastor continued. He was a man not entirely gray but past his prime, a contemplative man, a pillar of the community, and someone who wouldn't join the hunt because of his pastoral duties. But this service, the calling for community worship, was as much a part of the hunt as the making of homemade bombs and the fitting of sealskin boots.

"May the bowhead thrive as they pass by in migration at this festive time. May the government quota-makers understand there are bowhead enough, and it's all in God's plan. May we come together in ways we haven't in recent years. And may we one day meet again, for eternity, on that great ice shelf in the sky."

There were piles of parkas at the ends of pews. From his library research Jacobs had read that the Inuit loved summer best of all, and while he realized that most of the materials he had come across were about his people as they lived one-hundred-and-fifty years ago, he supposed this simple fact was still true: that the people who lived in the Arctic appreciated the warm sunny days, and they longed for them when they were gone. This being the start of spring, spirits were high, and the layers of clothes were coming off.

A teenage boy who had been sitting next to Yuq got up and read from the Bible at a side podium. The story was "Jonah and the Whale," which everyone had heard hundreds of times, but they listened with joyful antici-pation. Jacobs realized he hadn't paid much attention to this story before—why would he?—but he was able to make sense of it. Jonah hadn't listened to God, so a storm came and drowned the people he sailed with, while Jonah was swallowed by a whale for three days and brought to shore, mercifully. It was a parable, and Jacobs tried to work out the Christlike similarities. Like Christ, Jonah walked on water, *in a way*. He was out there with fisherman, *though he hadn't saved anyone*. And the three-days motif was uncanny. Jacobs remembered that the story predated

Jesus, from the Old Testament, and he wondered about Bible stories and threes.

Yuq's kid was well-dressed and he stood tall, his inflection clear and precise. He was the inheritor of the tribe, and prosperity would come to him. He had no fear of whaling, and he was a future leader. He'd been groomed for it. After he came and sat down in the pew with Yuq, the kid brought his flat palms together in an outward sign of solemnity, conscious all eyes were on him now. For the men this was another opportunity to steal glances at Yuq's wife. Most of the Inuit women put on weight by middle age, but Yuq's wife looked like a TV news anchor from Iceland, with bright green eyes, full pink lips, and a straight sure posture.

The pastor came to the podium and paused. He relished the silence after a favorite Bible story, and he let them wait before he would breathe new life into it.

In the Bible there are times of plenty and times of famine. In each, God provides. He moves the heavens to protect the worthy. The unbelievers, he smites. But God also forgives. And he summons his animals to serve.

Anybody here watch *Shark Week*?

Those were some good shows. The beauty and danger of sea creatures on display night after night. Did you hear how they said the story of "Jonah and the Whale" might have been a great white shark? That the Bible translation is "fish," though it's open to interpretation.

I believe the Bible was written with all of us in mind. God knows us before we're born. And for us, who find it hard to imagine what life in the desert might be like, we understand that forty days on the ice shelf would make you come to terms with yourself. Or three days in the belly of a whale. It would be quite a feat, and you would come back purified. We understand this Bible, though the people who lived it, and the people who wrote it, didn't even know the Arctic existed. They may have never even imagined snow.

And so I believe "Jonah and the Whale" is one of *our* stories. And it *is* about a whale. Because if a shark swallowed you whole, how would you breathe? They didn't talk about that. And wouldn't you like to watch *Whale Week*? They haven't thought of that one. They think people want blood. And that channel is for kids. Kids wanting blood.

But a whale is bigger and he breathes air. He holds in air, and he is intelligent and aware, not a voracious killer, but a friend to us, and known to be kind. A whale would listen to God.

Is it sinful for us to eat such intelligent, godly creatures? PETA thinks so. Greenpeace thinks so. The government quota-makers think so. But it is not sinful if we are aware of the bounty of God's gifts and if we remain grateful. We have heard stories of white men, once they were among us, lost in the Arctic wilderness and facing death—how they turned on each other and ate one another. Did God judge them? We can't know. Was human flesh a gift God allowed? And what about you? Would you eat your neighbor? None of us can say without actually being there. Because hunger is a powerful motivator, and we have all seen the most graceful of malamutes brought low over scraps.

We were hungry last year, and that hunger isn't yet forgotten. We were also brought low. We celebrated with bear meat, and seal meat, but I heard it spoken that there was the feeling that the Chukchi Sea had dried up. I heard talk of *uggianaqtuq* from Sila—or that God made this *crazy-weather*. That the heavens affected the bowhead migration, and we would soon find ourselves among the extinct. And I heard it said that infighting in our clan kept God's creatures away.

We can't know what happened. But we can pray. We can be thankful for what we do bring to the table. And we can stop this bickering.

Would you blame God for withholding? Nobody said he had to save Jonah, who didn't deserve God's mercy. But Jonah soon understood the errors of his life and the terrible greatness of God. We are given these words as a warning. It is nothing short of miraculous that the Bible was brought to us by men of good intention. Our ancestors nearly slaughtered those first white missionaries because we had too often dealt with the shiftless white whalers. But those men of God, those first missionaries—they were faithful and true. They staked everything on us and believed in the mission enough to live among us. We owe our Christian heritage to them, and we thank them for recognizing the godliness in us.

May we come together in a spirit of brotherhood, and may many whales please us with bounty. We pray for a successful hunt, brought about through cooperation and respect for the whale. In God's name, we pray.

After the service Jacobs followed Toni and the captain out the side entrance of the church. Snowmobiles were started and left idling as groups congregated. One by one they walked over to Jacobs and called him Jonah. Jacobs corrected them at first but decided the name might suit him. They also called him *Tanik*, but it seemed more a description than a name. They didn't really introduce themselves but said, "Jonah, good luck," or "Jonah, God is with you." Q laughed and shook his head. And so, thanks to the pastor's sermon, Jacobs had won them over, and he would be Jonah.

Yuq and his wife and son remained aloof, but Jacobs decided Yuq's approval was important, since warm Sunday feelings might be short-lived, and he also wanted to meet Yuq's wife.

"Your father told us how he lost his eye."

"That old story," Yuq's wife countered. "And Akmaaq wonders why people don't respect him."

"But you were there," Jacobs said to Yuq. "You saw the white whale."

"Believe what you want to believe," Yuq said. "The ice plays tricks."

"Then what really happened?"

"We were hungry and exhausted. My best friend fell out of the umiaq and he died. My father didn't make *that* up."

Yuq's family got into his white Jeep Cherokee and drove off with the windows whited over.

John remembered his promise to Jessica, and he had seen votives in a side vestibule. In the Catholic churches Jacobs had grown up in, the tradition was to light a candle for the deceased, and in Point Halcyon the custom was probably the same. John supposed Jessica didn't know about votives. Her approach to God was more like talking to herself in a daydream. When she lit a candle and prayed for the dead bird, he wondered what the Catholics would have thought. And while he liked being called Jonah as a sign of acceptance, he also found the name foreboding, since Jonah wasn't so lucky after all.

Jacobs excused himself from Toni and the other Point Halcyoners, and he went back into the church through the side entrance. Toni looked at him like she wanted to follow. The night before, Jacobs had asked her questions about what Inupiat men were like. What did people admire about her husband? What would a whaler like her husband think of a white Eskimo—*taniayaaq* she had said was the word, or *tanik*. Or of his son, Q, who was even more racially mixed—*taaqsipaiyaaq,* she had said, or *taaqsik*. Toni knew people expected her to light votive candles for her husband

and to dust the snow off his grave, but she was tired of being the widow and of praying over a leg. Mostly she wished there were more single men in Point Halcyon.

Kneeling in front of the candles, Jacobs saw they weren't candles, but small porcelain reservoirs of seal fat. When a match was lit, the match was leaned to become a wick, and the votive burned until the pat of blubber melted and eventually extinguished. Jacobs knew he was supposed to leave something in the offertory basket, but he didn't have money, so he believed what the pastor had said—that he'd come to bring bounty through the sacrifice of his efforts at the risk of grave danger to himself. He didn't give money, but it wasn't like he didn't give.

Kneeling in front of the array of small oil lamps, he lit a match, placed it in the ball of fat, closed his eyes, and thought of Jessica. He'd grown fond of her since he'd left. He understood some of the hurt he had caused, and he was now resolved to remain faithful. Though he couldn't help fighting off the mosquito notion that if Toni looked more like Yuq's wife....

He remembered the Hail Mary, but the prayer didn't seem fitting, so he let his thoughts wander. He started off by addressing Jesus, God, and the Spirit. And Mary, since he didn't want to leave anyone out. Jacobs wondered what was appropriate and could he ask for the killing of a whale? He thought of Toni's husband, Ilguq. He knew what he looked like and how he had died. They'd never met, but Jacobs wore his boots. The idea of God and Jesus and Mary left his imagination and he concentrated on Captain Ilguq, Toni's dead husband. The snow whale had thrown him from the umiaq, and he had died in the frozen ocean. Jacobs asked his spirit for help, so he might land a whale for the family Ilguq left behind.

Jacobs daydreamed about the hunt and his mind conjured the enormous terrible snow whale that stared with its malicious and ancient black eye. Jacobs imagined a cavernous mouth that could swallow him whole, lined with large jagged teeth that would chew him before spitting him back out into freezing waters. "Please protect me," he whispered to the spirit of Ilguq. And so the good intentions of his original prayer were a ways off. There was no longer any thought of Jessica or Jesus, and Jacobs was left pleading for the protection of his own hide. "Please don't let me die."

Akmaaq stood behind him and reached over Jacobs's shoulder to extinguish his prayer lantern, but he missed and reached into some of the other cups. Eventually, he zeroed in on the one Jacobs prayed over by holding his hand flat and feeling for the heat. He put out the flame with a sizzle and it sent up a ribbon of sweet smoke. Jacobs wanted to say, "What did you do that for?" but he recognized Akmaaq was his captain and his chief. Jacobs wasn't about to object, and he would hear him out, though he felt the man was being disrespectful.

"Don't buy the hocus pocus," Akmaaq said. "Spirits are not obligated to help."

"Why do you want to die?" Jacobs said. Akmaaq couldn't deny the accusation, though this was the first mention of it between them.

"I want to go the only way I know how," he said. "Back to the sea. No amount of praying is going to prevent that, so why not accept fate?"

"I'm not ready," Jacobs said. "I'm too young."

"Q is young. You've lived. The question is: *how* have you lived?"

"I'm only beginning. The truth has been kept from me."

"I'll teach you," Akmaaq said. "But we stick with traditional Inupiat ways. I don't want to see you praying on your knees." He reached into one of the unlit cups, pulled out the ball of lard, and popped it into his mouth.

"What about Q?" Jacobs said. "You can't keep *him* from praying.."

"We won't need to," Akmaaq said. "If the whale sees him, it's coming right for him. Your son will get his chance."

Outside the church, parishioners continued to loiter. Toni and Marta had walked home, and there were two snowmobiles left idling, one of which Akmaaq said Yuq was letting him borrow. Then Jacobs saw something he'd seen a hundred times, so at first it didn't register as uncommon in Point Halcyon—a police car with a black kid in the backseat drove away. Then he remembered everyone here was Inupiat. And he remembered Q.

"They'll keep him overnight," Akmaaq said. "Builds character."

"That's my cameraman," Jacobs said. Then he corrected himself: "That's my *director*." Then he corrected himself again: "That's my *son*."

"I'll give you a lift," Akmaaq said, and they both climbed onto the snowmobile.

But they didn't follow the police cruiser, which drove off slowly. Instead, they went toward the ocean, and they passed the landing strip along the way. Jacobs held on to Akmaaq, impressed by the old man's physique. Akmaaq didn't wear his parka, despite the temperature being frigid, and his shoulders and chest were solid. On the ice near the shore, he didn't slow down, and Jacobs couldn't tell if they'd gone out over the water. With the ice beginning the yearly thaw, he felt uneasy, as if the sea ice might suddenly give way to deadly freezing water. They drove out to where the land ice met the sea ice, then northward along the rim. There was so much floating ice that a dazed driver might head straight out.

When the whales came, they would walk their umiaq out to the lead, where the ice opened into a channel, and then they would paddle. Jacobs wondered if they might damage the sealskin boat against the mini-icebergs along the way. And he wondered if there would be enough insulation between himself and the water. Would he succumb to hypothermia through the sealskins without ever getting wet?

Akmaaq parked the snowmobile. They looked out to where the sea met the horizon, and Jacobs hoped for the sighting of a V-shaped spout. He knew this would endear him to the clan, but he also knew it was too early. Otherwise, there would have been Point Halcyoners out watching.

"Because the air is dry," Akmaaq said, "the cold gets 'on' you but doesn't penetrate. You'll get used to it."

Along the edge where the land ice met the sea ice, Jacobs saw the ice was thick and he knew he shouldn't be squeamish, though the thickness along this ledge didn't guarantee that there weren't thinner spots elsewhere. Ice melted all around as it had for weeks, leaving standing pools, the ice polished and slick.

Akmaaq parked the snowmobile at the edge of the frozen ocean and climbed off. Jacobs remained on the seat and looked out. He was comforted by the solemnity of the white expanse, and he was confident he would live. He was at home here and he felt he'd been welcomed. Mike Schmidt was a fool staying in a hotel in the biggest city. Who did he think he was?

You had to give yourself over. You had to live it. He watched a pair of puffins that stood on an incline and stared back.

He was pulled out of his meditation by the sight of Akmaaq kicking over short snow totems that were in a row along the ridge. They weren't natural formations and were clearly left by human hands with some kind of intention. As he neared the puffins, they flew off.

"What are you doing?"

"I told you," Akmaaq said. "No praying. We have to stop them. Or the snow whale might not come."

So the old man wasn't a pragmatic traditionalist. Quite the opposite. He was superstitious and trying to draw out the snow whale with sacrilege. He wanted revenge, and he would risk the wrath of nature and the disgrace of the clan to bring him.

"Maybe you shouldn't do that," Jacobs said.

"Jonah," Akmaaq said, "let's go get your director."

The Inupiat had called him Jonah earnestly, while Akmaaq was mocking. Names mattered. Jacobs was pleased that the Point Halcyoners were able to accept him and annoyed that Akmaaq could joke.

On the ride back into town, Jacobs doubted his partnership with the old man but there was no other way. He wanted to bring back a bowhead as much as Akmaaq wanted the snow whale. It was important and would be his validation of the DNA test, of his leaving Jessica and quitting his job. Landing a whale would mean he really did have this special heritage. That he really could start over and accomplish anything.

On a day when she felt she couldn't avoid it any longer, Jessica put on her gardening gloves, hit the button for the garage door opener, and wheeled the push mower out onto the drive. John's Sunfire was there, and the poor vehicle looked dejected without him. It didn't matter that he'd stopped driving; he'd once been proud of that car, and there the Sunfire stood, a testament to how much he'd changed and a reminder he was gone. She wished more than anything that he were there to mow the lawn for her, something she'd never imagined herself doing.

"I didn't sign up for this," she said to herself. She unscrewed the gas cap, then went back into the garage to get the gas can. She stood back, to take in the mower and all of its parts. As she approached the mower, she wondered if she was supposed to do something with the spark plug, which she had located, and was proud for knowing what it was. But she'd never seen John do anything with the spark plug, so she filled up the gas tank, which was easy enough, except the gas rushed out too quickly and spilled over to make a toxic puddle on the driveway. She saw there were simple directions on the handle with primitive illustrations, a step-by-step guide of how to start the mower that anyone could follow and understand. She read through the sequence, and reread all the panels before she performed each task. She was reassured at no mention or graphic of the spark plug, and she choked the motor with a small lever, as described. When she came to the step that instructed her to pull the rip cord, she mentally focused all of her strength, she tugged as hard as she could, and the mower yielded the length of the cord with a disappointingly slow response. She'd never start the engine this way. She paused, concentrated more intensely, pulled with a grunt, and the motor coughed. She felt better about this but wasn't confident she was getting anywhere. She looked around to see if anyone was watching and also so she might enlist help. She felt silly in her white shorts and sneakers. She had never played tennis but would have described her outfit, with a pink pullover blouse, as tennis attire.

Jessica was sure Jodi watched, which led her to believe Nat was also a spectator of her struggle. Jodi could have sent her husband over, like when Jessica needed him to dig the bird's grave. Or Nat could have done the gentlemanly thing and offered to cut the yard when he saw the grass had grown tall. Since she and Nat had flirted with a forbidden encounter, she felt her expectations of him were justified. With each successive pull of the rip cord, she became more and more angry with Nat, until the engine finally turned over. Per the illustrated instructions, she released the choke; the engine revved, and then it died.

"Goddamn it, Nat!" she shouted. Then she collected herself, took a deep breath, and with one easy pull, the engine was running.

With her first row of grass cut, she was feeling independent and having doubts about a rendezvous with Nat. With a second pass, she broke a sweat and was exhilarated. She imagined Nat watching, and she put some sexy in her walk as she cut the next two rows. Then, before long, she didn't care who was watching. Really, she hoped no one was. She was hot and uncomfortable, dripping with sweat, and thirsty. Her husband had left her without a thought about what she might do when the grass grew, and she'd proven she could take care of herself. She was a fighter. She was strong. And she'd stand up to anyone who treated her indifferently.

Akmaaq parked on a street that was new to Jacobs and pointed at the only municipal-looking building in town. There was no sign, but there was a police car in front of the house next door. And the architecture was unmistakable, the place like a small square brick bunker. There couldn't be too many cells in there and Jacobs imagined the jails he'd seen in old Westerns, a sheriff's office with a stand-alone cage in the middle of the room. Akmaaq said he wasn't about to wait, so he gave Jacobs directions to his igloo, and also to Toni and Marta's, where they would meet up later.

Jacobs went to the door of the square brick building, which he expected to be glass and open to the public, but the door was steel, seemed fortified, and was securely locked. So he knocked. And he knocked again.

Eventually, a white sailor opened the door. He had a buzz-cut and wore a blue uniform. The room behind him was dark, and there were two more sailors seated, manning a wall of monitors and electronic equipment. The building didn't have windows. They all wore headphones, which accounted for why they'd taken so long to answer the door.

"It's a white guy," the sailor said to his mates. "What do you want?" he said to Jacobs.

"This isn't the police station?" Jacobs said. "I was looking for my son."

"Next door," the sailor said and pointed.

The police station did have a painted star on a sign, but it was easy to miss. The house next door was also where the police car was parked, but other than that it looked like the rest of the houses on the block. Until Jacobs also noticed there were bars on the windows.

"Cold enough for you?" the sailor said.

"I'll get used to it," Jacobs said.

"You want to come in?" the sailor said. "We don't see many white guys around here. You a teacher?"

Jacobs walked into the room, and as his eyes adjusted he recognized maps of the coast near Point Halcyon and of the Chukchi Sea. There were speakers in the room that broadcasted the repeated, hypnotic tones of sonar.

"You're the sonar post," Jacobs said.

"Technically, we're not supposed to let you in here," the sailor who had let him in said.

"Top secret," one of the others added. "But nothing will happen. Russians are our allies."

"That's one of our boys," the other seated sailor said, and he pointed at one of two blips that pulsed with the rhythm of the sonar. Then he pointed at the other: "And that's a Ruskie."

"So close?" Jacobs asked.

"Doesn't really matter," the sailor nearest Jacobs said. "Here." He handed over his headphones. "They're talking about *American Idol*."

"I can hear them talking," Jacobs said as he put on the headphones. "But you understand this?"

"We speak Russian. It's how you get the job."

"Is this going out over the radio?" Jacobs asked. "Are we intercepting their comm-link?"

"Sound travels really well underwater," the standing sailor said. "We're picking them up with microphones."

"You want something to drink?"

"You guys drink on the clock?" Jacobs asked.

"Why not?"

"Don't drink that piss the Eskimos give you. We only get the good stuff."

"*I'm* Eskimo," Jacobs said.

"No shit," the one who had pointed out the subs said. They all squinted their eyes and looked more carefully at Jacobs. "We aren't supposed to let you in here."

"But you just said—"

"Look," the one who had opened the door said. "Just don't get too close with them. Trust me on this one."

"Why don't you come back tonight?" the nearest one said, taking his headphones back. "We're playing cards. You play poker?"

"I might," Jacobs said, but he didn't like the way they had been talking about his people. He wondered what they meant about not getting too close. Surely these men couldn't be so educated they had learned Russian but maintained their prejudices?

Back outside it took a moment for Jacobs's eyes to adjust. The overcast sky seemed bright and the snow covered everything but the roads, which were a mud and gravel mush. He walked to the police station and let himself in the front through the glass door, which was unlocked, just as he had expected. There was an Inupiat cop at the desk, not Jamo, but the one he hadn't met, Peter Pence.

"You must be Jonah," the cop said.

"I came to pick up my son," Jacobs said. "Is he here?"

"We don't got any white kids," the cop said. "We got a brown one."

"That's him."

"You're kidding me?"

"He's my kid."

"So what's it like," the cop wanted to know.

"What do you mean?"

"You know," he said. "What's it like . . . with a black lady?"

Jacobs realized he didn't know. "Women are the same."

"They're not," the cop said. "Even I know that."

"What's the charge?" Jacobs said.

"The black kid?"

"My son."

"We're holding him to be sure nothing turns up missing."

"You can't do that."

"I was shitting you. That's a joke. He was filming without a permit."

"You can't keep him on that."

"We're Inupiat. You can't just film us willy-nilly. You going to bond him out?'

"How much?"

"What do you got?"

"I can get liquor."

"I don't drink that piss."

"The good stuff," Jacobs said. "From the white sailors."

"They *do* get the good stuff," the cop said. "So Jamo was right about you."

"How so?"

"They don't give *us* anything. And we're neighbors. But you can pass for a white guy. *Tanik.*"

"We got a deal?"

"You get us the good stuff and the *taaqsipaiyaaq* goes free."

At Akmaaq's Jacobs put his own boots back on. Ilguq's slipped around on his feet and he was starting to blister. Though his own boots weren't broken in yet, so he was likely to continue to feel pain.

"How much you pay for all this junk?" Akmaaq said as he looked over their gear. When Jacobs didn't answer

Akmaaq added, "You should have just given the money to me."

"I *do* have something for you," Jacobs said, and he went over to his pack. He came back with one of the desk doodles and he set it on the table. They watched as the goo did its thing. Jacobs turned the desk doodle back over and they watched again. Then Akmaaq turned it over, missing on his first grab, but feeling around and getting the desk doodle turned over once more.

"I used to sell them," Jacobs said. "That was my job."

"No wonder you left," Akmaaq said. "The whole world has gone crazy."

"I didn't think nothing of it," Jacobs said.

"You can paddle a boat?"

"I think so," Jacobs said. "But isn't there more you want to show me?"

"From here on we pretty much wait," Akmaaq said. "The snow buntings should arrive first. Then the beluga migration. We can hunt beluga for practice. They travel in pods and aren't as dangerous. The smaller bowheads will show up first, with the larger ones following a few days later."

"Do we get Indian names?"

"What, like White Bear and Black Bear?" Akmaaq laughed.

"I don't know," Jacobs said. "You're the chief. Can you teach me to throw?"

"*I'm* the harpooner," Akmaaq said, "but why the hell not? You came all the way up here. You probably want the full experience. We can throw some at Marta and Toni's."

"I'm playing poker at the sonar post."

"They invited you?"

"I need to win a bottle to exchange for Q."

"White men bartering with liquor," Akmaaq said, and he shook his head. "It's a good thing you didn't offer Jamo beads."

"They shouldn't be keeping Q in the first place," Jacobs said.

Akmaaq's sod house rose up in back not unlike the head of a whale breaching water. They stood at a distance and took turns chucking harpoons into the snow-covered earthen mound. Even when Akmaaq counted his paces, he tended to misjudge the distance, and he threw past the house or short of it. But he talked as if he never missed, he critiqued Jacobs's form, and he made suggestions to correct stance or follow-through—though Jacobs hit the house time after time. Jacobs glared at the snowy mound and released the shaft with the full force of his being. He felt stronger. If those cops could see him now, they wouldn't go messing with his family. He was Inuit. Throwing the harpoon came naturally to him, and he imagined himself standing in the umiaq.

"You throw like a girl," Akmaaq said. "They have to go deep."

Jacobs reared back and threw with more intensity, but he lost his balance on the follow-through and fell face-first into the wet snow.

"Now you're dead, White Bear. You just fell in the water and froze to death. That's why I'm the harpooner."

But Jacobs persisted, so Akmaaq continued to coach.

"Aim with both eyes," he said. "It's not a rifle. Keep your feet planted, but fall to your knees if you start to slip. The boat can absorb the shock as long as you keep your gravity low. But fall in the water and you're a goner."

Jacobs issued a primal grunt with each throw, and he let out something long submerged. He imagined the Ruskie sub floating by and the harpoon tip putting a hole in its side. He imagined spearing Jamo and Peter Pence, the fat Inupiat cops. He scored hit after hit, and the head of the harpoon went deep—until Akmaaq had to actually tell him to let up. "Save it for the whale," he said, and he patted Jacobs on the back.

He had done well. He was learning. He was becoming a man.

"You got an e-mail," Akmaaq said. "I wasn't going to read it, but you left your mailbox open, so I thought it was for me. You should have someone spy on that wife of yours. She sounds frisky."

"You *read* it?" Jacobs said.

"Easy, White Bear," Akmaaq said. "You're living two lives. You want to go back to selling trinkets, be my guest. I'd shack up with Toni if I was you. She's a good-enough woman. Around here you settle on looks. Yuq went away to college to get his girl. She's not one of us. She's an Inuk, but she's from Canada. Grew up around Newfoundland somewhere—but an Inuit girl is an Inuit girl, and an Inuit girl makes up for the cold."

Back in the sod house Jacobs read his e-mail. Jessica had changed, and Akmaaq was right to pick up on it. She said she missed John, but nothing in her e-mail gave him that impression. Joining the Catholics was the least of it.

"You got a picture?" Akmaaq said.

Jacobs did a search for her web page and saw she'd updated the content. She'd changed the single photo of her face to a new one with her hair dyed—still nothing to brag about. There was a new list of favorites and even a coat of arms. Before Akmaaq came over, Jacobs clicked away from her site and back to his search results. He selected the other

Jessica Jacobs, the one with the MySpace page. She'd also made updates and she was pictured with a hip-looking guy her own age, an urbanite with a goatee. There was music playing, some kind of neo-punk, contemporary and white. Jacobs was embarrassed and he paused the player.

"Nice," Akmaaq said when he saw the other Jessica, but then he pointed at the picture with the new boyfriend. "See what I mean? With Toni you wouldn't worry."

"That's her *brother*," Jacobs said, and he started to describe an imaginary woman who was a composite between his own wife and this stranger, this alluring and much more interesting stranger.

"I thought your wife was black," Akmaaq said.

"Me and Q's mom didn't work out," Jacobs said. "He's sensitive about it though. So don't say anything."

Jess:
I lit a candle and prayed we'd be together soon. Isn't that funny, both of us praying? But I'm feeling something I can hardly describe, and when I come back you won't recognize me. Today I learned to chuck a harpoon, and I know we'll be blessed with bringing in a catch. I feel it.

I showed the picture from your website to the chief. If you saw your counter go up, that was us visiting. He said I should send out spies, or someone would steal you away. I explained you weren't that type, and our bond was strong. It might not have always felt strong, but it was. It is. We were meant to be together. I know this more than ever. The Inuit girls don't do anything for me, not even the Canadian ones—and they're my people. You'd think I'd be attracted to them, at least a little, but I'm not. I'm faithful to you. Not that I even needed to bring that up. You always knew, didn't you?

I met some white people. They're sailors. They're here to listen for Ruskie subs. It sounds like Ruskies are a lot like us.

They like the same things anyway. Funny to think we almost destroyed the earth hating each other all those years. And there are Inuit across the Bering Strait over in Russia too. More cousins of mine. I never would have thought there were Russians in the family. And I may have relatives stretching all the way to Newfoundland. Just goes to show we're more alike than we might think.

Don't tell his mother if she calls, but the kid, Q—he somehow got himself into trouble. I'm going to have to get him out of jail. I don't know what he'd do without me. This kid needs me.

OK, that's it for now. I think of you every night. We probably weren't intimate often enough when we were always around each other, and now I miss you. We haven't lost each other, but I suppose under different circumstances we might have. Light me another candle, but don't go over to the Catholics wholesale. Sooner or later they'll try to make you feel guilty. And they'll try to get our money.

Everyone in the clan calls me Jonah, and my chief calls me White Bear. I think I like it. I can't wait to tell you in person about all I have seen. And, likewise, I'll want to hear about you.

Love,
Jonah

Before he went to Marta and Toni's, Jacobs put on the sealskin boots. There was no cure for his blistering, and Ilguq's boots were broken in at least. Marta was upset but not surprised that Jamo had taken Q into custody and that they wanted a bribe to get him out.

The largest of the malamutes came over to Jacobs and sniffed him up and down. The dog looked suspiciously at him. Jacobs had been around white people at the listening post, and he thought maybe the dog knew.

Jacobs took out another of the desk doodles and he set it on Toni's table for her kids.

"Look," he said. He flipped over the desk doodle and they watched. Then he flipped it over again.

"Let me try," the youngest girl said.

"Me next."

But before long the kids wandered the house, bored. Toni fried fish while Marta and the chief passed the bottle of yellow liquor. The TV was loud, a police drama, with bass notes in a catchy rhythm whenever someone broke the law. When no one but Jacobs saw, the malamute went up to the table and took the desk doodle in his mouth. Then he flipped it over and watched the goo.

"Do that again," Jacobs said, but the dog went back to his spot and lay down.

"What if you lose your poker game?" Toni said.

"I haven't thought that far ahead."

"Sailors are good at poker," Marta said. "They play all the time."

"Do you have any more of those things?" Akmaaq said.

"The desk doodles?" Jacobs asked. "I only brought two, and I gave you the other one."

"They might trade one of those for a liquor bottle," Toni said.

"You kidding?" Jacobs said.

"They might," Toni said. "You can take that one."

"You don't want it?" Jacobs said.

"Not really."

"It was for the kids," Jacobs said.

"I don't think they care," she said.

"What about the dog?" Jacobs asked.

"Which dog?"

"He was staring at it."

"Trust me," Toni said. "The dog doesn't care."

Chapter 7

A letter addressed to John Jacobs came from REI, the sports gear outfitter where he bought his supplies. Jessica didn't know how long he might be gone, so she opened it. A salesman identified a number of items found in the store as having been John's, and his address was obtained through the credit card company. As per store policy, a refund would require the in-store receipt, but an exchange for the items, totaling $1,109.47, would be honored if the credit card used to make the purchase was presented along with picture ID. Jessica knew John had done irreparable damage to the bank account, but was pleased there would at least be a slight recoup. He'd given her an excuse to go shopping, and she drove with the letter out to the mall.

She was surprised at the size of REI and that a store that large could have escaped her notice. She was doubly surprised that such a large store had nothing for her. At the front entrance there was a climbing wall and an open area with display tents, canoes, kayaks, and inflatable rafts. Jessica was drawn to the shoe department, but even there, all the wares tended toward ugly and durable. Nearly all the shoes were brown and she couldn't see wearing them for any occasion other than walking up the side of a mountain. There were backpacks, coils of colored rope, water purifiers, electronic GPS trail-map locators, flare guns, binoculars, and display case after display case of pocket-knives. The clothes had too many floppy pockets, zippers, hoods, and drawstrings. Mesh was in this year. There were aisles of freeze-dried just-add-water meals and protein bars. She saw they also proudly displayed first-aid supplies, and this reinforced the notion that she would never, ever, participate in the kinds of activities this store championed.

Then she saw it. Hanging on a wall with the off-road bikes was a bike she couldn't stop staring at. The color scheme and frame line of this bike reminded her so much of the moonbike it was uncanny. She approached slowly, in a kind of trance that the mountain man salesman recognized, and he swooped in behind her.

"The Luna Expedition Special Edition," he said. "Our premiere mountain bike."

Jessica knew *luna* meant moon, so the likeness could hardly be accidental.

"Can I try it?" she said, and the mountain man was quick to get it down for her.

"Lightweight but sturdy. The Luna company is known for their alloys. It's an eighteen speed, which will give you more options going up and coming down."

"I'm a street rider."

"It's good for that too," he said, and he adjusted the seat and handlebars to Jessica's height.

She sat on the bike and really had to fight the urge to pedal through the store.

"If you want a test drive," the salesman said, "I'll go out to the lot with you."

"I'll take it," she said.

"Will you need a lock? A helmet? A rack for your car?"

"I hadn't thought of that," she said. "I guess I do."

At the listening post, Jacobs and the three sailors sat at a table in the middle of the room. Each of the sailors had the headphones half-on, so they talked and played cards, but they also remained attentive.

"They're rooting for the black chick," one of them said.

"*American Idol*?" Jacobs asked.

"They can pick up our local station from their base," the sailor said, "and a videotape comes in on their supply ship."

"I hate to break it to them," another said, "but the black chick lost."

"They also like the blonde."

"Everyone likes the blonde."

The room was dark except for the glow of monitors and it took time for Jacobs's eyes to adjust. The pulsing sonar was tranquil and the room was lit like an aquarium. The gruff voices of the Ruskie sailors were miniaturized to mousy whispers, and occasionally one of the sailors transcribed the conversation with his laptop, or he scribbled on a pad of paper while he noted the time. Jacobs had the sneaking suspicion there was more than *American Idol* being discussed on the Ruskie sub, and the *listening post* sailors only befriended him because they needed another hand in their poker game.

Jacobs understood the basics of poker, but they preferred variations of the game that didn't much resemble five-card draw. He kept forgetting the rules, and he suspected they changed them or made them up as they went along. Jacobs only won hands when one of the sailors pointed out a card combination he hadn't seen, but the whiskey flowed, and the whiskey was good. They played for pennies and Jacobs quickly ran out.

"Have you seen one of these?" Jacobs said, and he set the desk doodle in the middle of the table. All of the sailors watched silently as the goo glowed in the light of the monitors. The balls of goo rolled slowly in a row down the spiral maze like angels descending a staircase. Until the last one came to rest. Jacobs waited, then he flipped the desk doodle back over. He'd observed desk doodles for over a decade, and he had to admit the dim light of the room and the sound of the sonar increased the meditative effect. The card game came to a halt and the Ruskies were heard, sometimes laughing.

One of the sailors said, "That's awesome."

"Really cool," the others agreed.

Jacobs had to make his offer before they got bored with the desk doodle, but he also didn't want to seem too eager. He waited until one of them turned it over again and they all watched.

"Would make a great Boggle timer," one of them said.

"I can let you have it," Jacobs said, and they all perked up, "for some of that whiskey."

"The stuff ain't cheap."

"I used to sell them," Jacobs said. "And I happen to know this model is going out of production. These will be collector's items."

"You got anything else?"

"The liquor wouldn't be for me," Jacobs said, softening his pitch, "but for the cops. I've got to bond out my friend. They picked him up for being black."

"Those racist cunts."

"I just don't understand racism."

"OK, we'll trade you," the one with the biggest pile of pennies said. "But don't tell them where you got it. We don't want them coming here." And he flipped over the desk doodle again.

In silence, as they watched the desk doodle do its thing, Jacobs noticed a change in the tone of the sonar and he realized he'd been hearing it for a while, not sonar, but another sound, a rising and falling staccato tone.

"What's that?" Jacobs said, and as soon as he asked he also knew he knew the answer. They were listening to *whalesongs!*

"The bowhead migration," one of the sailors said. He got up and walked over to a monitor and pointed to a spaced line of faint slow-moving blips that would pass near Point Halcyon before long.

"Last year the ignoramuses nearly missed it."

"If anyone ought to know about global warming, you'd think it would be Eskimos."

"The whales migrate earlier every year."

"No shit?" Jacobs said. He was proud and indignant all at once. Tonight was the night. He was whiling away the time and the whales might have gone unnoticed. "Why the hell haven't you said anything to them?"

"We told you. What we do here is top secret. We aren't up here in service of some tribe. Our job is national security."

"They can buy an early tracking system," one of the sailors said. "There was a guy up here a couple of years ago trying to sell them one. He also had night-vision goggles and scopes, GPS. They ran him out of town. They wanted nothing to do with him."

"You know they don't have jobs," Jacobs said in his clan's defense. "And they need the meat."

"There's plenty of fish. They don't need to whale. The bowhead are endangered. For me or you to kill one would be a felony. We'd go to jail."

"I'm Inuit," Jacobs said. "And I'm sorry to bust up the game, but I've got to go."

"Just don't tell them how you found out," one of the sailors said.

"Yeah, it could be our asses."

"Come to think of it," the one with the biggest pile of pennies said, and he grabbed the bottle from the middle of the table, "I don't know how comfortable I am with cops getting drunk."

"We could be accessories."

"A deal's a deal," Jacobs said.

The sailor looked at Jacobs, and Jacobs looked at the faint row of blips on the monitor as they moved nearer to Point Halcyon. Then he locked eyes with the sailor. They had made an agreement and the sailor handed over the bottle— from one white guy to another.

"You don't have an unopened one?" Jacobs asked.

"They'll take that one."

The fat cop, Jamo, sat at the desk. Jacobs wondered how they did it, only two cops for the whole town. If one was on duty and the other manned the desk, that didn't leave them time to sleep. So probably there were times with no one at the desk and no one on duty.

Jacobs plunked the bottle down on the counter and said, "I had a deal with your associate. He said this would bond out the kid."

"The black kid?"

"Why does everyone focus on his race?" Jacobs said.

"This bottle's been opened."

"It's what they gave me," Jacobs said, and he added, "a deal's a deal," though he knew with this fat Inupiat cop that approach wasn't going to work.

"How do I know you're not trying to poison me?"

"I'll drink one with you," Jacobs said.

"We'll take it," Jamo said. "But the kid doesn't have a permit, so we're keeping his camera."

"How do we apply for a permit?"

"You get an OK from the chief."

"You need to call the chief anyway," Jacobs said. "There's bowhead in the lead. There's been a sighting."

"Why the hell didn't you say something?" Jamo said, and he stood up and let Jacobs walk around behind the counter. "You wait here. I'll get the kid."

Q came out angry.

"Where have *you* been?" he said. "You left me in here."

"Why'd you get yourself arrested?" Jacobs countered.

"That cracker said he was giving me a ride."

"I *did* give him a ride," Jamo said.

"It was cold," Q said. "I was tired of waiting around."

"The wait is over," Jacobs said. "There's bowhead in the lead."

"I'm not going without my camera," Q said.

"It's too dark," Jacobs said. "You can't film tonight anyway."

"You hired me to film," Q said. "Not to fish. I ain't going out there without my camera."

"Call the chief," Jacobs said to Jamo. And as Jamo dialed, Jacobs remembered Akmaaq didn't have a phone.

"Yuq says you can film," Jamo said.

So Yuq and his crew would be first on the ice to meet the migration. Jacobs tried not to let this bother him. He knew his ego shouldn't get in the way of what was best for the clan. He knew that anyone bringing back a whale was good for everyone. But he wanted to prove himself to his people, he wanted the validation that he was one of them.

"I thought Akmaaq was chief," Q said.

"Akmaaq is *inugluk*," Jamo said. "It means like a friend acting strange. Like the weather lately, which we call *uggianaqtuq*, for *crazy-weather*. The weather and the sky we call Sila. This is the realm of God, who is everywhere and nowhere—the Great Living Breath—who is not a who but the atmosphere and the spark of life within us."

Jamo walked to a storage closet and took out the camera. Q stood behind him and eyed the loot. There were bags of marijuana, a sawed-off shotgun, night-vision specs, and several sticks of dynamite.

"Is this what I think it is?" Q said, picking up the night-vision lenses.

"One of them sailors was a perv," Jamo said. "After we arrested him they shipped him back to prevent an incident. He was spying on girls through their windows. He was trying to sell us this stuff, but one perv was enough."

"Crazy person," Q said.

"Or horny," Jamo said. "Sailors are cooped up with men. It's not natural."

"There's no telling what they do inside that bunker," Jacobs said. "Or what their *real* mission is."

"They're spying *on us*," Jamo said. "We're not really Americans, you know. We are but we aren't. Because we're the *first* Americans, and they hate that."

Q picked up the night-vision specs. "All the way up here to peep."

"Will it work?" Jacobs asked.

"On the camera?" Q said. "It's worth a try."

"Can we take the TNT?" Jacobs said.

"Just don't tell anyone where it came from," Jamo said, and Q and Jacobs stuffed their parka pockets.

Jamo locked up the station, and Jacobs and Q ran toward Akmaaq's. Jamo got in his cruiser with the lights going, and he went up and down the streets broadcasting over his PA, "Bowhead sighting in the lead. There's bowhead in the lead."

Lights went on in houses all over Point Halcyon, and snowmobile engines were heard idling as the men and boys gathered outside and the women made preparations. The church bells tolled. A snowmobile zoomed off, then another. It had been set in motion, what every Inupiat boy longed for, and Jacobs also felt the anticipation.

"Whatever happens," Jacobs said to Q as they ran.

"Whatever happens, what?" Q asked, but Jacobs didn't mean to complete the phrase.

"We did our best," Jacobs almost said, but it felt halfhearted. "*We will be remembered,*" Jacobs said confidently, and he knew it was true. Whatever Q's life had been to this point, Jacobs had now given him that.

But Q wanted to know, "Remembered by whom?"

"Our people. Our clan."

"Let's go get this film made," Q said.

At Akmaaq's, the borrowed snowmobile was gone. His dogs ran out of the entry tunnel and Jacobs and Q went inside, but the house was empty. For a moment Jacobs wondered if Akmaaq might have left without them, but he knew he couldn't. Akmaaq needed them as much as they needed him. And so they filled their backpacks with whatever they could carry and they ran.

When they arrived at Marta and Toni's, Akmaaq was in front of the house tying gear onto a dogsled behind the snowmobile. He'd dragged out the umiaq from the garage and tied it onto its own sled. Akmaaq wore the caribou snow pants, the sealskin boots, and a parka, with his face wrapped in a scarf. In the furry pants Akmaaq looked like some kind of squirrel or fox walking upright.

"Where the hell have you two been?" he said. "There's bowhead in the lead."

"I know," Jacobs said. "I'm the one who spotted them."

"What were you doing out there? It's dangerous. You should be more careful."

"We brought boomers," Q said, and he held a stick of TNT in each hand.

"We've got to get going," Akmaaq said. "Are you ready, Black Bear?"

Q said, "I need to call my mama."

And Jacobs: "I need to call my wife."

Jessica opted for the roof-mount bike rack, and she loved the way the Jetta looked with her new moonbike standing on top. She had the good sense to park outside the garage, because she would have missed clearing the garage door by a few inches, which would have spelled the end of the Luna Expedition Special Edition, and might have even damaged the roof of her Jetta. She took the bike down, noting how light and sturdy it was. She parked the Jetta, removed the bike lock from its packaging, hit the garage door opener so the door rolled down, and she ducked under with the bike helmet in her hand. Jessica strapped on the helmet, got on the bike, and she stood up to pump the pedals as hard as she could. As she picked up momentum and rode into the street, the air around her became suddenly alive, and the sense of motion was invigorating. Without slowing down, she jumped a curb, which jarred the bike, but she laughed and did it again as soon as she'd built up speed.

She was young again, she felt free, and riding her new moonbike was like flying. While she'd always bragged that dancing was such good exercise, and that it worked the glutes, she knew riding the bike as enthusiastically as she did was even better. She breathed hard, she felt muscles back there she hadn't felt in a while, and she loved it. She didn't know why she'd never bought a bike. It was so obvious, but the routine of their days kept her inside. She'd forgotten who she once was. And while it wasn't exactly fair, she'd have probably never bought the bike with John around, and so she blamed him for their tame ways. She had a lover now, and she'd finally found an aerobic exercise that wasn't absolute torture. John had better come back on his hands and knees. He had better come back apologetic and flattering. Because it would take more than a steak dinner to win her back. She was happy and attractive. Her new life had just begun, and before long, maybe by the time he came back, she would be out of his league.

After a rousing circuit around the neighborhood, Jessica stopped in the driveway and planted her feet on the ground, which was solid, and she felt connected. She was a conduit of libidinous energy and lightning was coursing through her.

In Toni and Marta's house the TV was off and the kids sat at the table quietly. The dog with the smarts came up to Jacobs and nudged his hand approvingly. He petted the dog, then he leaned over and tongue-kissed Toni in front of her children. It wasn't a kiss good-bye but a loving kiss and a promise to come back. She gave him a white fur mitten and told him to hide it somewhere on the boat. Jacobs took her phone off the table without asking and went into the back bedroom.

> Jess, I know it's late and when you get this message I'll be gone. The whale migration arrived tonight and we're rowing out to meet them. This is more dangerous than anything I've ever done. But the Inuit have a saying: *Don't begin if afraid. Once begun, don't be afraid.* And I'm one of them because that's how I feel. I have a clear sense that I may die, but there's no question that this is what I was born to do.
>
> I've accused you of not understanding, but you *do* understand. Rather than fight me, you let me go, and I'm grateful.
>
> Know that I love you. I really do. And I'm coming back.
>
> Meanwhile, keep praying. It may be days or weeks before you hear from me, but I'll call or write as soon as I can. I love you.

Jacobs handed Q the phone and Q called his mama.

"No, I'm not in trouble," he said. "There's a time difference is all."

"We're going out on the water and it's dangerous.

"No, Mama, killing whales is not illegal. We're just making a film, I promise."

Marta gave Q a fox fur belt that she tied around his waist. She handed them packets of frozen fish, a bottle of the yellow liquor, and two skins of water she told them to wear under their parkas and against their bodies. When the water skins emptied she said they should fill them with snow. She embraced each and called them by an Inupiat word, *nafiitchuq*. She told them she believed in them, and that they were brave.

Jacobs patted each kid on the head, and they went out to meet Akmaaq, who paced and spat at the frozen ground.

"It's too early in the season," he said. "This is *crazy-weather*. There's no snow bunting. No beluga. It's all backwards."

"But they're out there," Jacobs said.

A flare shot up from the direction of the sea ice.

"Thar she blows," Akmaaq said. "They're confirming your eyes, White Bear. We need to get going." He lashed the last of the supplies to the dogsled and also tied a rope to the sled, with the umiaq on it to drag along behind. Q stood around looking for something to do. So he tried filming through the night-vision lenses.

"Too much feedback," he said, and he flipped around the miniscreen of his video camera to show Jacobs and Akmaaq the distorted green haze that was caused by the interference of the two video sequences.

"Did you get a good night's sleep?" Akmaaq said to Q, and he laughed.

"Those crackers got nothing better to do than pick on kids."

"They weren't crackers," Jacobs said.

"Cracker means cop," Q said.

"Crackers are white people," Jacobs said. "The only crackers around here are in the navy. And they stay indoors. You've got those crackers to thank. Or you'd have stayed locked up longer."

"I ain't thanking nobody. Ain't you a cracker?"

"I keep saying—but no one seems to get—that I'm *Inuit.*"

"He's an Inuk," Akmaaq said. "And so are you."

"Right," Q said. "Like everybody's Irish."

"I really *am* Inuit," Jacobs said. "Why's that so hard to believe?"

Q just stared. He packed up his video camera but kept out the night-vision specs. "These should be useful, at least."

"We need to make a stop at your igloo," Jacobs said. "So we can get the rest of our supplies."

"I've got everything we need," Akmaaq said, and he climbed onto the snowmobile. "You two go lie in the umiaq and stay low. I don't want the thing tipping over."

There were two bearskins along the bottom of the umiaq to insulate against the freezing water. Jacobs and Q each lay on one, facing up, and they watched the formless overcast night sky.

There were several snowmobiles parked along the ridge where the land ice met the ocean ice. Q scanned the coastline and the ice-covered water. "I see boats, but I don't see any whales."

"Watch for spouts," Akmaaq said, and he told Jacobs, "Unlash the umiaq."

Akmaaq kicked over more snow totems left by the other crews before they set out.

"I wish you would stop doing that," Jacobs said. "It seems rude."

Q went over to the old man and tugged him away from a pool of water. He caught him before he nearly slipped and fell. "Come on, Captain."

"He thinks he can attract the snow whale," Jacobs said.

"Yuq lied to them," Akmaaq said. "No one else was there, and Yuq is a liar. I should be chief. We have to kill the snow whale so they know. Are you ready to face him?"

Jacobs looked out at the dappled expanse of sea ice, with a chill wind blowing and an overcast sky. They walked out onto the frozen ocean and dragged the umiaq with a rope to the lead, the wide channel of water that ran along the coast like a river. As they neared the lead, the support under them gave, and they splashed through puddles. For the last stretch, they held onto the boat as they pushed toward the ice edge. Soon they were all in the umiaq and they launched into water, with the packet of food, their backpacks, several harpoons, coils of rope, the inflated sealskin buoys, and two canvas bags filled with sticks of TNT and Akmaaq's homemade bombs.

The flow of the Chukchi Sea propelled them as Jacobs and the captain paddled. Q nestled in the middle of the wide bone-frame canoe and he looked out with the night-vision specs. Jacobs muttered to himself, *"...Holy Mary, Mother of God. Pray for us. Now and at the hour of our death...."* He tried to wipe everything from his mind: all memories, all grace, all sacrilege. He was a blank slate paddling. He saw no stars, he felt no discomfort or fatigue, and there was no meaning in anything except that he should go out to meet the whale. And then, instinctively, or with the help of Akmaaq, he would know what to do.

Chapter 8

Distant sounds chimed across the frozen ocean like none Jacobs had ever heard. The crews chanted songs meant to attract whales, atonal melodies blown in from farther out that also echoed back from Point Halcyon. The men sang minor keys in the upper ranges, layered over the noises from ice sheets cracking apart and large ice blocks that rubbed against each other in the floes, random sharp tones that popped and knocked as the constant wind sang low, a permabreeze that chapped their exposed faces. Jacobs and Akmaaq exhaled clouds as they stroked and pumped along the open channel of the lead. Despite a faint glow from the overcast sky and the white sea ice all around, there was a vast, disorienting darkness. The white of everything that blinded during the day was felt more than seen, and the umiaq rolled to-and-fro. With so much white and so little light, the world was formless and the imagination conjured hostile forms. The temporary river in the sea ice gave them the only sense of direction and they paddled out toward nothing, to where the water opened wide.

Jacobs imagined the Ruskies nestled and warm somewhere deep beneath them and they watched the same programs as nearly everyone else on Earth. He thought of Jessica and was depressed that, as a couple, they had also succumbed to the same distractions, so many eyes watching the same things, yet each viewer was solitary and apart.

Akmaaq sang low and in English, presumably for the sake of his crew, who were ignorant of the traditions and the language. *We hear you near. Follow us to meet the first whale and to return home. Fill your belly in the Chukchi Sea, rise to the surface and breathe free air. In the upside-down time before the beginning, men were animals and animals were men. Like the first whale, you will walk on land with legs. Like the great land whale, you will take a wife. Your wife is here with us. Come meet her and breathe free air. Ask and she will be shown to you. We have seen her. We know where she lives. Our waters are thick with prawns. And we remember you. We have known you a long long time.*

Q and Jacobs rowed while the old man stood in the boat. The noises that blew in off the floating ice were unsettling and strange. Akmaaq sang from somewhere ancient inside. His song borrowed the same rhythms as the other crews, only slower, accommodating for the English words, and his singing gave the crew something to ponder. After the fourth time around, Akmaaq sang softly and Q joined in, ad-libbing his own verses. *Strut on land, walking whale. Attract a female. We know her. She's here. We're pimps with the women. Come say what you got. Show us what you got.*

Jacobs recognized they might paddle like this all night, and the singing would pass the time, so he added his own verse. *I have seen the ice mountain, so tonight I'm happy. I may not get there with you, but together we will. We have no fear. And we are happy. Come follow us back to Tikigaq.*

They sang until the songs of the other crews were near. And shouts were heard. Another flare was fired, and Akmaaq said, "A whale is struck."

There had been no rest, but Jacobs and Akmaaq paddled harder while Q took up the night-vision specs and pointed the way. The lead opened into an expanse where even a whale would be easy to miss. The skin-boats had spread out with the hope that a whale would surface near enough to strike. But now the crews all paddled in the direction of the umiaq that had fired the flare.

"If the whale is killed," Akmaaq said, "the harpooner who struck first gets the first share. Otherwise, we spend all night rowing after him. And tomorrow we wait for the next ones to follow behind."

"How many are there?" Q said.

"They follow each other and surface in the same places. We need to be waiting with harpoons half-cocked. They'll come one after another. We may be out here weeks."

Q said they were close to the boat that had sent up the flare with nine strong men and a boy paddling in unison. Jacobs saw how severely disadvantaged they were, with just the three of them. They could hope for the luck of striking the first blow and the others coming to help, but he wasn't optimistic about the three of them—an old man, a boy, and himself, who had been an out-of-shape middle-aged white guy from the suburbs—pursuing and catching a whale.

The other boat sped past before Jacobs and Q could take in what was happening. The whaling crew had appeared a vision in the night and they were gone. Then another umiaq rowed behind them, equally outfitted and swift—and it nearly sideswiped Akmaaq's crew. Jacobs had seen kindness in the faces of the Inupiat in the Piskipulut church, but now the men displayed a ruthlessness he couldn't quite come to terms with. They sacrificed to feed the community, but there was competition and a single-mindedness that Jacobs hoped not to get in the way of.

Akmaaq stopped rowing, and so Jacobs stopped too, not out of frustration, but because with only one paddler they would go in slow circles. Akmaaq took a flashlight from the pile of gear and moved the beam of light across the water.

"There's an oil trail," he said. "The whale outpaces them, but he will have to surface." There were slicks of oil on the water that reflected a dull yellow shade.

"We can't keep up with them," Jacobs said.

"The whale is faster," Akmaaq said. "But he's hurt and pulling drag-floats. He may become confused. He may slow down. When he surfaces he will take fifteen breaths. Don't give up. There's a chance for us."

"What about an outboard motor?" Q asked. "Have you thought of that?"

"The whales would hear the propeller," Akmaaq said. "Many of the whales are old enough to remember the white whalers in their diesel ships, and even the steamships."

"No shit?"

"Besides," Akmaaq said, "you know how much an outboard costs?"

"Do *you* remember the cracker whalers?" Q asked.

"I didn't have Yuq until I was forty. I had other children, but he's the only one here."

"You're eighty?" Q asked.

"Seventy-nine. There were days when our men lived to be one hundred."

"You can make it," Jacobs said.

"I don't want to."

"I'm surprised you made it this long," Q said. "This shit is dangerous."

"Not as dangerous as going without food," Akmaaq said.

"They are going to *love* us at The Black American Film Festival."

"At the *what?*" Jacobs said.

"You heard me. BAFF. We got a good chance. With a prize I could make my own movies."

"But we're not making a black film."

"I'm black," Q said. "I'm the director. The *black* director."

"Black Bear and White Bear make a film." Akmaaq laughed. "For the Black American White Bear Festival."

Akmaaq scanned the waters with his flashlight. "The drag-floats," he said, and they bobbed on the surface a ways off. One of the sealskin buoys was decorated with a brightly colored face. Otherwise the dark gray of the sealskin was difficult to spot against the sea, and Jacobs and Q had seen how some of the buoys in their own boat were also painted with masks, so they knew what they saw and what it meant. Akmaaq told Q to take his place with the paddle in the front of the boat, and Akmaaq moved to the middle and picked up the hunting rifle. The buoys floated wildly as the waters became turgid.

The whale lifted up, a large black mass barely seen against the dark waters. Its blowholes expelled, and Akmaaq fired. The crack of the gun rang out and they heard an instantaneous slap as the whale hide absorbed the bullet. The other crews cheered in response, and they rowed back in the direction of the rifle report.

"You got him," Q said. The whale rolled and sent a wave toward their umiaq, the wave dissipating over the distance, but the boat rocked.

Akmaaq fired again and one of the sealskin buoys popped, the one that had been painted. This was not good luck since the drag was reduced and the whale would be harder to spot. Even so, the whale stopped midroll and flopped sideways, now facing Akmaaq's umiaq, and with its next roll moved closer.

Akmaaq dropped the hunting rifle and picked up one of the harpoons. The whale rolled again and they saw its features. The whale was slick, black, and enormous—the head above water thirty feet long. Now the bowhead came right at their umiaq. The whale didn't charge; it was just too immense and they were in the way.

Jacobs and Q quit rowing, which was useless, while Akmaaq stood with a harpoon. At the last possible moment, he threw. He overshot by a good distance, but the harpoon line came down on top and spooked the animal. They heard the two blowholes slap shut, the whale arched its back, and dove deep. The tail was fifty feet behind, but it followed and the flukes raised fifteen feet, then also submerged. The whale pulled a great surge of water down behind it, and Jacobs and Q held tight to the sides of the boat. They were relieved, because they were in the path of the whale and about to be capsized. Akmaaq, however, was disappointed and upset. He wasn't yet used to the decrepit state of his body, which he seemed incapable of accepting. He slumped in the middle of the umiaq and shook his head. If the bowhead was committed to this dive and not just evading them, it may not resurface for another twenty minutes, and miles away. And if the other whalers saw how Akmaaq shot the painted buoy, this accident wouldn't sit well with those who seemed to think he was too old to help, too dangerous to be around, and that Akmaaq should retire from the hunt.

As Jacobs watched Akmaaq throw, he also felt this. Jacobs had thrown the harpoon confidently in Akmaaq's yard, and he wouldn't have missed. They had been close enough he didn't think he *could have* missed. But the old man wasn't about to give up his idea of himself as harpooner, and Jacobs was in no position to give orders. And so Akmaaq began the hopelessly repeated futile action of rowing after the harpoon shaft and retrieving it. But his harpoon line disappeared underwater and became taut, the harpoon line entangled with the sealskin buoys, and the whale pulled the ropes down as it dove. Akmaaq fed the line so his rope wouldn't catch on the oarlocks and tip the umiaq.

"Hold tight," he said. And as the rope was nearly let out, he said, "Come help."

Jacobs and Q both moved to the middle where all three held the line and braced themselves as the whale dragged the umiaq. Akmaaq took a paddle under his arm and let it dangle over the edge, so the paddle blade was dipped in the water as a rudder. He steered as their boat skimmed over open water, even faster than the umiaq with the crew of nine men. They left a wake, and the direction of the wind was no longer felt as they moved quickly through the cold night air.

They soon passed the other umiaqs, and each crew cheered in encouragement as they tried to follow, but Jacobs noted how they also looked on with trepidation because Akmaaq's umiaq was poorly manned and the three of them were doomed.

"When will he come back up?" Q asked.

"Dragging us is no fun for him either," Akmaaq said. "Maybe half an hour. Maybe sooner."

The whale carried them out into the night sea. Jacobs was disoriented and had no sense of how far they'd traveled. He suspected miles, but they could have been turned around at some point. Jacobs didn't know how long they'd been on the water, though he watched the sky for clues and estimated there were still a few hours before the first light of morning. The cloud cover had broken up and dense patches of stars shimmered. Their eyes had also adjusted to the darkness, so the reflective surface of the black water and the blank white of the sea ice were more distinct.

But seeing wasn't reassuring, because they headed toward an ice field that seemed to have no end, other than the spots where the flat ice had broken apart to form channels or where it had thawed to form ponds. This floating shore of ice was still several minutes away, but they moved straight for the inevitable and massive obstacle, and Jacobs wondered, when it came to that, if Akmaaq would have them let go of the rope.

There were smaller pieces of floating ice along the way, and they sometimes bumped into formations as big as the boat. The umiaq was either dragged across, or they slowed for a merciful moment while the ice block added to their drag. Until the floating boulder was pushed out of the way and the whale pulled faster. When Akmaaq was quick enough, he would extend his paddle to soften the collision, and on Q's side he did the same. But sometimes the bone frame of the umiaq cracked hard and threatened to snap. Jacobs was terrified of freezing to death in the waters and of dying in the night sea. He remembered what Yuq had told him about making offerings and praying, and he found it to be true. He wished his time in Point Halcyon had been better spent, and he wished he hadn't been paired with the reckless ex-chief who defied God and everyone else. He wondered what Q thought but decided the kid had ways of dealing with fear, though Q had to be afraid.

In the last moments, as they approached the line where the ice shelf met the open sea, they faced a ridge that was thirty feet high and stretched for miles in both directions.

"Should we let go?" Jacobs said. And the ice ridge came closer.

"Do we let go?" Jacobs said again. And he and Q both continued to hold on, against reason and with no expectation other than to crash and capsize the umiaq. Akmaaq didn't say anything but he held on tight, they all held on tight, and the bow of the boat struck the hard white wall. Jacobs expected the frame to shatter, or even for them to be pulled into the black water beneath the ice. Instead, the rope became slack. One of the drag-float ropes rubbed the underside of the ice shelf until it snapped, the dragline and the harpoon line untangled, and the seal buoy surfaced. If the lines hadn't frayed apart, the umiaq would have been pulled under.

"Come on," Akmaaq said, and he pointed with the flashlight toward a spot where they could dock. They rowed over, and the slope was more gradual and the ice not as slippery as Jacobs had expected. They were able to climb to the top of the ridge, and they pulled the umiaq onto the ice behind them by its rope. They took turns with the night-vision specs, but the clouds had broken up, and a white sliver of moon shed light over the plane of ice. They rode on a flat floating sheet that had boundaries they could see, now that they were at a better vantage point. There were small ponds from the thaw that dotted the surface and a large dark hole that went through to the seawater. Along the far edges, rivers of seawater opened and closed, depending how the long flat berg drifted.

"There," Akmaaq said, and he pointed to the hole that was open to the black waters. "He will surface there."

"I say we head back before we fucking freeze," Q said.

"You don't get to say," Akmaaq said.

They pulled the boat down off the ridge and safely away from the water. They tipped the umiaq over and Akmaaq stuck one of the long paddles straight up and down into the snow, so they might better see it on their return. Akmaaq grabbed the bag of explosives and a tent, and they each took a harpoon, the lines coiled and draped over their shoulders, with the sealskin floats trailing across the ice behind them.

Akmaaq showed them how to use the shaft end of the harpoon as a walking stick to sound the ice before advancing. He sometimes took them wide of the most direct path, or they stepped through puddles instead of spots where the ice was dry, because the ice was thicker and more sure. Jacobs and Q both slipped and fell, and so they moved slowly, but the old man's quick boots planted firmly. Before they reached the open hole, Akmaaq dropped the tent at a spot he said would be among the last ice to melt. At the edge of the large round hole, Akmaaq instructed them to spread out and ready their harpoons. The hole was big enough to contain the whale, and standing apart as they were, the whale would be within striking distance of at least two of them.

In the moonlight, at the edge of the hole, the seawater rose and fell with the weight of the flat iceberg. At times they stood a few feet above the surface of the water, which occasionally surged high enough to lap over the edges, and it left the ice clean.

"The sea is melting the ice," Q said, "from below."

"Like Al Gore explained in his movie," Jacobs said.

A sheen of whale oil spread over the surface of the water, and it coated the ice along the edge of the open hole as the water rose and fell. Jacobs could smell the grease of the whale, and he realized he was hungry. They'd left their food in the umiaq and he didn't want to have to trek back for it.

He'd traveled great distances and was standing on the Chukchi Sea. He held a harpoon with his arm cocked and was about to repeat a gesture celebrated by his ancestors. Genes long dormant were crawling out of sleep, and he relished these last moments of adolescence before finally becoming himself. He'd been a somnambulist, numb and slumbering.

The waters swelled up forcefully and disrupted the rhythm set by the sea—and the lone seal buoy surfaced and bobbed. Then the whale breached, a black behemoth that spouted a vapor cloud and absorbed two harpoon blows from each side in the same moment. Jacobs and Q had both struck, while Akmaaq's throw went wide, coming close enough to Jacobs that he dodged and nearly fell. Jacobs and Q jumped up and down. There was little skill in what they'd just done but great joy. Anyone could strike the whale from such close range. But they had to get all the way out here, and they risked everything, so the effort felt magnificent.

The blowholes slapped shut and the whale rolled, entangled in several lines and dragging the floats. The giant rolled again and kicked its tail, sending a wave at Q, who was quick to get out of the way, but he also kept hold of the line. When the whale submerged the water level fell and a wave peaked in the middle of the round pool, where the floats all met and offered a brief resistance before being pulled down. The three backed away from the edge, and Q and Jacobs let out rope while Akmaaq used his line to fish for his floating harpoon shaft.

There was a minute or two of silence while Jacobs and Q let out more and more rope. Meanwhile, Akmaaq strapped a stick of TNT to a harpoon blade, secured the blade to the harpoon shaft, and readied a Bic lighter near the long fuse. When the last of the rope was about to disappear into the water, the lines went slack, and the white Eskimo and the black Eskimo were quick to react and coil their ropes on the ice as they pulled them back in. Akmaaq waited, then he lit the fuse and readied his harpoon.

The buoys surfaced. Then the whale appeared. And the whale gave them a knowing look. It rolled and breathed, only becoming more entangled in the lines, and it rolled and breathed. Akmaaq threw his harpoon, and again he threw wide. Jacobs dropped his rope, turned, and ran. The harpoon was lodged in the ice at the edge of the hole not far from him; he let out a scream as he leapt, and he dove to the ice along the same path they'd walked. The explosion rocked the night and lit up everything around them with the flash of an orange fireball. Ice chunks and water were thrown in all directions. Jacobs stood up and dusted himself off as he watched his harpoon line slip into the water and become entangled with the whale as it rolled.

"Heads up," Akmaaq said, much too late. But then Jacobs understood the danger hadn't passed. A loud cracking was heard as the iceberg shuddered and a line formed in the ice that started at the hole and followed the path they had walked. The crack passed right beneath Jacobs and split the ice apart as seawater puddled around his boots. Again he ran, screamed, and dove, this time landing near Akmaaq, who helped him stand up. Akmaaq patted Jacobs on the shoulder and laughed.

"Don't stand there!" he said. "Throw a bomb!"

"Are you crazy?" Jacobs said.

"Do it," Q said. "Kill it." Q continued to reel in or let out his harpoon line in response to the whale as it rolled and bobbed.

The animal breathed sporadically through the two blowholes and the water became clouded with the blood that seeped out of the harpoon wounds. It slapped its tail, slower and with less force as it watched and waited. It opened its mouth to let in water and the massive tongue forced seawater back through the stripes of baleen. The whale made a clucking sound and it moaned.

"He's tasting his blood," Akmaaq said. "He's deciding whether to fight or let us finish him."

The whale watched the hunters and opened and closed its mouth once more. It pushed the seawater back out with its tongue and produced an oily bloody sea foam that floated on the surface. Akmaaq, Q, and Jacobs each lit a stick of dynamite and let the fuse burn down. When the whale opened its mouth they threw. Jacobs's landed near enough that it was sucked in through the stripes of baleen and the bomb went inside the whale's mouth. Q's landed near the dorsal fin, the animal resting on its side. Akmaaq once again overthrew, and his stick of TNT landed in the pool above the crack created by his first bomb. The lit dynamite sank into the crevice and became lodged.

Akmaaq's exploded first, and again, ice and water went everywhere while the whole sheet of ice was lit orange. Jacobs's went off underwater, illuminating the large round hole in a flash, and the body of the whale was seen in shadow, an enormous black mass that produced a large belch of fire and smoke. The whale rose up and rolled as chunks of lard floated, and the slick of blood and oil thickened. The whale was coated in its own fluids and wrapped in harpoon lines. It slapped the surface of the water feebly with its fins and tail. Its jaw was open and bleeding, with a gap left in the stripes of baleen. Q's stick of dynamite exploded on the surface and covered them all with oil and blood.

There was another loud foundering as the crack that stretched away from the large hole grew longer, spread apart farther, and threatened to split the plane of floating ice in two. Jacobs was glad the old man was satisfied and they wouldn't be throwing more explosives anytime soon. And all three jumped up and down and shouted, because the whale, though not yet dead, had given up.

Akmaaq retrieved the harpoon shafts from the water. He used one to sound the ice and he found a solid spot to set up the tent. He put together the small A-frame they would barely be able to sit up in, with just enough room for them all to lie down. Then he tapped the harpoon shaft on the ice to find a good place to drive in some stakes to secure Q's harpoon line. The whale wasn't going anywhere, though if it tried to make a break, these tent stakes wouldn't slow it down. The idea was to keep the rope from falling into the water as Jacobs's had, and Akmaaq drove the stakes into the ice with the side of a pick.

In the glow of dawn, Q took out the camera. They were all covered in whale grime, but the sight of the field of ice in first light was glorious. They were like grubby nothings wandering around in heaven. The whale too had been brought low. Q shot some footage of the animal, though not much. He seemed embarrassed to film the whale in such a state. The majestic mammal was now maimed and covered in filth. Q narrated the night scene from the hours before, and he pointed the camera at the different spots where they each stood, but he couldn't do justice to what they'd seen. After a while, he rolled a large snowball to build a snowman.

Jacobs sat at the edge of the waterhole with his expensive Arctic sunglasses on, too exhausted to do any work. They had been up all night, and he looked forward to lying down. Akmaaq said they could sleep before walking back to retrieve the umiaq.

The whale stared without seeing. They would wait for it to die. And they would wait for the sun to melt an opening that would allow them to paddle out. Jacobs couldn't imagine the three of them towing the whale with the umiaq, and he felt sure Akmaaq had brought them out here with no intention of coming back. But they had surprised Akmaaq with their success, and they had given the captain a reason to want to live.

Q set his camera on a pedestal of packed snow, stood with his snowman, and pretended to interview him.

"I'm speaking with a real live Eskimo," he said. "So tell me, Frosty, how cold does it get?"

But before Q was allowed to ham it up long, Akmaaq kicked over the snowman and carried back an armful of the packed snow. He dropped it next to the tent, for bedding, and to insulate against the ice.

"That was my first snowman," Q said in protest.

"You've never seen snow?" Akmaaq said.

"It snows where we live, but never enough. Not like this."

"You got snow now," Akmaaq said. "Make all the snowmen you like. But help me carry this over."

When they had moved enough snow, Akmaaq picked up the tent, the poles held together with elastic cord, and placed it on the rectangle of packed snow. Then he went around and drove the stakes into the ice with the pick. Jacobs thought leaving the umiaq might be an error in judgment, but he couldn't imagine walking back now, and he supposed the ice would last through the day.

The sun came up over the white horizon, the clear skies brightening, with the dawn pinks giving way to hints of blue. As Akmaaq and Q crawled into the tent, Jacobs stood outside. The patterns of footprints in front of the tent looked to Jacobs like the fox-trot that was painted on the dance floor of Jessica's studio. For a moment he was taken back to when he glided with her around the room and she'd complimented his form, their bodies pressed together and they looked past each other over the shoulder, in the classic closed hold. He remembered how she projected a genuine smile, not her routine dance-instructor smile. She really liked him then, and he knew it. In those days it was easy for them to have a good time.

Inside the tent, Akmaaq told them to take off their dirty clothes but to keep them in their sleeping bags. Their skins of water they should fill up with snow and wear next to their bodies. They had been moving and exerting themselves but now realized how cold it was. They wouldn't want to wake up to find their water and their clothes frozen solid. If they had to relieve themselves they should take the harpoon shaft and sound the ice as he'd shown them. They'd left the waste pot in the umiaq, but it was best to keep that clean as long as possible. He told them to take the ice pick and walk as far from the camp as was safe, and to keep away from the edge of the water. Dig a hole and bury the waste back over with snow. Whales avoid the stink of humans. Jacobs didn't really see the point. The whale they'd caught had been enough of a challenge. But

Akmaaq was serious about how to do things on the ice, so they listened.

Q took the camera and a harpoon shaft, and he tapped on the ice as he walked away from camp.

"Get some sleep," Akmaaq said.

Q answered, "I can't. I have to get this shot. I've missed so much."

"Sleep. There'll be another dawn."

"I have to do this," Q said. "I don't have anything else.

"You can just die," he continued, "and that's OK. Or you. Go back to your wife or whatever. For me this is a one-shot deal. When else am I going to find a producer? I didn't come up here to find myself. I came here to film."

"You don't have to film everything to make it real," Akmaaq said.

"Let him," Jacobs said. "It's a brilliant shot: the sun coming up over the plane of melting ice." And he added, "Who needs sleep? What's the saying? *I'll sleep when I'm dead.*"

"You've got it wrong, White Bear. Spirits are restless. Spirits roam."

"Let him roam," Jacobs said, but Q was already gone.

"You're his father," Akmaaq said.

"You're his captain," Jacobs said.

The sun struck the tent with all its radiance, and there was so much light Jacobs had difficulty drifting off to sleep. At first he listened to his own teeth chatter, but before long, the sleeping bag did its work, and for the first time since they'd set out, he was warm and he was comfortable. His muscles and joints felt like weights that settled into the packed snow, and he tried to relax for some well-needed rest. But his mind drifted in and out of dreaming and wakefulness, and he sometimes opened his eyes to see the brightly lit beige roof of the tent just above him. He could hardly believe where he was and what they'd done. There was still the rougher half of the journey ahead of them—towing the carcass of the whale through the frozen ocean. But they had been lucky, and they had managed that rare feat: they'd killed a whale in pursuit.

When the president of the neighborhood association returned to the white domicile where John and Jessica lived, he was prepared to take legal action.

"We haven't gotten a response," he said, "and I've been fielding complaints on your behalf."

"My husband has been out of town," Jessica said. "Can you wait until he gets back?"

"We've been very patient."

"He'll take care of it when he returns."

"We can get someone out here tomorrow," the man said. "All I need for you to do is sign. And then we'll contact your husband about remuneration."

Jessica felt there was no way out. She wanted to get on the moonbike and just ride away. But the easy thing, the thing she had to do now, was to sign his paper.

As soon as he was gone, she walked into the front yard of the house across the street. She saw their house as their neighbors saw it, a white blot on the backdrop of brick copies. And she saw the house as her husband had seen it, a cry for something genuine and something more, the expression of a suppressed urge to go backward in time and far, far away. She knew no one else would see it that way, because John had erased the brick and made the house ugly. The white brick emphasized the cheapness of the neighborhood, since it negated the elegance of brick. The charming, homey, and stylish connotations the homes once inspired were mocked by the white ghost of a house. She could see how her neighbors must hate seeing it, and for this she was proud. After he graduated from the advanced ballroom dance class, John had done seldom else to stir emotion. He'd been a follower.

Jodi saw Jessica, and she came out.

"They're going to sandblast it," Jessica said.

"You don't actually *like* it?" Jodi said.

"I could go either way."

"Did Nat do all right? He's pretty handy."

"Thank you for letting me borrow him. Men are good for a few things."

"Where *is* John?" Jodi said.

"He's finding himself. In the Alaskan wilderness."

"No shit?" Jodi said. "He doesn't seem the type."

"He's not," Jessica said. "But then something happened and he's all brand new."

"He get hit in the head?"

"Yes," Jessica said. And she was confident that had happened in one of his caveman lives. "He did."

Between sleep and wakefulness, Jacobs listened to the cries of the bowhead dying. He could hear the low plaintive whalesong through the ice, and he felt disoriented from the movement of the ice plane as it shifted over the water. The inside of the tent was bright with daylight, and Jacobs knew an overwhelming sadness from having to listen to the whale in pain. He had known the triumph of defeating

Goliath, but now he was sorry. The kill was unnecessary. The whale was rare and gorgeous. Jacobs should have been satisfied with seeing one alive and up close. He was too tired to crawl out of the sleeping bag—as Q and Akmaaq snored—but the cries of the whale had woken him, and he couldn't fall back asleep.

So he listened. His regret seemed to betray his ancestors, but he said quietly over and over, with the hope that the whale would somehow understand. *I'm sorry. I'm so sorry.*

The edges of the giant ice sheet they slept on rubbed into other bergs. And he was aware of the flow of the water beneath them, sometimes gurgling. But then as he listened, he also heard a second whalesong. The second whale was distinct, the song in another register and carried over a great distance. The sailors in the sonar post had said songs could travel hundreds of miles, and he knew by the long pauses between call and response that the second whale was some ways off. The dying whale and this other whale talked, though they might be days apart. So their whale, though he was in pain and he was dying, at least he wasn't dying alone. Jacobs was comforted by this thought. He listened to the whales sing back and forth to each other, a conversation without words. He was convinced he understood their emotions. And the distant whale told the dying whale something that changed the character of his cries. The dying whale actually sounded like he cheered up. And they sang together. And Jacobs eavesdropped until he drifted back into sleep.

Akmaaq woke up his tentmates after a few hours to retrieve the umiaq before the sun went back down. He had his glass eye in his mouth and Jacobs was startled and confused before he realized what he saw. The old captain rolled the glass orb around in his mouth, and as he spit out the eye, it appeared to watch them from Akmaaq's pursed lips.

Q and Jacobs dressed slowly and put on the dirty parkas, caribou snow pants, and sealskin boots. They felt the painful soreness of their muscles because they'd rowed all night, but they also felt a deeper soreness from the shivers they'd learned to ignore. They'd gotten more used to the cold, though they still shook from it.

A ceiling of low flat clouds had rolled in to blot out the sun, the temperature warming. The hours of morning sunshine had accelerated the thaw and the water hole had tripled in size. The long crack had also lengthened and widened into a canal that had grown considerably from the melting ice and the force of the giant flat berg rocking on the ocean.

They walked to the edge of the water hole and saw that the whale was dead. It floated in the sea without life, and Jacobs crossed himself.

Akmaaq saw him and slapped Jacobs's hand before he completed the gesture. "I thought I *told* you."

"But the soul of the whale—"

"Why should the soul of the whale be at peace while I live to suffer?" Akmaaq said.

They pulled on the harpoon line to bring the dead whale to the edge of the ice, which took a great effort, and Jacobs was aware of the soreness in his muscles and his joints. Q framed the shot and walked back to the tent to retrieve a new tape. Akmaaq cut into the whale. He sawed his knife to get through the blubber, he reached in, and he cut out a piece of meat. He took the whale steak and divided it.

"Why couldn't you wait until I was rolling?" Q said. "I need a little more cooperation."

The raw meat tasted like blood and gristle. When Jacobs swallowed, he felt a rush. The meat soothed his hunger, and he wanted more. Akmaaq cut out another steak, then another. The mood lifted and Q asked questions as blood and oil ran down their chins and stained the fronts of their parkas.

"Should whaling be illegal?"

"It *is* illegal," Akmaaq said. "And it is our right. This arrangement is the only way. The whales were stolen for industrial products. For school lunches. For profit. But *we* have a sacred bond with the whale."

"And Ronald McDonald," Q said, "has a sacred bond with..." But Q didn't finish his remark because Akmaaq slapped the camera, which made Q chase after the old man, who was faster on the ice. Q filmed and held out his gloved fist, intending to hit Akmaaq if he caught up with him, except he was too slow, especially since he tried to film it.

"Don't touch the camera," he said. "We've only got one."

Akmaaq held up his hands for a truce, and Q saw that he still had the bloody knife. Akmaaq went back to carving raw steaks from the carcass. When they could eat no more, they walked toward the umiaq, sluggish from the high-calorie meal.

"Digesting raw meat warms you," Akmaaq said. "The body works hard. Blood pools at your center."

They dragged the skin-boat back across the ice, and soon they would bed back down for the night. A second channel had opened on the sheet of ice and on their walk back they saw where new water holes had formed. The ice melted rapidly and they knew now that Akmaaq was right. They could just wait another day or two, then row back with the carcass of the whale. They also saw how Akmaaq had selected the right spot for their tent. Their camp was far enough from the places where the ice had thinned that they would be left floating while the rest melted away. Though to be sure, they tied the umiaq to one of the tent stakes.

Q made three large snowballs for them to sit on, and he asked Akmaaq for his pipe. Q produced a bag of marijuana, packed the pipe, and they smoked and passed it around.

"Did you bring this on the plane?" Jacobs said.

"Nah," Q said. "Was in the closet with the night specs and dynamite. I nabbed this while that cop had his back turned. You were standing right there."

"Do you know what I went through to get you out?" Jacobs said.

"It was my birthday."

"You turned eighteen?" Jacobs said. "You didn't say anything."

"There wasn't time," Q said. "I'm saying it now."

"Well, happy birthday."

"Black Bear is a man," Akmaaq said as he took the pipe.

They watched the orange clouds on the horizon darken to rose, then magenta, while Akmaaq talked. He puffed on the pipe and told of the snow whale while Q kneeled to get a close-up of the storyteller for his film.

A whale needs to breathe. And we need meat. We live together in harmony and are grateful to one another. But the snow whale has bloodlust. Whales evolved at the top of the food chain, so they are mostly docile. Only in the past one thousand years have whales known what it is to be hunted. The snow whale takes great offense at being hunted, and he fights back. He doesn't live to play. He is a living whale on this earth, but also a spirit, and a protector. When the white men came with steamboats and harpoon cannons, they knew no bounds. They had no respect for the whale and the snow whale followed the white men here from other waters. The snow whale was a curse from the tropics and he hates the cold. But he stays because he thrives on hate. And the whites have stopped hunting whales. So he haunts *us*, and *hunts* us, wherever whales are defiled. When we revere the old traditions the whales shed life willingly, and the snow whale keeps away, with respect for our ways. But when we forget, the snow whale returns.

He has brought the tropics with him, and that's how we know he is here. The snow whale has upset the natural order and disturbed Sila. The snow whale is the cause of *uggianaqtuq,* this *crazy-weather.* Sila is the air and sky— also that which breathes life. Our ancestors were closer to nature, and closer to the wisdom of the heavens. But when the missionaries came, we changed. This new generation is trying to take us back, but they don't know all we've lost.

The snow whale is an abomination and has upset Sila's order. The snow whale carries the early thaw as cover for the bowhead. Without the sea ice, there will be boundless waters where whales can surface. And we won't be there. The seas will rise and Tikigaq will become submerged. Tikigaq, the first whale, will swim off with us on his back. The upside-down time will return, like in the song, and men will be animals again, and animals will be like men.

You think I'm a superstitious old man. You think it's the pot talking. But it's true. Great changes have come. This thaw is out of season, and one day soon there will be no more ice. We will float off on the back of the first whale, and the snow whale waits to hunt us. And Sila—the skies and the air—will forever torment. The storms have increased—we've seen lightning here—and it's because we've lost our way.

Our journey is not complete, hunters. We killed our whale, the snow whale is coming for us, and we must kill him. Not so an old chief can save face with his clan. Not for them to believe my story. But to save Tikigaq and all our lives.

Our courage and our strength are yet to be tested. The mind is attuned through privation and suffering. This is the way back to the ancestors, and the way to wisdom. God will put us through it. Are you ready, Black Bear? Are you ready, White Bear?

To stop this *crazy-weather* we have to kill the snow whale and bury his bones in Tikigaq—to return his white flesh and his evil spirit to the first whale.

Chapter 9

The first full day on the ice, they waited. Jacobs, the wood gatherer, had nothing to collect. Much of the sea ice on the horizon had turned to black water, and the length of the enormous flat iceberg they'd slept on was being overtaken. Elsewhere on the white plane, ice had liquefied into puddles. Their encampment was at the high end of a slope, and the hole where the whale carcass floated wasn't as wide as it appeared, because seawater had spread over the rim, but a white ring of ice remained below, where it hadn't melted through.

On winter camping trips, John's father would whittle with his knife as he smoked. John would stand with his hands in his pockets and watch while his father carved facial expressions into the deadwood. The idea was to make a pile of shavings, for kindling, but the sculpted relief faces brought the broken branches to life. And so John had to go get more wood, because he didn't want the carvings burned.

Jacobs couldn't remember the last time he'd had time alone like this. He knew he should pray. He was in awe of where they were, and of what he saw, but he couldn't find the words. Q sat apart, on the snowball he'd rolled for a stool, also staring out, except he looked bored.

"Were you a Boy Scout?" Jacobs asked. He didn't have to raise his voice, though Q was some ways off, because the sound carried.

"A Ghetto Scout," Q said.

"What was ghetto about it?"

"Officially, we were Boy Scouts, but there was only one kid with the uniform and no one listened to him. We had copies of the official handbooks, with the covers torn off, all these illustrations of white kids and the white idea of Indians. We weren't about to swallow that. Mostly, we saw it as a manual for tying knots, so in the church basement, we took turns tying up the kid with the uniform, practicing our knots."

"You learned knots, at least."

"I can tie someone up," Q said. "I'm not sure it's quite the same."

"Did you ever whittle? Make Pinewood Derby cars? Go canoeing or camping?"

"We weren't allowed to have knives in the church basement," Q said. "A knife was what you took to school. Our troop disbanded when the ghetto leader got arrested for not paying child support. He had two sons who lived in another city that he never saw. He started the troop because he missed them."

"Not enough to send them money."

"Nobody had money. In our neighborhood money came and went, but it never stuck around."

"You don't blame him?"

"The city sucks," Q said. "Everyone knows it. No one is saying it. Supposed to be this great accomplishment.

People piled on top of each other. Everything's expensive, the buildings are old, and in the summer it smells like garbage."

"What do you think of *here*?"

"We should be filming," Q said.

"These could be outtakes," Jacobs agreed. "Ad-libs from the director."

"We're not supposed to be here," Q said. "We ain't Eskimo. We ain't even on land. We're floating on the frozen ocean, and sleeping on ice. Who *does* that?"

"*We* do," Jacobs said. "And we killed a whale."

"So do I get a merit badge?"

On the second day, the whale floated out of reach, in the middle of an ever-widening pool of seawater. Akmaaq had cut enough of the whale meat that they didn't go hungry. The wind picked up, they talked less, and they chewed and chewed. The wind howled to remind them they may not survive, and the ancestor spirits joined the chorus. Jacobs kept his hands between his knees, or he paced, to keep warm.

The sea ice had returned overnight, but the long flat berg continued to melt. Sometimes when he looked out he couldn't distinguish the white sea ice at the horizon from the white overcast sky. Up and down blended. His sense of self dissipated, and for long stretches of time he thought about absolutely nothing. He was a living breathing animal that nature didn't care enough about to spare.

Q filmed the wind. A snowdrift accumulated at their tent until the berg rotated, the wind shifted, and the same gale blew the ice bare. Q filmed the old man huddled in meditation. Q filmed the whale carcass that rolled or drifted in response to stirring gusts.

The wind was an irritation that mocked their sense of ease. The wind brought atheist torments. And the constant wild air vanquished these recently proud hunters.

They put in early and crawled into the small tent that billowed and shook, so that when night came, the white Eskimo and the black Eskimo were unable to relax, the winds whistling and the alien rants of the icy ocean loud in the dark.

"How come you don't have kids?" Q asked Jacobs.

"I've wanted them," Jacobs said. "I worry about money. I worry I won't do it right."

"All you have to give them," Akmaaq said, "is your name."

"Mine didn't even give me that," Q said.

"Is that a saying?" Jacobs asked. "An Inuit saying?"

"I'm saying it," Akmaaq said.

"But have others said it? Have you heard it said? *All you have to give them...*"

"Are you quoting?" Q clarified.

"I know what a saying is," Akmaaq said. "At Tikigaq a saying can be a thousand years old, or forty. No one can know for sure."

"But you've heard it?" Jacobs said.

"Why does it matter?"

"It's my heritage. It's what I'm owed. It's why I'm here."

"*Don't eat the yellow snow,*" Q said.

"Very funny."

"I *have* heard that one," Akmaaq said.

"Tell us *something*," Jacobs said. "We want to know."

"You really want to hear it?" Akmaaq said.

"We do."

"Then listen," Akmaaq said. "You've heard the wind all day, but have you listened? Sila talks. The Great Living

Breath. Who gives life. Who is indifferent to us. And who is not a who. If you listen, you will know. There's no city. No wealth. No modern. No facts. Your sayings are garbage. Listen."

"You told me we would only follow Inupiat ways," Jacobs said. "But you also said the snow whale came when there was disregard for the traditions. So which was it?"

"We followed the old ways," Akmaaq said. "But the snow whale will come because I've brought a white bear and a black bear. I'm not saying it's right, but our people will never fully accept you. And the whale has eyes."

"I'm Eskimo," Jacobs said. "I have proof."

"The whale has eyes."

On the third day, the men busied themselves through morning. They ate, then washed off the blood with meltwater and a rag. They tore down camp and tied the tools and implements to the bottom of the boat. As they digested the raw meat they became warm enough to unzip parkas. Jacobs saw the fox fur belt that Q wore, a band of white that played in the breezes, and he remembered his mitten from Toni. He untied the mitten from under his seat in the umiaq where he'd hidden it, and he rubbed the fur of the white rabbit against his stubbled cheek. He caught a whiff of musk and decided Toni had doused the mitten with perfume. He occupied himself with the pleasant sensation of the soft fur and he breathed in the sweet aroma.

The ice horizon had broken apart, and there were branching veins and large sections of the ice plane that had buckled under and were carried away. Akmaaq's plan was to head toward open water before nightfall and to land at Tikigaq in the light of morning. They would use bombs where the channel met a dead end, and the carcass of the whale would keep the ice from closing back on them.

Akmaaq spoke of the possibility of a south wind, or "woman wind," that pushes together the pack ice in the lead and closes it. But Akmaaq believed the snow whale had brought the early thaw, and the tropical air that followed the snow whale would keep the lead open, even with a "woman wind."

Q held the camera and he filmed the old captain.

"What do the whales do," Q asked, "if the pack freezes over? How do they breathe?"

"They can break through ice a foot thick," Akmaaq said.

Q slowly panned and noted the thinning ice. "If the whale were alive, there'd be nowhere safe for us."

"Don't think he wouldn't know," Akmaaq said. "But a bowhead might have mercy on you."

"Even after we harpooned him?" Q said.

"When the snow whale comes," Akmaaq said, "you will know the difference."

Before they set off, Akmaaq advised his crew to empty their bowels one last time, to wipe out the waste pot with snow, and to bury the snow in a hole away from the edge of the water. They ate again and cleaned themselves. They dropped the umiaq in the water, retrieved Q's harpoon line, and rowed toward the open channel. The rope strained against the weight of the whale, and they rowed to gain inches. Once the whale moved, their progress was easier, though they had to paddle hard to keep up momentum. Jacobs looked back at the whale and sympathized with what the animal must have felt when it pulled the drag-floats, though he knew that what the whale had to contend with could hardly compare with the resistance they experienced in the umiaq.

"This is when it would be nice to have the outboard motor," Q said.

At different times throughout the day, Q had taken out the video camera and made observations. They had seen a bazaar of murres land near them and dive for fish in the water. The birds were like large gulls, only with plumage in a black-and-white penguin pattern, and they could dive deep. Jacobs wondered if the footage would amount to much, but he supposed the sight of the dead whale was worth something. He hadn't seen that on the nature shows, and he also knew the three of them would make an impression in their animal skins covered with blood.

He had taken a piece of rope and made a necklace with Toni's mitten. He wore it around his neck, tucked into his parka, and every now and then he smelled the perfume. The mitten was a token of love and good luck. He knew their stamina would be tested through the night, and he knew his people depended on them.

He thought of his wife, Jessica, in bed and watching television, and he wished he'd been more assertive with her. Too many times they'd drifted off to sleep by the light of *The Tonight Show*. Too many times he left in the morning to sell desk doodles though he wanted to stay with her in bed. This was the routine, and there was nothing sacred or elemental to his getting up and going to the office. Jessica needed John, but only for her comforts. And she was made glad by him, but only because his company was better than being alone. He wished he could make her feel more of a connection and hoped he would live to try again.

Jacobs counted strokes to remain focused and he kept his gaze centered directly ahead. He refused to look back at the sixty-ton mammal that fought them still. By turns he convinced himself to row harder or to conserve his strength. By turns he sweated in his parka or he caught a chill. By turns he felt the pain of his joints and the aches in his muscles, or he felt capable and strong, driven by his dead ancestors, the spirits who haunted Tikigaq.

When the ice shifted and the canal closed up, Akmaaq tossed lit sticks of dynamite and they all ducked down and covered their ears. Eventually, the ice obstacles were removed and the lead was near, the channel of water that ran along the shore, the way open and only blocked by one remaining ice boulder. Akmaaq gave two sticks of TNT to Q. He pointed the best path for him to walk across the ice and explained where to plant the bombs.

"I told you a boy is handy," Akmaaq said.

"Who you calling boy?" Q said.

"I only meant that you weigh less," Akmaaq said.

Before Q climbed out of the umiaq, he asked Jacobs to film him, and he gave him instructions on how to frame the shot. Q moved step-by-step until Akmaaq shouted that he was close enough. He planted the bombs, he lit the long fuses, and he walked away as quickly as he could without running. The ice was disturbed by his movement, and they heard it crack apart. Q hadn't yet made it back to the umiaq, they listened for the successive explosions to go off, and the ice surged upwards. A giant white glistening creature surfaced between Q and the boat. The sudden appearance of a whale was enough of a surprise, but the sight of the white whale, under any circumstances, was unsettling. The snow whale saw the dead body of the bowhead in tow, and as his giant black eye darted from man to man, he seemed to project hateful accusations at Akmaaq and his crew. Q was forced to move back in the direction of the booby-trapped ice boulder, and at the first explosion, everyone screamed. The white monster turned, an effort that broke apart most of the remaining ice, and when the second bomb went off, the snow whale dove back underwater. His white tail lifted up, his head went under, and the flukes followed ever so gently for a creature of such unimaginable girth. When the smoke cleared, Q lay on a flat piece of ice not much bigger than himself. He bobbed on the ice mattress that threatened to tip over in the wake of the white whale. Q shivered and screamed but was unable to move, since any movement might dump him into the water.

The snow whale was longer and larger than the bowhead. His skin was as white as the ice, but there was also a grayish cast that made him look aged. Unlike the bowhead, he was covered with imperfections. There were barnacles on him, long scars, and swollen-over harpoon blades. His head and his body were a uniform and enormous elongated box. He lifted half out of the water with little effort and his mouth opened wide. He could swallow the boat whole, and his square yellow teeth were spaced apart and nestled in blood-red gums. His single blowhole exhaled a fume of angry air, and as he smacked his jaw from side to side the boulder-sized teeth ground together and his lips made a sneer. By contrast, the bowhead had recognized the hunters with a look of fear, and the baleen-striped jaw of the bowhead appeared to shape a natural smile, even in death. The snow whale bulged with his own weight, and he looked out with an ancient and boundless hate.

The white whale was a shocking and terrifying sight. He had appeared a flash of white, obscenely large and powerful. As the seconds passed, they were given the opportunity to examine him, and as they understood he was real, he became more grotesque. Then, as soon as he had appeared, he was gone.

Akmaaq cut the rope to the dead bowhead in order to paddle over to Q, who screamed. Q was in pain and would soon freeze to death. He hugged the piece of floating ice and he was soaking wet. They had to move quickly before his vital functions shut down and he would start to die. Jacobs was torn between filming this sequence and being able to lend a hand. He was sure he'd gotten a glimpse of the snow whale on the tape, and he was sure, if they could only get back to shore, that this footage was priceless.

They pulled Q into the boat, Akmaaq told Q to strip down, and he wrapped him in one of the bearskins. Q shivered while Akmaaq and Jacobs wrung out his parka and his clothes.

"What *was* that?" Q said.

"You know what that was," Akmaaq said.

"I thought the whale was a story. Some myth."

"Like Smurfs?" Jacobs said.

"The curse is real," Akmaaq said. "The whale spirits and the spirits of the ancestors are real. Tikigaq is real."

"How do we stop him?" Q said.

"Like we stopped the last one," Akmaaq said.

"But he's bigger," Q said. "He has teeth and he's trying to kill us."

"You did good, Black Bear. You outran him."

"What about next time?" Q said.

"Next time toss a bomb," Akmaaq said.

They returned to the bowhead carcass, secured the line, and started to row. The way out to the water was now clear. The ice boulder was free and had floated away. In the lead, the action of the waves sometimes made the whale's weight resist them more, while at other times the line went slack as the dead whale threatened to roll over on them and capsize the umiaq. Akmaaq pointed the way, but the sun was making its descent, and before long, they would have to paddle in the dark.

In late afternoon light, with the sun going down, Nat Jorgenson was watering his rose bushes when he saw Jessica standing and pumping the Luna Expedition Special Edition like a kid racing home from school. She dismounted and stood in front of her garage to catch her breath. Nat placed the end of the hose at the base of a bush, and he walked over.

"That's quite a bike," he said.

"I love it," Jessica said, and she took off her helmet and hung it from one of the handlebars. "I can go really fast."

"Have you ever ridden a motorcycle?" Nat said.

"Aren't they dangerous?"

"Not if you know what you're doing. I suppose a lady might be better suited to a motor scooter."

"I like the exercise," she said.

"I used to own a bike until Jodi made me sell it," Nat said. "Her excuse was the insurance, which wasn't that much. But I sold it for her."

"You regret it?"

"I was under her spell," he said.

"How are things," Jessica said. "Between you?"

"We're not getting divorced, if that's what you mean."

"Would you want to?"

"You think because you and me? . . ." Nat said, and he gestured that there was a connection between them. "We haven't even really done anything."

"Would you want to?"

"Are you asking me?"

"I think maybe I am."

"You could still be friends with Jodi?"

"I don't see why not."

"She'll be gone for three hours tomorrow."

Three hours. Jessica decided that gave them two hours. Not a date, but time. She looked at Nat's hands, which were strong but well-manicured. She tried to project the relationship well into the future and drew a blank. She tried to visualize him dancing but couldn't. She felt a thrill because she'd never had an affair. She had somehow started something that she was incapable of stopping. She had no idea where it might lead, or even if being with Nat was what she really wanted. She took a step toward Nat, who leaned back, afraid she might try to kiss him where Jodi could see. And more than anything, more than any sense of what was right or wrong, Jessica blamed her husband. John was the one who had left. And while she couldn't imagine telling her husband what she planned to do, Jessica also knew she would be dying to, just to set things straight.

She gave Nat a lusty look, which was unpracticed and awkward, and she said, "I'll leave the door unlocked."

At night as they rowed, Q sometimes stopped to scan the water with the night-vision specs, but before long the batteries died, and he put the specs away in their case for good.

Jacobs and Q didn't know how far out they were or how much farther they would have to go. They had paddled miles to meet the whale, and on the ice they had drifted miles. Akmaaq knew by his compass the way to point the umiaq, and when they eventually sighted the shore, he would recognize where they were. But for now, there was the open black sea with the redundant broken ice and the endless formless overcast night sky. With the three of them rowing they kept the harpoon line taut, but seemed not to move. The floating ice passed by them, and they appeared to remain in place. There were no sounds other than the wind and the lapping waters, and they didn't have the energy to sing.

The bowhead settled on his back with its face under-water and the tail flukes raised up. Or it would roll onto its side. The drag-floats shifted and strained as the whale became waterlogged and the whale was beginning to sink. The resistance from the whale increased as more of it settled under the surface. And as the whale sometimes swung out and turned sideways, they could tell from the ice chunks they had already passed that at times the bowhead dragged them backwards. There was nothing to do but row.

Jacobs had set out wearing ski mittens, and he had gotten used to them. But when he saw that Akmaaq did everything barehanded—he rowed, he reached into the water, he pulled on the harpoon line, his hands callused over and his skin dark from prolonged exposure to the elements—Jacobs felt the old man knew something, and rather than protect them, his hands should be made to adjust. So Jacobs did likewise. Blisters formed, broke open, and reformed. Eventually, his skin became desensitized and tougher. His nails had grown long, and he noticed, but then that didn't matter. At first the aching soreness of the open wounds on his palms nagged, and the numbing pains from the cold bite of the sea air made him grimace, but then he was able to ignore the discomforts and he simply rowed.

In a few short days his body had changed. He was leaner, he was stronger, he sat straighter; his bones were more perfectly aligned and his awareness sharpened. He couldn't believe the way he used to live. His hapless and unquestioned purposeless days. His dull nights. The predictability of the trajectory of his accomplishments, so piddling and meaningless. He'd had no courage or virtue other than politeness and staying out of the way of others. He had managed to avoid offense, but now when he looked back at himself with the eyes of a hunter, he was deeply offended. How dare he expect so much and give so little. How dare he wallow in waste. He had been a lustful coward and a plebe.

And he saw changes in his mates. Q was a man who had witnessed unparalleled natural beauty. He had pitted himself against the currents and the winds. The old man had proven what he had left, selflessly and with no expectation of success. But they did succeed, and they would succeed. Akmaaq no longer had youth, and his ego had been damaged, but this season's would be his greatest catch. He had set out, virtually alone, with a crew of half-breeds. With nothing but muscle and will. They would return with whale meat for the celebration and the hope of success in future seasons. Lost in thought, they paddled with a constant stroke, and the hours passed slowly, but they passed.

They approached what looked like a sunken iceberg. Jacobs saw a white form under the surface and he couldn't tell quite how deep it was or how large, because of the darkness and the refraction of light, but they rowed along for a while before he realized that the submerged white mass moved alongside them. And then he also remembered that ice didn't sink. It was only the sheer weight of icebergs that caused most of them to be underwater, while there was always a point that penetrated the surface. As they kept rowing, he watched, and he could make out the shape of the whale. They were too near for Jacobs to see the entire silhouette at first, and when he recognized what he saw, he was overcome with panic.

He wanted to say something to his mates, but he was afraid that calling attention to the creature would bring wrath upon them. He had the feeling that this was probably the end for him and he had been stupid to follow in this course. He had just thought how profoundly he had changed and how he couldn't imagine his life without this experience. And now he was going to die. Cruelly, he had been shown the way only at the last moment, right before being snuffed. He thought he could make out the black eye of the devil, and the giant seemed to smile. The snow whale toyed with Jacobs and fed off his panic. And no one in the boat did anything but row with a steady stroke rhythm.

"Captain," Jacobs finally said, but Akmaaq didn't hear, and Jacobs had to repeat himself.

"I see him," Akmaaq replied. He stopped rowing and crawled slowly to the middle of the umiaq, where he prepared a harpoon. He opened the bag of bombs, and he readied his hunting rifle. Q moved into the bow and took Akmaaq's place. All would have been achieved without notice, except Q looked nothing like the captain.

The whale slowly rose and surfaced. The waters from underneath the umiaq swirled then lifted up, and they were on the back of the beast. Akmaaq stood and put all his weight into a thrust that went deep into the white hide of the leviathan, and the creature raised his head, arched his back, lifted his tail, and shuddered with a roar. Akmaaq had struck the giant with a pinprick. The old captain shouted as his harpoon went deep into the whale flesh, past the shaft, and the whale twisted and flapped as the boat was thrown off its back. The waters peaked, and the tail slapped the surface near enough to tilt the umiaq while a wave passed over them. They were each splashed but minimally wet. And for an Arctic night, the air was relatively balmy, though they didn't know the temperature. Of all the things they could have brought, a thermometer was simple enough. Probably, REI had a digital one that would also measure wind speeds.

The snow whale dove deep and nearly disappeared. He became smaller and smaller, and the boat tipped slightly as Akmaaq put his full strength into guiding the harpoon line. The snow whale would surely bleed and spew oil. By now, Q knew the drill, and he set his paddle down in the boat while he moved to the middle to help Akmaaq take hold of the line. As the boat picked up momentum and skimmed over water and ice, Jacobs cut the line to the dead bowhead. He didn't want to, but he imagined their small boat torn apart between the weight of the two whales.

"He's taking us back out," Akmaaq said. But that was obvious. They could expect no luck, and should they survive the encounter, with or without the snow whale, rowing back to Tikigaq was an ordeal they would gladly endure.

Jacobs felt a sense of loss as they were pulled away from the dead whale. There was nothing left in the umiaq for them to eat, and the killed whale would go to waste. Eventually, the seal-floats would become waterlogged and sink, and the bowhead would return to the sea with his gift of life gone. Jacobs felt a dread only overpowered by the will to live and a fear of death.

Their line became slack again, and the snow whale surfaced. He had doubled back and just might come for them. There was no surviving in the water for more than a minute, and this whale was experienced: he knew how to rid himself of the nuisance at the other end of a harpoon line.

Jacobs and Q reeled in the rope while Akmaaq aimed with the hunting rifle. The white whale was behind them, between the boat and the dead whale. Akmaaq fired off rounds as quickly as he could cock and reload the chamber. Chunks of flesh exploded from the cheek of the snow whale as Akmaaq's bullets landed. When he missed, the bullets sunk into the flesh of the dead whale beyond the white whale, or they ricocheted off the ice and water. Akmaaq aimed for the creature's eye and came near enough that the whale turned and slapped the water with his tail. Now the men were completely wet, and Q bailed out water with the waste pot while Jacobs cut open one of the drag-floats and used the sealskin to bail too. There weren't enough drag-floats, harpoon blades, or sticks of dynamite left to kill a second whale. Their best hope was survival.

With the white whale below the surface, Akmaaq let out the line, and Jacobs and Q picked up their paddles and rowed back toward the dead whale. But this action provoked the snow whale, and he appeared again.

"Help me pull us toward him," Akmaaq said, which didn't sound at all like the thing to do.

Jacobs and Q hesitated but dropped their paddles, and all three drew in the line as the umiaq moved in the direction of the white monster. Akmaaq let Q and Jacobs man the rope as he took a harpoon and waved it over his head.

"I'll frame a sod house with your bones," Akmaaq shouted. "And we won't return your head to the sea. You'll forever wander in the cold nights at Tikigaq, where your soul will never rest. The ancestors you killed will torment you, and when I die, my spirit will poke out your spirit eyes."

Jacobs and Q continued to pull the umiaq closer. They were within harpoon range, and the wait was unbearable. The snow whale appeared cognizant of Akmaaq's curses, and he reared up. They were much too close to the angry whale, but Jacobs and Q were tired of seeing Akmaaq overthrow and miss his target. Their only hope was a blow that struck near the heart.

Again, Akmaaq aimed for the eye, and again he missed, but the harpoon entered the animal's cheek. When he opened his cavernous mouth, the harpoon shaft broke apart, but the blade had pierced all the way through. He dove and bit down but missed the umiaq, so the boat was sent backwards in a wave. And when the crew righted themselves, Akmaaq gave the second rope to Jacobs, who took in the slack, but there was no sense approaching the creature again, or of hitting him with more drag-lines, because only a fatal shot would save them.

They couldn't escape him, because they were tied to him. They let out the two lines when he swam away, and brought in the lines when he swam near. The whale circled but kept his distance. He slapped the ice and water to threaten them, but he didn't come closer. Meanwhile, the dead whale had drifted off.

"Give me the camera," Q said, but there weren't enough hands.

Q crawled over to their gear, grabbed the strap of the camera case, put it over his shoulder, and crawled back to help Jacobs with the rope.

On what was an otherwise beautiful night—with the winds calm, the water on the open sea flat, and the temperature rising—the quiet was too much to take. So Akmaaq provoked the snow whale again.

"The whites are coming back," he yelled. "There will be swarms of whites on the seas, and no one will stop them. White whalers with Inuit ancestors have come, and the government can't stop them. Your curse won't stop them. They won't quit until the last whale offers up his parka, and at the last celebration we'll parcel off the last morsel of whale flesh. I only hope I live to see it."

The snow whale dove, his tail rose and followed him under, and the ropes became slack. He doubled back under the umiaq and they could see him, a white mass that moved below with the drag-floats hanging off him like baubles. The harpoon lines followed under the umiaq and Akmaaq yelled, "Turn the boat," but Q wasn't strong enough, and the boat was too big for him to maneuver in time. Akmaaq screamed at Jacobs in the last moment, "Drop the line," and he slapped at his hands. Both ropes disappeared into the water and followed where the snow whale had passed under the boat. The whale was free of them, and Jacobs and Q were glad to see him go.

In the silence that followed there was nothing else to do but row back to the dead whale. The meat would stay preserved for as many days as it would take to tow the carcass back. And though they were feeling beaten down, they would return with the bowhead, and that would make them esteemed in the eyes of the Point Halcyoners.

When the umiaq brushed against the dead whale, Jacobs retrieved one of the harpoon lines. As Q watched the expanse of floating ice and black water, Akmaaq cut into the flesh and pulled out another meal. They chewed until they were full. Akmaaq gave the knife to Q and instructed him to climb onto the animal. Q gave Jacobs his camera, he used the harpoon lines to pull himself up, he crawled with his belly against the whale, and he sat atop the floating island of flesh.

"Cut off Yuq's float," Akmaaq said. "It's that line over there."

Because Akmaaq had explained that the first harpooner got the first share, this was cheating his own son. The captain had told him to do something he ought not do, but he did cut the rope, and Yuq's remaining sealskin buoy floated off. From Jacobs and Q's perspective, they agreed with Akmaaq that if they managed to bring the whale back, after all they'd been through, then they deserved the credit. While the first harpooner might be luckiest, and while he also deserved a share, he wasn't always the one who worked hardest.

"Get a shot of me up here," Q said to Jacobs, but he only joked because the night was too dark for the camera.

Before he could climb down, he pointed to Yuq's float and said, "He's still out there."

Their own floats surfaced nearby. The white whale rose up, bit down on Yuq's buoy, and disappeared back underwater.

Akmaaq jumped into the bow and shouted to Jacobs, "Let's go!"

"But the kid," Jacobs said.

"He's safe up there."

And so Jacobs and Akmaaq rowed back out, but Jacobs kept the line of the dead whale in the boat for as long as he could. He felt responsible for Q, and despite what Akmaaq had said, he didn't want to leave him stranded on the dead whale.

When they neared where Yuq's sealskin buoy had been swallowed by the snow whale, the harpoon line that connected them to Q had nearly run out, so Jacobs cut loose one of the few remaining drag-floats in the umiaq, and he tied it to the end of the rope that stretched back to the dead whale.

"What are you doing?" Akmaaq said.

The drag-float would make the rope easier to retrieve, and Jacobs thought this was obvious, so he didn't answer.

Again, the buoys popped up, the whale surfaced, he opened his mouth, and he swallowed the drag-float Jacobs had just released. They were close enough that Akmaaq threw but missed, and the harpoon shaft skimmed the water in front of the whale.

"Hold on," Jacobs shouted to Q, and the harpoon line that led back to the bowhead leapt out of the water and became taut. The white whale towed the dead whale as Q screamed, and the carcass rolled and shifted as it moved across the water. But then the rope went slack, and the sealskin buoy popped up again on the surface.

"He's playing with us," Akmaaq said, and he cut another drag-float loose as Jacobs had done. He tied a stick of TNT to the short rope. He waited for a sign of the whale, and when the drag-floats reappeared, he lit the fuse, swung the buoy over his head, and he let the bomb-and-buoy fly. The snow whale came up, opened his mouth, and the drag-float was swept in. He dove under with it, and the three Eskimos let out a shout, with Akmaaq especially pleased at his own cunning.

There was a flash down below, smoke bubbles effervesced on the water, and they hoped to see the carcass of the white whale also float up. But he didn't surface and Q screamed because he was the first to see what Jacobs and Akmaaq soon realized. The snow whale had survived and was maybe even stronger. He charged directly at the bottom of their umiaq. He wasn't playing this time, and he wouldn't miss.

There was one last harpoon shaft left in the umiaq that lay near Akmaaq but on the same side as his glass eye. Jacobs slid the harpoon back to the stern of the boat without the old man noticing, and Akmaaq felt around for the remaining harpoon but there wasn't time, so he grabbed a stick of dynamite and the flashlight, and he stood up.

The white whale breached in front of them and rose up. If Akmaaq had had the last harpoon, he could have thrust it into the white wall of flesh without throwing. But Jacobs couldn't have known, and he didn't want the captain tossing out their last spear. The animal tilted back so his head leaned out of the water at an angle. His mouth was open and chunks of bleeding blubber hung from charred lips, the tongue blackened and smoking. Blood and oil floated on the water around him. The creature was seriously wounded and seemed to have been sapped of strength. Akmaaq pointed the flashlight directly into the large black eye and blood seeped from under the eyelids, blood leaked out, and the animal stared back with a dull red pupil.

The explosion in the mouth of the whale may have given him a concussion, or it may have damaged the eye-socket from within, but the creature couldn't see. He was next to them now, Akmaaq shined the light in his eye, and the white whale didn't react as the blind eye stared back at nothing.

Akmaaq lit the fuse of another stick of TNT, and he just couldn't help himself. He shouted at the whale and gave away the location of the umiaq, "Welcome to *my* world. How does it feel? *Die,* you old devil!"

Jacobs was in the stern with the last harpoon. The snow whale—despite his being stunned, and despite the wounds around his jaw—slowly smiled. Akmaaq continued to shout, and Jacobs lay down in the back of the boat. He had the presence of mind to hold on to the last of the drag-floats, should the whale dump them from the boat.

The whale twisted his head and bit down on Akmaaq. Jacobs could hardly believe what he saw, but he watched as the white whale chewed on the old man, and as the bomb Akmaaq held blew smoke and fire out of the mouth and blowhole of the enormous creature. The whale was alive but stunned. Jacobs rowed up to him, raised the last harpoon, and thrust it with his remaining strength near one of the flippers, where he guessed the heart might be. The whale's mouth and blowhole continued to smoke, and blood poured from where Jacobs harpooned him.

Sluggishly at first, but with increasing force and speed, the white whale slapped his tail where the umiaq had been. Jacobs paddled as quickly as he could, but the whale's reach was great, and the umiaq was too big for Jacobs to make anything but slow progress. The snow whale's tail landed hard on the boat and the whalebone frame of the umiaq snapped to pieces. Jacobs remained conscious but was suddenly treading in the icy dark waters with the tail flukes raised above him. As the tail slid back under and the animal swam off, Jacobs hugged the last of the inflated sealskins. He floated and let out a scream. He sometimes bobbed under, in the residual waves from the tail smacks. His nerves reacted at once to the overwhelming cold, and he felt sharp pains shoot up his limbs, accompanied by a tingling numbness. His stomach seized. He screamed until his lungs emptied. He was in a state of shock, and even though he swam on the surface, he was unable to breathe.

Jacobs hugged the drag-float and the toothy face of the dead seal stared back at him, one of the buoys without a painted mask. Once Jacobs realized where he was, he kicked furiously in the direction of the dead whale. He heard Q root for him but couldn't make out the words. His mind raced with panic. He could see the dead whale and knew he was too far off, though his kicking legs helped keep him warm, and the seal-float raised him at least partially out of the water.

Jacobs continued to cry out and was unable to stop. After he kicked for what he decided had already been a minute, he was relieved with the hope that he might actually live to reach the dead whale. He kicked happily. He might die soon, but he couldn't believe all he'd experienced. He was overcome with a grateful joy as his surroundings faded, and Jacobs became himself at age six. He kicked in a pool with a kickboard. He was learning to swim at the city pool in June. He was a motorboat.

When the rope on the sealskin buoy went taut, he didn't know what was happening and he continued to kick. The resistance from the harpoon line pulled him backwards. Then he disappeared underwater with the drag-float.

Chapter 10

Jacobs was submerged in the freezing water, his arms clenched around the seal-float like it was charged with an electric current, and he kicked involuntarily as he went deeper. The ice floes on the surface above him seemed square clouds that lit up a flat ceiling of night sky. Jacobs screamed from the penetrating pain of the icy waters, but the pain passed quickly. He was numb and losing awareness, though he continued to shout, "*Help!*" and "*Please, God, help me!*"

Soon his lungs ached to breathe, and he felt he couldn't stand the weight of the water on his ears or the dull cold pain as he convulsed and continued to go deeper. The darkness glowed with a red tint, and warmth emanated from the core of his body, where whale meat had settled, undigested. There was a buzzing as his head cleared. Then he heard a whalesong. And the repeated ping of a sonar pulse. He remembered one of the listening-post sailors explaining that sound carried hundreds of miles under-water, and he heard him say it now, like hearing him in a dream. Jacobs was out of breath, but able to breathe. The seal was alive again and he rode its back. He no longer kicked, but the seal swam deeper and Jacobs hugged the seal like they were companions at play.

He had a premonition of the direction the seal would swim. A line in the water projected ahead of the seal and touched an isolated white moving cloud. He heard screams but no longer associated the sounds or the emotions with himself. He had no sense of the present, but time had loosed. Even as things were happening they felt like memories. Jacobs thought the seal had screamed and the seal needed help. And he was concerned. But as soon as he felt compassion, the thought dissipated. There was something ahead of them. It was no longer a cloud but a low-flying white dirigible, an oblong balloon on fire, with a trail of flames. Or this was the great seal mother, an enormous white seal. Jacobs saw groups of seals that swam alongside and behind. Seals that screamed. They needed help. They came closer and he saw seals with human faces, seals with broad-lined bright iconic features like the masks of opera singers. Below the white mother, Jacobs saw something dark, moving, and colossal, an object that couldn't be contained with the eye. What he saw was long, and perfectly rounded. He thought of the first whale and remembered the white whale. He became aware of the seals, the deep, and the icy waters.

Jacobs looked up and saw a flock of white angels swimming in the water above him. There were at least one hundred of them and they gave off a glowing light, like tall strong men in rippling robes. They were a beautiful sight to behold, and Jacobs felt at peace. The choirs of angels had come to meet him. He had been worthy of God's recognition, he had been true to himself, and he had lived his purpose. Then as an angel came near, Jacobs recognized a large white porpoise. This was the beluga migration. He was pulled deeper, and the belugas passed. And the white cloud ahead of him became the snow whale in the next moment. Wounded, the snow whale made a cloud of bloody red water. The snow whale came toward him with enormous mouth gaped to envelop, and the seal-float Jacobs embraced wasn't alive after all.

The first whale rose from below the white whale. The first whale was black, three times as large, and mathematically symmetrical. There were few features: a dorsal fin and a small tail, without flukes. The first whale hummed and swam with little effort. The first whale didn't bend and there was no mouth or eye, his blowhole sealed with a mechanical wheel. Jacobs saw foreign lettering on the side of the first whale, and what seemed a flagpole that rose straight from the giant's back. What harpooner would have the guts or inclination to throw at the first whale, he wondered? What would Akmaaq have done had they come across this titanic whale out in the open ocean?

But the jaws of the snow whale clamped down, and the great tongue pushed and moved Jacobs around as the freezing waters receded. Jacobs lost his grip on the inflated sealskin that was chewed and popped. The numbness was replaced by deep prickling stings as Jacobs's limbs thawed. He was unable to move, and he was in utter darkness. As he was tossed around, the body heat inside the cavernous mouth of the snow whale brought Jacobs back to life. He coughed, he spat, he breathed. He had taken in seawater and felt turned inside-out. But he was breathing. He was overcome by a fit of coughing—*but he breathed.*

He also screamed. He was unable to control the screams. As his body settled into a soft warm space, and as he found himself able to move again, his awareness of what had happened returned. And though he thought his situation inconceivable, the pain lessened, and he was all in one piece. He was panicked but coming to terms with his place and his condition. He was alive and should be dead. He realized he had survived, though his mates probably hadn't—and this seemed as good a time as any to pray. He had forgotten to pray. There was no way of escaping the snow whale. He was still in its clutches, and the creature might yet chew him up.

A match was struck, and Jacobs saw Akmaaq seated on the back of the whale's tongue. The cavity of the whale's mouth stretched and disappeared into shadows. Akmaaq held the match to his pipe and puffed. He sent up a cloud of smoke and the cavern was lit brighter as the captain inhaled. Jacobs lay in the front of the mouth, near wounds in the whale's gums that bled, and the air inside the mouth cavity was damp and smoky. Jacobs became aware of himself in a pool of blood, conscious that the tongue might move if the whale felt him, or that he might be spit out or even chewed if he remained where he was. He shivered as he remembered the extreme cold he had just survived, and he moved as quickly as he could, crawling along the gumline toward Akmaaq. He climbed onto the back of the charred tongue, which rolled but couldn't brush them off, and they were safe.

Akmaaq held out the match to let Jacobs take in the scene. The living cave was comfortable enough. They breathed freely and it was warm. Akmaaq stared back without his glass eye. His eye socket was a dark open hole, and the old man smiled. Above them somewhere was the blowhole, and the creature vibrated as they heard his whalesong from within.

"That's the death knell," Akmaaq said. "We've killed him.

"We've saved the world from a disastrous fate," Akmaaq continued, and he held out the pipe. "Our people are now free to hunt and to live as we please."

Jacobs took the pipe, and Akmaaq said, "Black Bear gets good weed."

"He gave you some?"

"I nabbed it when his back was turned," Akmaaq said. "You were standing right there."

"He's not really my kid," Jacobs said. "I owe him money, and I guess he'll never see it."

"He came on his own," Akmaaq said. "He's Inupiat, though, don't doubt that. He'll show them the video and we will live on in the stories. They will welcome him. They'll see him as one of us."

"*I* had the camera."

"You *lost* the tape?"

"The whale smashed our umiaq."

"You sank my boat?"

"Q's up there floating on a dead whale."

"Then there's hope for him," Akmaaq said. "But they'll never believe his story. Not without the tape. White Bear they might have believed. *Him?...*"

"If they find the kid, maybe they'll find us too."

"Not a chance," Akmaaq said. "You saw what the whale was doing. He popped the drag-floats with his teeth. He's dying and he'll swim to the bottom to sink. We're stuck here, and this is where you die."

"Don't you mean 'we'?" Jacobs asked.

"For all you know," Akmaaq said, "I'm already dead."

In the morning, Jessica tried to recall what she knew of Nat. He was just some man, and that was the best she could come up with. He happened to be the man next door. And

Jodi—*was* she a friend? She could only come up with the same answer: she was the woman next door. Jessica was about to steal a dance with someone else's partner, which was awkward, against propriety, and unscrupulous. The point of ballroom dancing was to partner as a unit that moved through the crowd. To share a familiar moment, joined, but looking elsewhere, attuned to the drift of other couples. Nat was not her partner and she'd made him a promise she couldn't keep. She hadn't yet gone through with the infidelity, and she knew she didn't want to, because she was already terribly ashamed.

So she didn't unlock the door, and she'd remained in her satin pajamas all morning out of a paralyzed sense of helplessness. When the doorbell rang, she wanted to hide, but she decided she had better face her fate.

The man at the door was in coveralls and work boots, and he held a respirator. He didn't seem at all surprised to see Jessica in her nightwear.

"I'm here to take off the paint," he said. His white van was parked in the drive with the name of his business on the side, and written underneath was the phrase, "Sandblasting for all occasions."

"Can I get you something to drink?"

He said, "Just please stand clear of the windows."

Once the motor was started and the man went to work, there was a rumbling low vibration throughout the house. Jessica couldn't help creeping toward the front window to look out, and she saw the man in the respirator as an anonymous force who wore away their home. He was too focused on removing the white paint to notice her spying, and his arms held what looked like a silver rifle attached to a gray hose. He rocked the gun up and down, or back and forth, and the stream of compressed air and sand responded in a hypnotic dancing arc. She was over-whelmed by the excessiveness of the response of the neighborhood committee, and she was transfixed. More than anything she wanted to continue to stand and watch. But she saw Nat leave his house and cut across the lawn, and she decided to meet him in the garage.

"Look at you," he said, and he reached around behind her to stroke her back. "You're wonderful."

Nat wore a polo shirt and shorts. He wore cologne. This was his clubhouse look and he acted the part of the rich spoiled bachelor.

"I've been thinking," Jessica said.

But Nat said, "I can't hear with all that racket," and he took her by the hand and pulled her inside the house.

In the kitchen, she tried to begin again, but Nat latched onto her and kissed her neck.

"I'm not sure I can do this," she said.

To which he responded by standing straight. He held her by the shoulders, leaned back to look her in the eye, and said, "Of course you can."

"I don't think I can."

"I know you can," he said. "Remember yesterday?" He leaned in to kiss her but she dodged him and broke free.

"I'm afraid I led you on."

"You're not really afraid."

"That wasn't me."

"I know," he said. "I *love* the new you. I've been up all night, practically."

Nat followed her, he found her, and he felt her body through the sheer satin.

"Have you lost weight?" he said. "Not that you needed to. But you look great. You *feel* great."

"I lost a little," she said. "I've been riding the bike."

"John doesn't even know how good he has it," Nat said. "Does he appreciate you? I mean *really* appreciate you?"

"You know how it gets."

"But it doesn't have to," he said. "*I* appreciate you. And *I'm here.*"

"That's true," she said. "I told him not to leave."

"I love what you've done with your hair," Nat said, and he ran a hand through it. He pressed against her and pinned her to the kitchen counter. Meanwhile, the guy outside had worked his way around back so the nearest wall moaned and vibrated as it was sandblasted. Jessica found herself in an alternate reality where her neighbor felt her up in her kitchen while the house threatened to collapse. And she resisted, though she wanted Nat. And she resisted, as the resounding outer wall grew louder. And then as Nat sought her out with persistent hands, she lifted herself onto the kitchen counter, and she gave in.

Jacobs was belched from the beast into daylight and he swam to the surface where he bobbed in the floating ice. He shouted, and other voices called back. He saw an aluminum pontoon boat that sped toward him and kicked up a wake of seawater and ice. An enormous submarine had surfaced, and the white whale lay across the black hull like the body of a fish in a market display case. A flagpole in the middle of the submarine displayed a wide tricolored red-white-and-blue banner, and there was a small crowd of sailors on deck snapping photos. The sailors in the pontoon circled back and tossed Jacobs a lifesaver line. He grabbed the white ring and held on with the last of his

strength while the boat powered down beside him and
three sailors pulled him aboard and smothered him with
blankets. They spoke Russian to him with excitement, and
Jacobs blacked out.

When he roused again he screamed, held up in a shower
stall by sailors as steaming water jolted his nerves and his
core temperature rose. He was alive aboard a Russian sub,
and they had saved him. The body of the white whale had
been found, so the Inupiat would know what Akmaaq had
done.

The pain passed and he became himself again, only
exhausted. When he remembered all that had happened
the past few days, he tried to communicate that Q was still
out there, but the Russians didn't understand. He repeated
himself and got upset, until he eventually asked for food,
which the sailors understood and were happy to provide.

Jacobs sat near the shower drain and propped himself
against the wall while hot water coursed down on him with
the curtain left open. Eventually, a sailor reached in and
turned off the knobs. "Enough," the sailor said.

In an elongated room with an iron mesh pathway between
four small bolted-down stainless steel tables, Jacobs and an
interpreter sat facing each other as he drank hot
soup. Jacobs was clean-shaven, his hair wet and slicked
back. He wore one of the blue standard-issue navy
uniforms. His own clothes were ruined, and he only kept
the rabbit fur mitten, which had dried into a hard piece of
flat leather, with the tufts of white fur mangled. The
interpreter brought Jacobs a laptop, and Jacobs spoke to a

representative from the U.S. consulate through an encrypted Internet video feed while the interpreter mostly listened.

The diplomat looked to Jacobs how he had imagined the rich and powerful bank executives. The diplomat was gray, but fit and extremely sharp. He took charge—with no doubt about his decision-making capabilities—and he was apparently well-compensated for his service.

"We want to avoid an international incident," he said. "So I'm going to explain what happened. You memorize the story and never deviate in your telling. Is that understood?"

"Or I'll disappear?" Jacobs said. "Are you giving me some big CIA threat or something?"

"Or we leave you there," the diplomat said. "You are costing your government millions in resources and you'll do what we say. We saved your life, and you owe us."

"The Russians saved me."

"Who do you think phoned them?" the diplomat said. "This is top-secret information, and I'm not even supposed to tell you this, but some of our agents at a coastal monitoring station picked you up on their mics. They heard you. They saw the Russian sub in the vicinity and sent word up the vine. I got a call in the middle of the night and forwarded your location to the Russian base just in time. Our guys knew there was a sub in the vicinity, and the Russians were your best bet. If I'd stayed asleep, if those sailors hadn't been doing their jobs, or if we didn't have good relations with the Russians—you'd be dead. But you don't have to thank me.

"You should thank our guys, however, and this is what you say: 'I am deeply indebted to my government and to the Russians for their extraordinary efforts. I want to apologize for recklessly putting myself at risk in international waters, and I would like to thank everyone involved in my rescue. I did a stupid thing, and I promise I won't ever do it again.' You got that?"

"They *heard* me?"

"We've got sensitive equipment. Sound travels under-water."

"What's the story?"

"You didn't kill the whale. The Russians were pursuing it for scientific purposes when they accidentally struck your umiaq. They managed to capture the whale alive, but it died while they were tagging it. They're keeping the whale and we're sending you back home."

"The kid is still out there," Jacobs said. "You've got to find him."

"There was nothing left of the boat," the diplomat said. "There were no other survivors. Give us the names, and we'll contact the families."

"He wasn't on the boat," Jacobs said. "He's floating on the body of a dead whale."

"He's what?"

"He's on a bowhead. He's out there floating on a dead bowhead whale."

"We'll send out crews," the diplomat said. "I'm meeting you at the base tomorrow. We're flying back to Seattle together. When the press approaches us, you let me do the talking."

"I need to return to Point Halcyon," Jacobs said.

"You aren't making this easier."

"I'll give them your story," Jacobs said. "Just let me stop on the way back."

The interpreter logged and saved the conversation, he flipped the laptop closed, he got up from the table, and he walked away. He returned with a sailor in casual dress. The man had a salt-and-pepper beard and wore jeans and a blue T-shirt. He carried an aluminum tray over to the table and spoke through the interpreter.

In the tray were three harpoon blades. The first blade, Jacobs recognized as exactly the kind that Akmaaq had owned and they had been using. The interpreter said something about the likely origin, a manufacturer of agricultural equipment in Iowa. "They making of farm supplies and also for hunting," he said.

The second harpoon blade was larger and had imperfections. The metal was corroded and the hands of the bearded man in the tee shirt were stained with rust from handling it. He made the action of pretending to hammer the blade, and the interpreter said, "Making from hand. Much old."

The bearded sailor pointed out a series of letters and numbers that were stamped into the second harpoon blade, and he spoke with confidence in his thickly accented English, "Nan-tuck-y. Year of one-eight-three-zero."

"Nantucket?" Jacobs said, and the bearded sailor nodded.

The Russian took the third harpoon head and ran his hand over it in a sanding motion. The blade was a pointed chunk of black slate. Jacobs had seen that type of rock all over Point Halcyon, where there was slate and gravel in the patches that weren't snow-covered. "One thousand years," the bearded man said, "to five hundred years."

"Much old," the interpreter said.

The snow whale had been around the world. And the snow whale was hundreds of years old.

"But you'll be able to carbon date, right?" Jacobs asked. "You'll be able to find out exactly?"

"Much old," the bearded man said and nodded.

"Much old," the interpreter agreed, and they smiled.

The bearded sailor pointed to the two oldest harpoon heads in succession and said, "Russia Antiquities Museum. Russia Antiquities Museum."

Jacobs picked them up just to hold them. He held one and ran his hand over it as he contemplated the age of the blade and the fate of the hunters. "OK," Jacobs said as he set it back in the tray and picked up the second. "OK," he said again, and he set down the second blade too. Then he picked up the harpoon head that had been Akmaaq's. "Mine," he said and held it to his chest.

The bearded Russian shrugged his shoulders in a gesture that showed he didn't care. "You keep," he said. "Six more just like."

The ropes and seal-floats were cut loose, the whale carcass was secured by its tail, and the Russian sub towed it below the surface. Jacobs asked the interpreter if sonar could detect a dead whale, and he was shown the monitoring stations where those observations were made. Jacobs didn't want to become a nuisance, but the Russians were fond of him, as an American, and he had to find Q.

That night they watched a videotape. Jacobs suspected it was the same one he had heard in the listening post, and that they played this tape over and over until a new one was brought in with the supplies. The men took shifts eating in the small dining area while the audio track was patched everywhere on the sub over the PA. The video was a not-so-recent episode of *American Idol*, and the Russians who knew a little English kept asking Jacobs about black girls.

"She's going to lose," he said, though this wasn't what they'd asked.

"Yes, too bad for you," the sailors said back to him. Or they said, "I would very much like," as they nodded.

The rest of the recording was a two-hour Lawrence Welk special as part of a PBS pledge drive. Whoever had made the tape had cut out most of the philanthropy pitching from the station workers but got the show in its entirety. Jacobs stayed in the dining room as sailors came and went, and he conversed with them as best he could. Mostly, they misunderstood each other. He found the Russians liked the music well enough, but he was surprised to discover how much he really loved it. He tapped his toe and stared at the TV while he drank coffee, happy to be alive. From here on these songs, these versions of these songs, could be the soundtrack to his life.

"Polish girls, yes?" one of the sailors said. The backup singers wore candy-colored outfits and possessed a clean respectable sexuality. They were beautiful straight-haired blondes, or beautiful blue-eyed straight-haired brunettes. They were young, they were buxom, they were trim, and they had incredible legs.

"Yes," Jacobs said, though he knew all the musicians and dancers were Americans except Lawrence, and today the candy-colored girls were senior citizens who lived in Minnesota or Wisconsin.

Group after group of sailors came and went and enjoyed the show without any sense that the selections, the performances, the costumes, and the sponsorship—just the word *Geritol* that hung above the orchestra—were dated, whiter than white, and universally uncool. Jacobs wished he could enjoy watching like they did, unselfconsciously. But he carried the songs with him and he hummed as he walked around to check the sonar stations for any sign of Q and the bowhead. And he still had the songs in his head, and the images of the singing girls played in his mind as he lay down in a bunk to go to sleep.

Chapter 11

In the morning, after they docked, Jacobs met the diplomat at the Russian base, and they boarded a navy helicopter that sped over the Chukchi Sea to Point Halcyon. When Jacobs asked about Q, the diplomat said temperatures had hovered around freezing and he might still be out there, though his answer was discouraging.

Jacobs didn't understand how they could miss a whale. Then from the sky over the water he saw the sameness of ice floes where each ice chunk was indistinguishable, and the complexity of the pattern stretched to the horizon and made it nearly impossible to detect difference. And the sonar imaging encountered the same problem. Q was out there surrounded by white sea ice on a bowhead black as the dark waters.

They flew over the Chukchi Sea, and Jacobs couldn't quite grasp what he had been through. He had been out on that ice for days. He had slept on the ice, hunted on the ice, and eaten the raw meat of a whale. He had bonded with a black kid and an old Eskimo. All things the person he had once been could have never done. They had struck out courageously and he had survived. He was the sole survivor. And he might have just as easily met the same fate. And now, he could hardly believe that an area that had taken them days to travel by umiaq only took minutes to fly over.

The diplomat made Jacobs promise he would never set foot in Alaska again. He said hunting an endangered species was a felony. They could stack the charges and put him away for a long time if he tried to come back. "You've cost us a lot," he said. "And we never want to see you again."

"I'm Inuit," Jacobs said. "I have tribal rights."

"That's not in your file," the diplomat said.

"I have a file?"

"*Everyone* has a file," he said. "Don't you watch TV?"

"You can't put me in jail," Jacobs said. "Your white man's laws don't apply to me."

"We can bill you for the cost of your rescue," the diplomat said. "However you want it, we can make things difficult. All we ask is that you never come back."

The diplomat pulled up a contract on his laptop. He typed and made changes to it as they flew, so that the electronic form was no longer a plea agreement but a fee waiver, where it was stated in legal language that Jacobs owed nothing to the US government, so long as he remained in the lower forty-eight states. But all debts would come due should Jacobs ever return to the Alaskan territories. Jacobs typed an X in a box where the cursor flashed and verified his name and social security number, which he was informed counted as his electronic signature. Then he allowed the diplomat to scan his thumbprint. He was exhausted, and all he wanted was to return to his wife. He'd made his promise and would never whale again.

As they neared Point Halcyon, Jacobs spotted four umiaqs with full crews towing a whale. So they had been successful and there would be a celebration. He wanted to feel happy for his people, but he couldn't get over his melancholy. Akmaaq believed they had slain the curse of the snow whale and the *crazy-weather* he brought with him. He was willing to sacrifice himself, but the Point Halcyoners would remember Akmaaq as *inugluk, crazy-person*. Q faced a force of nature like none he could have imagined in the city, but he was probably dead. As a filmmaker, he'd captured never-before-seen footage, but all was lost. Jacobs had lived and hunted with his people, but after tonight he would be gone, and the whales they'd killed were also lost. There was nothing else but to go back to his wife, and to his old life. He wouldn't be the same, but in his time away from Jessica, he discovered he loved her. He only hoped it wasn't too late, or that he hadn't changed so much he would scare her off. Jessica had understood him once, and she would at least be there for him when he got home.

They landed at the airstrip, and Jamo idled in his police cruiser with the lights going. He helped them with their bags, and the diplomat sat in front while Jacobs sat in the back, separated from the diplomat and Jamo by a Plexiglas partition. Jamo drove them to The Point Inn, and Peter Pence, the other cop, dispatched over the radio. Peter Pence told Jamo that Yuq's kid had made it back with word that they had landed a whale. He was going to lock up the station and go out there with everyone else to divvy up the carcass.

The Point Inn, like all the businesses in Point Halcyon, looked just like another house. An Inupiat couple greeted them and took Jacobs and the diplomat up to separate rooms. The inn was their house turned into a bed-and-breakfast, and the couple slept in a room on the ground floor.

"Get some sleep," the diplomat said. "We've got a long day tomorrow."

But there was no way Jacobs was going to miss out on the celebration. There were deeds and dead men to be memorialized. This was his farewell to Tikigaq, and he was going to be an Inuk for the last time.

Jacobs wore the Russian seaman's uniform and peacoat. Like most of the homes in Point Halcyon, The Point Inn would be unlocked and he didn't need a key. The couple sat in the living room and watched *Law & Order*. Jacobs told them what he'd heard over Jamo's radio and asked if they would go out to meet the hunters on the ice.

"Seen enough of that," the man said.

"They'll bring a portion in the morning," his wife agreed.

Jacobs was familiar with the streets of Point Halcyon and he ran to Akmaaq's. The dogs came out to greet him and he let himself in. He set the harpoon point on the table as a gift for Akmaaq's spirit, but he didn't want to part with this souvenir, and so he put the blade back in his pocket, where he also kept the rabbit-fur mitten from Toni. He rummaged through his supplies and suited up in the gear he'd bought at REI: Gore-Tex boots, snow pants, and ski mittens.

He turned on the computer and saw a series of e-mails from his wife. The tone of them changed as the days passed. She sometimes sent three in a day. At first, she didn't seem to understand he was out of contact. He felt reassured when she missed him but disappointed when she focused on something of little importance. It was as if she either didn't understand or didn't want to face the dangers he lived with. He didn't open all her messages but went ahead and responded: "Jess, I'm safe and on my way home. Will call from Seattle. Watch the news and you may see me. I love you and look forward to being with you soon."

He ran to Toni and Marta's, and they were loading their station wagon. Toni embraced Jacobs and said, "We thought you were dead."

Marta was upright, proud, and didn't ask about Q. She was dressed in a ceremonial parka that was a clean white animal fur decorated with copper buttons. They packed the back of the station wagon with sealskins and loaded up the kids. Marta came over and embraced Jacobs. She said, "We thought you'd died."

Marta saw Jacobs was puzzled and so she explained, "Q got the whale. They sent Yuq's boy here as the runner. It's an insult to Yuq's family. His boy was supposed to be the great hunter. This season was going to be his manhood. Everyone on Yuq's boat had agreed to let his son be harpooner, though they had many capable men. But Q got the whale. Q spoiled Yuq's plan."

"Q's alive?"

"You were with him," Marta said. "What happened?"

"We were separated. And I was separated from the captain. The Russians saved me. So who saved Q?"

"They heard him singing," Marta said. "He was joined by the other crews, and they found him with the whale. Q doesn't have a wife, but he's my man—so we get the first share."

As Marta spoke, a small white bird with black accents landed in the road, pecked at a gravel pebble, and flew off.

Marta watched the clear sky for signs of others. Jacobs realized this was the first bird he'd seen on the mainland since he'd landed at Point Halcyon.

"Snow bunting," Marta said. She smiled but shook her head. She said, "Everything's upside-down."

At the ridge where the land ice met the sea ice, families parked automobiles and snowmobiles, then they walked out to the ice edge, where the bowhead carcass had been dragged up and was being butchered. The stain of red on white was unmistakable and seen from a mile off, the black mass of the whale flattened under its own weight. The men worked together to roll the body with ropes. They walked on the thick pink carpet of blubber and hacked with long knives. Blood streamed away from the carcass and brightened the waters. The men huffed vapor clouds and worked without parkas, to keep from ruining them. Most of the community gathered with dogsleds and sealskins, and Jacobs, Toni, Marta, and the kids walked out to greet them.

"They're waiting for us," Marta said, and she added, "for a change."

When Q saw Marta he came running, and he knocked her down with his embrace. Flat on his back he shouted, "So good to be alive," and he made a snow angel with his arms and legs.

Jacobs extended a hand to help him up, but Q declined and said, "You left me out there. You were my producer."

"It was the captain," Jacobs said. "I sent the US and Russian navies to come find you."

"Did you get the camera?" Q said.

"The boat went down. I was nearly killed."

"That was my film," Q said. "Is it really gone?"

"I'm lucky to be alive."

"We had that thing on tape," Q said.

"We killed him," Jacobs said. "It's over. The curse is lifted."

"You owe me money," Q said.

"I know," Jacobs said. "I'll get it."

"You owe me more than that."

"I'll get you your money."

Hand in hand, Q and Marta jogged out to the carcass. The men stopped working and stepped back. Marta sang to the animal and poured fresh water on the enormous whale lips from a skin, the ceremony to thank the whale for his gift of life.

But before Marta had finished singing a young girl was brought over, and Marta was pulled aside. The young girl performed the same ceremony while Marta watched, confused. The girl held the hand of Yuq's son, and she poured drinking water on the whale's lips as she sang. Yuq's son had been humiliated but order had been restored, and he was happy to take what was rightfully his.

"I told them about the seal-float," Q said to Marta. "The one the captain told me to cut. Should I not have done that?"

"Honesty is best," Marta said. "Something the old man could have learned."

Jacobs went over to Yuq and said, "Congratulations. For your son, I mean."

Yuq looked suspiciously at Jacobs, and no one in the clan acted glad to see him. They called him Jonah, but didn't slap him on the back, or embrace him. Jacobs had also been through it. He had helped kill the whale with Q. But they all thought Jacobs had left his son for dead.

Jacobs extended a hand, and Yuq shook it.

"I saw the spirit of your father," Jacobs said.

"How did you see him?" Yuq asked. "In a dream?"

"I met him in the belly of the whale. We killed the snow whale and your father is at peace."

"What? Are you some kind of shaman?" Yuq said.

"You don't have to believe me," Jacobs said. "The ice plays tricks."

"You think I'm cold," Yuq said. "That I should be mourning his loss. But his breath continues after the body. Akmaaq lives on because his grandson, my son, shares his name. He will also grow up to be a great chief and hunter."

Men were embraced by their wives and they kissed. The men hugged their women back with elbows as they held up bloody hands. The youngest children ran on the ice and threw snowballs, the area beyond the ice ridge always forbidden to them. The older children gave out cuts of meat, now part of the mature order. There was heartfelt laughter that carried across the plane of ice along with the excited yelps of dogs that sometimes broke into skirmishes over scraps. Members of the clan joined in singing, and the hunters handed out strips of skin and blubber for the women and children to chew. A group of men gripped a sealskin by the edges, and they threw a child into the air with it. The child screamed at the heights but landed safely on the skin and was tossed back up.

Yuq's wife was covered in a parka, snow pants, mittens, and boots, but she still projected the light of a beautiful woman. Her ceremonial parka was more colorful and ornate than any of the others, turquoise and magenta, and it looked like something shipped from Norway. There was a four-inch oval of exposed face beneath her beveled snow hood, where one might make out her nose, her eyes, and the line of her bangs—but only if she looked straight on. And if she returned the gaze of a man, she quickened his heart.

Snow fell intermittently at first, blown in off the ice-covered water, until the flakes coalesced and fell in clumps. Then the flurries gathered into a thick descending swarm. The blanketing snow brought silence and the flakes were heard striking ice and pelting parkas. Jacobs watched his people as the scene grew quiet, and he had never known such calm. He was reminded of the phrase about the pin dropping, because he had never experienced it, had been unaware that such a thing could be true. And now snow accumulated on the whale. And snow collected in their dark hair. And snow covered their tracks. After the whale was cut apart and packed away, the head was returned to the sea, so the whale's soul could finally rest.

Yuq raised a hand and the clan gathered. Jacobs recognized the Piskipulut pastor among them, but it was Yuq who spoke:

> The air around us and the heavens have never stilled. The Great Living Breath is eternal. We know and remember the dead in our small graveyard and the ancestor spirits who walk among us. And their breath continues, for we speak their names.
>
> My son, Akmaaq, received a gift from the sea. We rejoice. And one day, many years from now, he will meet the spirit of this whale to thank him.
>
> May the whale's clan forgive us and continue to bless us. May my son also breed life. May Tikigaq remain at peace and accept these whale bones, returned to their source, the earth body of the first whale. And may we live on here, and sleep here, with the wisdom of *the-everything-and-the-nothing* that is the Great Living Breath.

When I was a boy, my father handed me the harpoon, and I struck my first whale. Then, when I was grown, I witnessed many changes. I saw what was then and what is now. I had heard the stories of what had been before. When my son is grown and I'm gone, I hope beyond hope that the winds will shift back to what once was, and that his clan will live to see it.

But we all know the sea ice will disappear in our lifetimes, and with it the old ways. Our children are the last generation, and our thousand-year collective knowledge, our connection to the land, our understanding of the wildlife—it will all be gone. Tikigaq is dying and our children will bear witness.

May they find a middle passage, a lead in the ice between ancient and new, to return to the wise ways of the ancestors—who were closer to heaven, closer to the earth, and in greater resemblance of Sila's image—yet may they adapt to a world with no place left for them.

May we always remember the deeds of those who came before. And speak their names. And we will all live on, in the stories, for as long as Inupiat breathe.

At the end of his last day on the ice, after celebrating the blood feast with his people, Jacobs said to Q, "We're flying home tomorrow. Will you spend the night at Marta's?"

"I'm not going back," Q said. "I have another film in me. I'm an Inupiat director, and I have to capture this way of life before the sea ice is gone."

"We killed the snow whale," Jacobs said. "The curse is lifted."

"Nothing has changed," Q said. "That thing will come back."

"Can I mail you a check?"

"Give it to my mom," Q said. "The money was for her anyway."

As Jacobs walked back across the ice, he passed Jamo, who pulled a sled loaded with slabs of blubber and meat. He moved slowly and looked vulnerable outside his police cruiser. When Jacobs passed him, Jamo shouted out a greeting. Jacobs turned and they spoke.

"Your white chief wanted you back," Jamo said. "Your life was important to them."

"I was lucky," Jacobs said.

"It wasn't luck," Jamo said. "They moved the heavens for you. They used the whole white world."

At Toni's that night, Jacobs slept with her in her bed. They were naked and they held each other, but they didn't kiss. They ran their hands over each other, and though they wanted to, they didn't have sex.

"I'm leaving and I can't come back," Jacobs said.

"I know," Toni said. "Your wife."

"Yes, my wife," Jacobs said. "And the US government."

In the morning, he gave her back the mitten. He thanked her, and he expressed what he truly believed. That her token had kept him sane out there, that he had benefited from her prayers, and that her prayers mattered.

In the yard as he left, the peculiar dog whimpered and bit at Jacobs's ankles. He pet the dog and said, "Take care of them." And: "We'll know each other again."

Chapter 12

Jessica didn't meet John at the airport, and he was let down. He called collect from a payphone and she said, "Can't you take a cab?"

From the backseat of the cab, the Oaken Glens subdivision looked foreign. The winding streets were lined with old-fashioned posts like gaslights, except they were bright. The houses were lit up with floodlights, pathway lights, and their windows also gave off light, where in room after empty room the lights had been left on. Jacobs let the cabbie drive past his house before he realized the mistake, and he had to tell him to turn around. The house was no longer painted white, and it didn't stand out. He had to concentrate to remember where he and Jessica lived, but he saw his car in the drive. The Pontiac, like a shadow of itself, was ready to settle back into the earth, a flawed animal doomed to extinction, too heavy to go on.

At the door of the house, Jacobs fumbled with his keys, noting what strange objects they were. He'd always taken them for granted and also depended on them. It was a balmy spring night and he held the Russian peacoat draped over his arm. He looked closely at the brick façade and saw white paint in the crevices. There was sand on the front patio and sand in the grass. At first he thought he walked in a dream, with the house as he remembered it before the DNA test, but then he saw how they had sandblasted, and he knew he walked awake.

Inside the house he felt a chill as the air conditioner purred. He left his bags by the door and went upstairs, to the bedroom. Jessica was in bed watching TV. Surrounded by the white comforter and white pillows of their large bed, she watched him from a floating block of ice. She didn't get up to greet him and she didn't turn down the volume.

"Howdy, sailor," she said, a joke with sexual overtones, except she said it flatly.

"I'm home," he said.

"Can you get your job back?"

"I can try," he said. "Do you want to hear it?"

"Do I have a choice?" she said. "I'm tired, John. Your plane was late and I'm coming down with a cold."

Jacobs undressed and crawled into bed. "I've missed you," he said, and he pulled her close.

"You think you can be gone then just climb on top of me?"

"I've missed you," he repeated.

"I missed you too," she said. "But not tonight, OK?"

At UniqCorps, the security guard was one Jacobs didn't know, so he had to have Mike Schmidt come down to vouch for him. In the elevator, Jacobs asked if the bosses were hiring.

"That new kid's got everyone charmed," Mike said.

"But I wouldn't compete with him," Jacobs said. "The more accounts the better, right?"

The elevator slowed as they came to their floor, and Mike stared at the crack in the elevator door. "They might hire you to get rid of me," he said.

"I wasn't thinking of that," Jacobs said. "I just asked if they were hiring. I can find a job."

When Mike stepped off the elevator Jacobs stayed and rode back down. He had thought they might go out to lunch and have some laughs. He'd wanted to tell Mike his *Moby-Dick* story.

Before the elevator reached the lobby, another worker stepped on. She was one of the few African American employees at UniqCorps. The air was still between them, and Jacobs knew he would never see this woman again, so he was willing to wait and walk away for good. But the woman spoke.

"Weather's been crazy," she said.

"Things will be normal again soon," Jacobs said.

Then, in the silence that followed, Jacobs said, "I used to work here."

"I thought I'd seen you," the woman said. "Where do you work now? Somewhere better, I hope."

"I'm a film producer. Of documentaries."

"What do you film?"

"Penguins."

"In their natural habitat?"

"There's penguins everywhere."

"I'll keep an eye out," she said. "Who do I phone if I see one?"

"Send an e-mail," he said, "to Jessica Jacobs dot com."

"Is there a reward?" the woman asked, and the elevator opened to the lobby.

"The reward is seeing it," Jacobs said. "And getting there."

"You're not talking about penguins?"

"I guess not."

"Did you quit or did they fire you?"

"Both."

"They asked you to resign?" the woman offered, and they both stepped out of the elevator because there were UniqCorps employees who waited to get on.

"It was headed there."

"Good luck," she said.

"Thank you," Jacobs said. "But everything is fine."

On his way home, he decided to drive to REI and he saw so much green: spacious manicured lawns, old dark evergreens, and lime-colored well-placed shrubs. Jacobs was over-whelmed by the greenery. The humid air took an effort to breathe. The hot sun made itself felt, and Jacobs was nostalgic for the landscape of ice, which he might never get over.

In the parking lot, he watched himself in the reflection of car windows, and he was shocked to see himself as a stranger. He was a Russian sailor back from a tour in Siberia and desperate for a job. He was an oddball. But at REI they might like that.

He spotted the mountain man salesman and spied on him from behind a display tent. There was a couple at the climbing wall, the woman nearly at the top while her beau held the safety rope and shouted up directions from the floor. There were rich kids trying on ski boots as their confident parents hovered nearby. The parents could afford anything, and they waited passively as the rest of their children roamed freely through the store. One kid nearly tipped over a canoe. Another took a pack of Gator Gum and stuffed it in his pocket.

Jacobs loitered by the sunglasses and picked up the most expensive pair, like the ones he'd lost when the tail of the snow whale slapped him into the Chukchi Sea. He put on the glasses and admired himself in the mirror. When the mountain man salesman came over, Jacobs said, "I could sell these."

"You know something about them?" the salesman asked.

Jacobs produced the harpoon blade from his pocket and set it on the glass counter with a snick. He said, "I killed two whales."

"You're that whale guy," the mountain man said.

"I need a job."

"I'll get you an application."

"Did you hear what I said?" Jacobs said. "I killed two whales. I don't need an application."

"OK," the mountain man said. "But you have to pay for the sunglasses."

"Take it out of my check," Jacobs said.

"You haven't earned it," he said. "Do you want to be paid hourly or on commission?"

Jacobs scanned the store and saw the people as prey. The children were seal cubs and their rich parents couldn't protect them. He would kill them on the ice for their pelts. He imagined throwing harpoons into the adults and when they tried to swim off, he'd use phrases on them like, "if you can afford it," or "if you want the better brand." And he would always be in a position to recommend spending more.

On his way home, in the Russian sailor suit and wearing his new pair of Arctic sunglasses, Jacobs was surprised by his cell phone. He hadn't heard a phone ring in a long while, and he had to pause to remember what to do. He pulled over to talk.

Jessica wanted to make a pledge to PBS, and would he rather have the coffee mug or the book bag? So she was back. In her small way, she was including him in her life. Jacobs remembered his years of selling desk doodles and couldn't help thinking of the pledge drive as a scam.

"I've only just gotten a job and you're spending money?"

"You got a job?" she said. "It's only a pledge. They send an envelope and we pay them when we have the money. I think it's the right thing to do. I've been watching better shows since you left."

"Do they have DVDs?"

"I think so," she said. "But at the two-hundred-dollar level."

"Any Lawrence Welk?"

"You like Lawrence Welk?" she said.

"I didn't, but I do now."

"You *really are* a white guy," she said.

"I can be an Inuk and like Lawrence Welk."

"No, I don't think you can," she said. "But we'll get it. Would that make you happy?"

Q's mama came out onto the stoop, but when Jacobs explained he wanted to talk about money, she invited him in. The Pomeranian barked until Jacobs sat on the couch, then the small dog curled around itself on the carpet at Jacobs's feet. Q's mama brought Jacobs a tall glass of iced tea with photoworthy chiseled ice cubes that were large and square. He held the tea up to the light to appreciate the forms of ice as they shifted in the glass. He didn't know what kind of ice tray or ice-maker would produce them, and so he asked, "Where did you get your ice?"

"From the freezer," she said.

"Have you spoken to Q?"

"He says you owe him," she said. "And that he's lucky to be alive after going out there with you."

"He's staying," Jacobs said. "He thinks he's Eskimo."

"Who's to say he's not," she said. Jacobs remembered the mystery of Q's father, and Q's mama said, "He might be."

"We killed a whale," Jacobs said. "Eskimo or not, your son is a hunter."

"How much do you owe him?"

"We never set a price. I brought him along. I bought his gear. I got him up there."

"But you owe him a wage."

"He wants me to pay you."

"I know what he wants."

"The film we were making," Jacobs said. "It got lost."

"He says *you* lost it."

"The thing is," Jacobs said, "I've only just started working again. I won't get paid right away."

"You took him along, but didn't know if you could pay him?"

"He agreed to go."

"It seems to me," Q's mama said, "that you owe him quite a lot. He risked his life. He worked night and day. He killed a whale. And you lost his film."

"When you put it like that . . . "

"How should I put it?"

The little dog got up and found another spot on the carpet a few feet away. Jacobs took his first sip of the tea. He wanted to know where she got the ice but was sure she wouldn't tell him. Not now anyway.

"So what are we going to do?" she asked.

"I'll bring you something each week," he said. "And I'll keep doing that until it's paid off."

"And if you don't," Q's mama said, "I have your wife's cell phone number. I'm not meddling. I just want to be assured that you'll keep your obligation. If it comes to it, I'll tell her about that Eskimo woman you met."

Jacobs could hardly believe what he'd come home to. He would need his survival skills and his hunter senses in this cruel modern world. He'd always intended to pay Q, but he was backed into a corner, and he felt wounded. He was being accused of something he didn't do.

"It's illegal for Q to hunt whales," Jacobs said. "He could go to jail."

"*You* brought him," she said.

"He agreed to go."

"Are you trying to get out of paying?" she said.

"I'll pay," Jacobs said. "But I love my wife. Let me tell her. You weren't there, and it should come from me."

"You bring a little something each week," Q's mama said. "And you won't have to worry."

"Q is pursuing his dream to be a filmmaker," Jacobs said. "You should be proud."

"I don't see why he can't do that around here."

"*The world is a book*," Jacobs said. "*And those who don't travel read only one page.*"

"Are you calling *my life* one page?"

"I'm saying *his* life can be different."

At home Nat Jorgenson caught Jacobs in the driveway, and he came over.

"Get it out of your system?" Nat said, but Jacobs just stared. So Nat continued, "Jodi said you had a midlife thing. You took off."

"I went to Alaska," Jacobs said. "It wasn't a *thing*."

"No shame in it," Nat said. "I get the itch too. Somebody you met online?"

"That's not what this was."

"You don't have to talk," Nat said, and he placed a hand over his heart. "Sworn to secrecy.

"We're cooking out next weekend," Nat continued. "Jess said you like fish these days. I've been getting this new white fish from the Philippines. Tastes like butter. I'll smoke it over mesquite. You're going to love it."

"You've been talking to Jess?"

"Relax," Nat said, and he put his arm around Jacobs. "We talked about paint. They sandblasted your house and I wanted to let her know the approved colors. I can't blame you really. Everything's the same here. You feel like a number. You wanted to stand out was all. I feel that way too sometimes."

"I didn't want to stand out. I wanted snow."

"You do a white trim and they can't say anything," Nat said. "Would have the same effect. Place would totally stand out. I know a guy at the paint store will give you a deal. Let me know and I can help you."

"I don't want just any white," Jacobs said.

"They got all kinds of whites," Nat said. "You can find what you want, no problem."

Jessica sat up in bed with the pillows propped. A fan spun in the window and the house breathed. The TV was off.

This was their night together. She was open to John and ready to take him in her arms. She smiled and watched him lovingly.

"I took the DNA test," she said.

"What'd you find out?"

"Nothing exciting," she said. "I'm mostly Scottish. I put a coat of arms up at the website. It's not really mine. I just picked one I liked."

"That's OK," John said. "Probably it represents you well enough."

"Do you want to be with a white girl?"

Jacobs thought back to the beginning and reflected on their time apart. It was dark, but someone outside mowed a lawn. A neighbor's dog barked. They lived together in close proximity, on solid ground, in their tiny subdivision on this big green planet. He thought about Boy Scouts, turn lanes, and mailboxes. He imagined their place in it all and how time was short. He hated that the success of his marriage might depend on regular payments to Q's mama. She was shallow and he didn't trust her.

Jacobs took off his Gore-Tex boots and sat at the end of the bed. He didn't see God's mercy in the Jonah story, but the whale was sent to punish. Jonah had been faithless and proud. And he needed to be taught a lesson. Jacobs lifted his legs and curled himself into a ball. He stared back at his wife, who was patient. He enjoyed the silence between them, and he waited. When he spoke again, finally, he told her the whole story.

Acknowledgements

I would like to thank first readers Katrina Gray, Jürgen Fauth, Joe Gross, and Chetley Weis for their feedback and input; mentors Frederick Barthelme, Mary Robison, Stuart Dybek, and Jaimy Gordon for their depth and inspiration; and above all my parents for their material and emotional support.

ABOUT THE AUTHOR

John Minichillo lives in Nashville with his wife and son. This is his first novel.